BISHOP BEWITCHED

A Garfield Falls Mystery

A PREQUEL TO BISHOP TO QUEEN'S KNIGHT

By

Bartenn Mills

may happiness come back to you three-fold [handwritten signature]

ISBN: 978-0-9905412-3-3

Acknowledgements:
When your world is so full of wonderful people, how do you single out only a few to thank? Henry, as always, who reads, rereads, and reads yet again. Julie who maintains the faith. Wendy who critiques with me. Jamie who won't let me take the easy path. And Ken who didn't know me but read two books in one week. Thanks to all.

CHAPTER ONE

Vincent Bishop woke before dawn. Cold spring air blasted through his open window sending the curtains flying like the tail of a ghost. In that instant between sleep and consciousness he thought he saw Teonna standing there, waiting for the sunrise, the quilt he was laying under wrapped tight around her shoulders, her blonde hair cascading down her back. She turned. What had been solid in that moment of half-sleep became translucent and she seemed to curl into smoke. As her image dissolved, the starry sky behind her overcame the white and blue and green of the quilt until all that was left was the shimmer of what had been. Only the eyes lingered, bright with intelligence, until they too melted, leaving him the pain, red hot, like pokers thrust into his flesh.

Shoulder. Shoulder. Lung. Leg. Heart.

He should be dead.

No use pretending he could close his eyes and die.

No use trying to go back to sleep where dreams of her haunted him. Life went on. He rolled out of bed and stood in the shower letting the heat pull the stiffness out of his shoulder. He needed to run. The stretch of muscles, the pounding of his heart and the rush of his blood, would finish his journey back to accepting being alive.

He was downstairs tying on his shoes when the phone rang. It would be Shirley from dispatch. It would be their usual routine.

"Dead body."

"Give me thirty."

"I'll give you ten."

He could be out the door in five, but he'd never tell her that.

Only this morning it wasn't Shirley.

It was the Chief. "Bishop, I wake you there, boy?" Although he'd lived in the north for twenty years, the chief still maintained his southern persona, made people think he was dumb and easy going. Bishop knew neither was true.

"You need to get yourself a wife, Bishop, someone with a pretty voice that will sweet talk me while you go to the potty and get the important business of the day done."

"Yeah, I'll get right on that."

They both knew it wasn't going to happen.

"Anyway, I have a favor to ask." Now the Chief was serious, his voice low and soft. Bishop assumed so that no one else would hear, and the only anyone else that might hear was the Chief's wife. Probably didn't want to wake her. If Bishop had a wife he wouldn't want to wake her in the pre-dawn – not for police business.

"County's got a little problem. They should call in the state boys. But Hank hates to, not after the muddle they made last time. You know how it is, country folk don't like big city people parading around like they know everything. Makes 'em all clam up, act dumb when they ain't. Body's just a few yards out of our jurisdiction. Everyone could say they made a surveyor's error."

There was a long pause. They both knew Morris was up on rotation. They both knew Bishop didn't have to be in for another two hours.

"Probably nothing. Bunch of old women out in a field doing some voodoo spells. One of them dropped dead. Paramedics wouldn't touch her. You go in, see what's what. Do that thing you do, you know ..."

Bishop knew.

"...get the old witch to tell you what happened. It'll help Hank out."

Bishop left the phone next to his keys and quickly changed. Instead of heading through town, he went west to the county highway, then north on gravel, finally swinging back east toward the city. It was longer in miles, but shorter in time. Not that Garfield Falls was a city in any real sense of the word, but it was a good sized town, large enough to have two high schools, large enough to have a three anchor mall, large enough to have murders and need someone like him on the force.

The scurry of early morning workers driving into town slowed. At the rise of a hill, Bishop could see the lights of a patrol car turning like lighthouse beacons. Gawkers formed a long line as traffic crept past trying to see what tragedy had occurred, then, cursing their delay, speeding to their destinations. When he finally reached the squad car, Bishop swung onto the shoulder. Other vehicles had left tire tracks across the field of freshly erupting corn, even the ambulance had ventured through the furrows, but he doubted his ancient Subaru would go off road and back without something shaking loose that would cause him trouble and expense down the road, so he parked half-tipped into the ditch, and tromped across the field. Dirt, moist with dew, clung to his shoes. The sun sat sleepily on the horizon casting deep shadows. Lonely figures in brown robes stood against brown trees at the far end of the field. The moon, big and full, hung in the early morning sky.

How often did that happen, the moon in daylight?

He passed the paramedics lounging against the ambulance, no doubt waiting for the coroner's office to give them the okay to leave, than a county vehicle nosed further in. The county boys stood close to their sedan, their brown uniforms no longer crisp, the end of their shift slipping through their fingers and taunting them. First on the scene, they had already staked out a perimeter, and likely told the witnesses not to talk to each other, the brown robed women standing apart as they peered from between the trees.

Normally Bishop would have circled the area before asking any questions, get a feel for the land, avoid people who might contaminate his thoughts with their versions of the truth. Instead, he stopped next to a lanky older officer whose bearing declared he was in charge. Although they'd never met, they had talked on the phone now and again. Nothing unusual about the county calling for a little assistance on a homicide. They didn't have the personnel or the experience for anything too complex. But Hank had never asked him to come out to a crime scene.

"Bishop?" They shook hands. "Nice of the chief to offer your assistance. Looks plenty cut and dried to me, but you never know."

"What's all that?" Bishop tipped his head toward the women shivering in the dawn light, the quickly shrinking shadows adding a surreal element to an already eerie scene.

"Wiccan."

"What?"

The second officer rested his hand on his gun holster, and nodded knowingly. "A witch's coven. They come out here to greet the dawn. Dance naked."

Bishop hadn't gotten the impression that any of the women would soon be appearing in an issue of Playboy. Even from a distance he could tell they were mostly older, plumper.

Hank scowled at his junior officer. "Never caused any trouble before." Then turned to Bishop. "Some locals harass them. But freedom of religion, you know."

Bishop knew.

What else was there to say?

He shuffled uneasily, the chill of the morning working its way through the thin soles of his shoes and up his leg. Protocol gave initiative to Hank, so Bishop waited studying the topography of the land. The earth formed a natural bowl with the figures and the trees defining the high, outer edge. A fire pit, rimmed with smooth rocks, marked the depressed center. A white sheet, he assumed covering the body, lay close to where logs, too green to burn, still smoldered. A wisp, more like mist than smoke, lifted from beneath the logs and hung above the sheet.

The county officers continued to hang back, well away from the yellow police tape that clearly defined the magic circle the witches had laid down. Bishop wasn't sure what they were waiting for. The body called to him, piercing and incessant, like a siren's song to an ancient sailor. Unable to stand at the edge of the clearing doing nothing, the sun lifting higher and higher, he moved away from the other officers. Stepping forward, dipping under the yellow tape, Bishop answered the mystical pull of the dead.

CHAPTER TWO

Everything was still. Even the ever present wind had quieted to nothing but a whisper of a breeze. Bishop forgot that people were watching him. Like a jungle cat carefully judging the best angle to approach its prey, he moved closer, answering death's call. On light feet, he circled the area, moving slowly inward. A bit of fabric, charred but not entirely burnt, caught his eye. It fluttered in the breeze, snarled on an early wild flower just poking its head through the grass. Retrieving a tweezers from his pocket he lifted the bit of fabric, turning it to catch the sun. The toe of a sock, perhaps? Brown beneath the burn. Pulling a small evidence bag from another pocket, Bishop stored the sock and moved on.

A circle of stones, cleaved in half, the flat surfaces turned upward making tiny tables where candles had been placed. Had they intended to mark the points of a compass? Each candle was a different color. Maybe it meant something, maybe it meant nothing. The wicks were long and black, and thick ridges of wax cascaded down the sides forming puddles at their base. Someone had dumped water into the firepit and pools of shimmery liquid were caught in the low areas. The force had collapsed the delicate architecture of logs, knocking them flat. He crouched down and studied the mound of black ash and slag. It must have been a huge fire with flames leaping to the night sky, to the moon rising in the east, the dancing blaze making odd shadows of light and dark. The women, in brown robes, surrounding the bonfire, standing in one world trying to reach another. He used the end of his pencil to reach beneath a bridge of logs and stir the ash, revealing still smoldering embers and lifting hidden smells. Beneath the scent of burnt wood was the lingering odor of herbs. Sage? Marjoram? The bite of gunpowder? His shoulder twitched, and he pushed the phantom pain aside.

Finally, vigilant not to disturb anything, he lifted a corner of the white sheet. Beneath was a young woman. She wore the same odd robe-like garment he'd noticed the women standing amongst the trees wearing, earthen brown and gauzy, suggesting but not exposing the nakedness underneath. Her hair, the color of potting soil, had fallen across her face. He imagined that she was pretty. Had been pretty when she'd been alive. Now in death, her lips blue, her cheeks blotched red, dark veins making a road map across her face, she was frightening, the kind of witch to scare young children with on Halloween night. Bits of ash clung to her cheeks and eyebrows. Her features contorted in pain. It would take a good mortician to ease that death scream into a tranquil smile. Bishop bent closer, smelling the fresh green of the new grass and the rich promise of the wakening earth. Then he turned his head so that he could see the blank brown eyes, hollow without their soul.

He took a slow breath, inhaling the air she had last exhaled.

The air held her joy at being there, under the moonlight, waiting for the sunrise. Like a puppy she danced on nimble feet. Excited. Anxious to greet the sun. Unashamed of her nakedness. Reveling in the moonlight playing on her skin. She spun, round and round.

Bishop straightened. Staring at the ground, he found little patches of matted grass, all the stems twirling in the same counterclockwise directions.

Yes, she spins. Spins until she's dizzy.

Where are the others? Are they watching? Laughing? Enjoying her joy? Or jealous? Envious of her youth, her beauty, her zest for life? Resentful enough to kill?

He studied the grass around the fire pit. Dew formed undisturbed on the tender blades of green. There were only three patches of trampled grass. If she had stood facing east, someone on her left, someone on her right, she would have collapsed right where she was.

He stared at the women in the trees, there were at least three, maybe four, where had the others been standing? Slowly he shook his head. No, the others weren't there yet. It's just her, her and her two co-conspirators. He held the word, co-conspirators, letting the implications soak into his psyche. They weren't supposed to be there. They weren't supposed to be doing what they were doing.

She didn't care. With the abandon of youth she is one with the moment. Today she controls her destiny. She reaches to the waking sky. She opens her arms wide, and sings.

Words? Gibberish? A chant? A chant to the sky and the moon. A call to the goddess.

She holds something. A candle. A red candle.

Bishop bent down, searching. There, caught between two rocks bordering the firepit, a small red candle floated in a backwash of water. How could he have missed it?

He left it for now, focusing back on the girl casting her spell. She throws something into the fire. Smoke explodes into her face. She inhales the smoke and the magic it contains. One breath. Holding it. Releasing it with her song. A second. She fights to draw in a third. Now she can't exhale. Dizziness overwhelms her. She stumbles. Falls. The control she was so hungry for deteriorates, dissolving into the night, mocking her last attempt to reach out and grab it.

But what had she thrown into the fire? The sock? Would a sock burn like that? One big puff of smoke like a magic act on a stage? Or had she thrown gunpowder in thinking it would help things burn only to have them explode? He'd smelt the gunpowder, hanging in the thick, spring air, the humidity holding the scent. Maybe she'd stood too close and the flash had burned her. But those red blotches and veins marring her face weren't burns. Not burns he'd seen before. No, they were something else. More like an athlete that had given their all. Muscles strained beyond endurance. Lungs screaming for oxygen.

Bishop checked her palms – pinpricks of red showed that she'd fallen. And her robe – spots of blood at the knees, a slight tear.

So, now on all fours, she gasps, fighting for air.

This is not dizziness brought on by her spinning.

An ashy froth clings to her hair, is still in her mouth.

Smoke? Could the smoke have overwhelmed her? Not likely. Not that fast. Not even if she'd been right on top of the fire. Something else. Something in the smoke.

She claws at her throat.

He could see red scratches down her neck. Deep. Painful. Made with her own hands.

"Paramedics think it was smoke inhalation."

Bishop exhaled the victim's last moments, letting them drift into the day, then took a fresh breath, inhaling the rich scents of spring. Earth. Green. Sunshine.

"What's her name?"

She had a name. They all had a name.

"Jones, Pear Blossom Jones."

Bishop looked up. Detective Travis Sam handed

him a Styrofoam carry-out cup of coffee. Black, no cream, no sugar, no latte, no cappuccino, no espresso. Black.

When had his tall, lanky partner gotten there?

CHAPTER THREE

Bishop wiped the dirt off first one hand, then the other. He must have been on the ground. He didn't quite remember. He opened the cup's lid and took a deep swallow of coffee. The heat hit him first, then the caffeine, sending warmth and energy down his throat, dispersing through him, though never quite reaching his cold toes. Everyone had left, Hank, the county boys, even the paramedics. Only a plain white coroner's wagon waited in the daylight to remove the body.

"Okay if they get to work?" Sam slouched perhaps knowing that he was like a lightning rod out in the field. "Where should they take her? I mean, we're here but their coroner declared her dead before we were called."

"Our case, our lab."

He'd call the ME later, ask questions, hope for answers. Bishop glanced at the trees. The women were gone as well, melted back into the woods, like tree sprites, or will-o-wisps, vanquished by the sun.

"County boys did all the preliminaries, took names, addresses. One of them was the mother. She was pretty shook up. High priestess took her home. That's what the head witch is called, a high priestess."

Bishop didn't interrupt. Sam had done well. He'd make a good detective.

"Anyway, they've been a practicing coven for years." The younger officer glanced at his little memo pad, his plain, square printing neatly filling the pages with information. "A core group of three, several others come and go. The dead girl joined last year. Year and a day, actually. Several of them said that. Sponsored by her mother. They come here on regular holidays. Witch holidays. Samhain, Beltane, spring and fall equinox, summer and winter solstice, moon phases."

Sam carefully turned the page back to the next. "Today is Beltane. May first." He looked at Bishop. "Remember when you were a kid and you delivered May baskets?" His tone was friendly, inviting conversation. Bishop remembered. His mother would always have a big recital with dancers flitting about throwing flower petals, and him standing there being the May pole as his sisters, and all the other dance students tied him up in garlands. But he didn't say anything

"I guess the girl, Pear Blossom was her given name, but everyone called her Blossom, got here first. Then," Sam checked his notes, "Amanda. They lit the fire. Nobody said, but I got the impression they weren't supposed to. Blossom was being inducted – is that what you call it? Anyway, they were making her an official member of the coven. That's why they all knew she'd been with the group a year and a day. Something magic about it. Anyway, the land belongs to the High Priestess's former brother-in-law." Sam put his memo pad down. "Want me to bag anything?"

The tall officer relaxed and tipped his face slightly upward toward the early-morning sun, its rays sucking the chill out of the air, the warmth of spring finally arriving after a long winter that hadn't wanted to let go. Everything about him said that he expected to be told they were done. No homicide just an unfortunate set of circumstances. He looked everywhere except at the men hefting the body onto a gurney. Regardless what Sam expected, Bishop smelled murder in the soft spring breeze.

"You finished taking pictures?"

"Yeah."

Bishop pulled an evidence bag from his inside pocket and reached between the rocks. As best he could, he placed the bag over the red candle he'd noticed earlier. One side had melted against a rock, but the candle came away with a gentle tug. He handed Sam the bagged candle, then toppled several of the unburned logs. He used the end of his pencil to stir the ash, mixing the residue and making sure all the embers were out, before scooping a handful into an evidence bag. Sam groaned.

CHAPTER FOUR

The only car left near the field was Bishop's ancient Subaru, but Bishop made a big show of looking for Sam's white Corvette. "You walk?" It was meant as a joke. Sam chuckled. They both knew some woman had dropped Sam off. It happened to Sam a lot.

"Get in. I'll give you a lift to town." Bishop took a fast food napkin from the glove compartment and wiped the soot off his hand, then tossed it under the seat to reside with the remains of too many carry-out sacks and clusters of cups from too many late nights.

Back on the highway, Sam contemplated the field of corn they were leaving, the plants only a few inches high, their leaves bright green with promise. "Do we have jurisdiction out here?"

Bishop swung south toward the city. "Nope. County called the Chief, the Chief called me, I called you." Something tickled the back of his mind. Was that right?

Sam stared at a cow calmly munching a tuft of grass in a passing meadow. "Shouldn't they have called the state boys?"

"All about the politics."

Which bothered Bishop. Why had the Chief called him? On the surface it didn't even look like a murder. Hank didn't have any reason to ask for his assistance? Bishop normally only got a call after the investigation was in progress and the puzzle pieces didn't fit. Hadn't Hank said the Chief had called him? Were it April First instead of May First, Bishop would have expected someone to slap him on the back and good naturedly hoot – April Fools. He shook off the feeling, he'd known the Chief too long to let questions form in his mind. He pointed at a large boulder they were passing. "There's the old city limits. Hank usually takes anything to the north, but another thousand feet to the south and it would have been within the new city limits and our case. City line follows some turn-of-the-century estate. Railroad money. There's a spur from the main line almost to the house. Politics. The city wanted the tax income so they annexed it."

Sam nodded as if he cared. Bishop shut up. He knew too much useless information and it could spill out at the wrong times.

"So. It looks like an accident, do we just wait for the ME's report?"

Normally that's what they'd do. But again that tickle that something wasn't right. "Who's on that witness list? Anyone jump out at you when you talked to them?"

Sam shook his head. "Amanda, no last name, apparently they don't share last names, not even sure if that's her real name, or her witch name. Some of them use their real name, some don't, they choose a name that fits their witch persona." He must have realized that he was rambling, cleared his throat and looked at his notes. "Anyway, this Amanda left when the High Priestess, a Keisha Michaels, her real name, arrived and called 911. Only thing she could say for sure was that Amanda drives an older car and that it's red."

Bishop could hear the little quote marks around it's red and the disdain in Sam's voice. Civilians couldn't be expected to remember details, but it made their job harder when they didn't.

"When the paramedics arrived they had no response from the victim." Sam lowered the memo book that he'd been reading from. "They didn't even touch the body. Pretty obvious she was gone. Cold morning, lying on the ground in nothing but that thin shift. Rigor mortis was already setting in. They stood back and waited for a declaration of death. County shows up, then you show up, they left."

Sam flipped to the next page, and continued reading. "About five a JoAnne Dole and a Laura Jones arrive. Laura is the dead girl's mother. Got into a row with the paramedics because they weren't doing anything and wouldn't let her near the scene. Her words, not mine."

Yeah, if it had been his child, cold on the ground,

no one doing anything, no one helping, everyone keeping him from cradling her in his arms, he would have been tearing up the turf.

"Finally a Mimi Yreka." Sam adjusted his long legs, trying to find more room where there wasn't any.

"Did you ask everyone about Amanda?"

One ahead of Bishop, Sam nodded. "Amanda had only come once before. Blossom brought her. The others thought they had met at the University. Everyone said she was a nice girl, but they didn't seem to like her much."

"Why do you say that?"

"Oh, the way they frowned when they said her name, shook their heads, pursed their lips in disapproval."

Sam was getting it – people lied.

"So where do we start?"

Bishop would have liked to have started with Amanda. She was the one who broke the dynamics of the group. But with no last name and no address he couldn't go knocking on the door of every Amanda in the city who drove a red car. No, he'd have to wait. He'd find her. Or she'd find him. "Family first." That had been Frank's mantra. They had the most to lose, they had the most to gain.

CHAPTER FIVE

A dark van heading out of town, the windows tinted darker than was legal, and blowing thick, black smoke from the exhaust, passed them a little too close. Sam coughed and waved the smoke away from his face. Bishop tilted his head to get a better look in the side mirror as it pulled away. The chassis hung low from a heavy load. A bicycle tied to the back, its wheels spinning yet going nowhere, retreated from them.

Another vehicle approached, the wind rocked a chair roped onto the roof as if a ghost rode along with them. Like the other vehicle, it rode low with a heavy load, but its windows weren't as dark. Bishop could see the driver, older and heavy-set . When the car passed, the driver recognized Bishop and averted his eyes. A face pressed against a side window looked out. Bishop recognized the twelve-year-old going-on-adult peering out the window. When the first day of warm weather had melted the snow, the rental next door had seemed to burst its seams with kids. He'd caught that one in his garage clearing out the backlog of beer bottles Bishop had meant to take to recycling. They'd split the redemption money, then Bishop had given the kid five bucks for helping clean out the rest of the garage.

Odd time to be leaving. Even with the planting done there was plenty of farm work around the area. Someone must have whispered immigration enforcement. Not one of the city boys. They didn't check id's. Not unless there was an arrest. Before Bishop could consider what else might have spooked the itinerate workers, the car radio crackled.

"10-33 Garfield and Main." Shirley's voice, always calm and efficient, told not just them, but any officer on duty, and any civilian bothering to listen to the police band. Both of them recognized the address – the Garfield Falls State Bank.

Sam shook his head. "That's the third false alarm in two weeks."

"Maybe this time it's a real alarm." Bishop didn't believe himself.

"They should be fined." Sam glared out the window. "It costs the city a lot of money to check out a false alarm and..." he paused for dramatic effect, "...it takes manpower off the streets. We don't have nearly enough officers as is."

"Are you running for public office?"

"No, I'm just saying if the Chief's wife didn't work there it would be a different story."

But the Chief's wife did work there, and that was the story.

Sam's phone rang. "Yeah." There were several long pauses followed by nods of the head and affirming yeahs. Finally Sam snapped the phone shut. "Shirley was wondering if we'd swing by the bank until the Chief gets there. Shouldn't take long."

"Morris is up." Although Bishop often worked multiple cases, officers didn't normally pick up two cases at the same time.

"Called in sick."

Bishop shrugged off the inconvenience. There wouldn't be much to do. Filing a report for a false alarm didn't take long. The radio hissed Bishop's code as officer in charge.

A few seconds later the phone in Bishop's pocket rang. As he flipped it open he noted the number. The Chief.

"Morris can handle the 10-33, probably another false alarm."

"Called in sick."

There was a long pause. "How's that crime scene going? The dead witch talk to you?"

The muscles along Bishop's back tightened. He never knew if the Chief was serious or making fun of him. He wished that he'd never told his superior the dead seemed to speak directly to him, but the Chief hadn't always been in charge, once he and Bishop had worked cases together. If it hadn't been for the Chief ... Bishop pushed the thought aside. He owed the man.

"Did you sense anything suspicious? Don't want

you to leave before you're done."

"No, we're already heading into town."

"Can't have you taking all the cases there, Bishop, now can I?"

Bishop could almost hear the Chief weighing his options.

"I'm a little indisposed here, but I won't be long."

It didn't take much to envision his boss, sitting in the bathroom with his morning paper and the first cigarette of the day.

"You tell Jackie I'll be there as soon as I'm finished. She left a little mess here I have to take care of." There was that edge of annoyance in the Chief's voice. That exasperated, irritated, acceptance of the long married.

Bishop didn't want to know.

"Then I want you right back on that witch case."

When they arrived, Bishop expected to stroll in and have everything fading back to normal. He expected a cup of fresh coffee and a sweet roll for his troubles. Instead four extra patrol cars were in the lot. A large officer, his skin the shade of the coffee Bishop had been expecting motioned them to go around back. A short officer, his skin a sallow hue of ethnicity and the same shade as Bishop's disappointment at the lost cup of coffee, let them in. Jefferson and Muttley, where you found one, you found the other.

They walked, as usual, Muttley talked.

"The Chief's wife arrived at seven-thirty, same time she arrives every day. She didn't notice a man hiding in the bushes. He shoved her inside. Made her unlock the vault. She did what she was told. Gave him the money. He locked her in, then left. Bank president, a Gregg Outtmann, got here a few minutes later, Mrs. Johnson called him, and he set off the alarm. By the time the patrol got here the robber was long gone with a duffle full of money. No one's saying how much, and it's not my place to ask, but from the way they're acting it wasn't just a few pennies."

While they'd walked through the bank, and Muttley had filled them in, Bishop had assessed the situation. The lobby was full of cops, milling about, talking in hushed whispers of speculation. As employees arrived they were escorted to the back break room and held there.

"Where's Mrs. Johnson?" He never called her that. It was Jackie. He'd caught the garter at her wedding to the Chief. He'd held her hand when the Chief had flipped his car in a high-speed chase and lay unconscious in the hospital for two days. Just last summer he'd cooked burgers on their grill.

"Her office."

The blinds were drawn. Without hesitation Bishop knocked on the glass. Jackie opened the door. She was expecting someone else. He could tell by the flash of her eyes. Of course, she was expecting the Chief. Instead she got him.

"Bishop? I thought ..." She smiled, a quick cover my faux pas smile, "I'm glad to see you. I can't believe all this is happening. What are you doing here?" She looked behind him and Sam nodded at her, his hands thrust deep into his pockets.

"The Chief called, said he'd be here as soon as he could. He had a mess to clean up."

There was a flicker of a smile, that sanctimonious smile women get when they are right and you are wrong. Whatever caused the smile, Jackie let it go, and turned back into her office. The place suited her. It was neither small and unassuming, nor large and pretentious. The darker tones of the woodwork and desk matched the creamy black of her skin. Here and there bold flashes of color caught your eye, just as the shiny gold blouse beneath her boxy, navy jacket did. Or the bright white, lacquered bracelet that matched her normally bright smile.

"Are you all right?" He cared. She had been Teonna's friend. He would not forget that when others had condemned Teonna as a home wrecker, Jackie had stood by her.

"Of course."

She sat, her back to him, busily shutting down her computer and turning papers over. Privacy. Bishop understood. To avoid accidently reading the pages she was turning over, not for any other reason, he scanned the array of pictures and awards on the far wall. His gaze found Jackie's diploma. Masters in Banking. Summa Cum Laude. Only the snapshot wasn't there. Wasn't tucked in the corner where it always was, where it always had been. Taken when Jackie had graduated college. Teonna and Jackie, sorority sisters in their caps and gowns, laughing, arm and arm. Salt and Pepper. Two sassy girls ready to take on the world. Only sometimes the world won. He reached for the frame. What was he doing? What was he thinking? He wasn't. He stopped himself, and straightened the frame underneath, the one of her little two-seater airplane. A pale baby blue, like the Chief's eyes, Jackie was quick to tell anyone who commented on the color.

Everything put away, turned over, and turned off, still Jackie kept fussing at her desk. Bishop turned back to her, away from the missing photo, and the hollowness its absence left in his stomach. "It's easier if you talk about it." Not that he ever talked about Teonna. He reached for her hand, but unexpectedly, she jerked it away.

"I need to make coffee." She stood, the abruptness of her movement knocked over her desk chair. Before it hit the floor, Bishop caught it with one hand, and reached out to steady her with the other. Her skin was cold, and he could feel a tremble. That would be the adrenaline, first too much, now not enough. Her blood sugars would be low.

"I'll meet you in Gregg's office."

He didn't have to be told to get lost, that she didn't want to come undone in front of him. She fled the room, leaving Bishop to follow. He paused in the lobby. Among the mindless churning of police officers and bank employees, Sam hung back in a zone of stillness.

"Forensics here yet?"

Sam shook his head. "Everything's waiting on the Chief."

Bishop nodded. If he were still on a beat, he

would be as well. The Chief wasn't the kind of man you second guessed. "Get everyone's name and phone number. Find out where they were and what route they took to work. See if anyone's missing. If someone called in sick. On vacation. Post an officer at every exit." He paused, he shouldn't have to say it. "And remind everyone not to touch anything." Bishop pulled the only twenty from his wallet. "Have someone pick up something with a lot of sugar in it."

Sam straightened to his full height and stepped toward a female employee, an attractive blonde with a cute Cupid's bow mouth. She certainly looked sweet.

The woman looked up, and up, at Sam.

"How tall are you?" Her voice had that edge of breathiness that revealed she was interested in more than just his height.

Some men got irritated at being asked the same question over and over again. Obviously Sam was tall, but he had turned it into a plus. "Six-four, right at the legal limit."

"Legal limit? What do you mean?"

Sam bent down, sharing an easy, even smile. "Maximum height for a police officer in Garfield Falls. Any more than that and you'd have to put me under arrest."

She giggled, her gaze still on his face. "I don't have any handcuffs."

"You could use mine." They both laughed.

"Why don't I show you where the nearest donut shop is?" She smiled, and led the way to the door. "I've never ridden in a police car before."

Satisfied that Sam would have no trouble getting some sugar Bishop walked the few feet to the president's office. The blinds were open revealing a conservative, somber decor, likely chosen by a decorator to reinforce conservative bank president, than personalized with an array of football trophies and plaques. Bishop had meet Gregg Outtmann at one of the Chief's back yard parties. Jackie hadn't liked him much. Bishop doubted too many of the other guests had noticed. But he noticed these things. It was an occupational hazard.

As Outtmann talked on the phone, or more listened, he kept shaking his head in disagreement. He didn't appear to be your typical bank president. In fact he looked as if he'd just stepped off a campaign bus, all white teeth in an I'm your best friend forever smile, and thick, wavy hair a little too long, but not so long as anyone would be offended. He was young, closer to Sam's age than what Bishop would have thought a man responsible for millions of dollars would be. A man watching over other people's money should be old, and cautious, and stoop shouldered.

When Bishop entered the office, Outtmann hung up the phone. As if on cue, Jackie entered from the other door. She carried a coffee mug that said World's Best Dad. When she handed the mug to Outtmann his hand shook, but hers was steady as a rock. It hadn't taken her long to get it back together. Guess being married to a cop toughened you up.

She nodded seriously at Mr. Outtmann. "I'll go cancel my vacation. I can't leave with all this going on.

Maybe I can still get some of the deposits back." She said the last to the air rather than her boss, but the bank president was quick to jump in and naysay.

"No, no, Jackie, all you've talked about for months has been this trip, when the FBI get here everything will be fine."

Who exactly had called the FBI?

Bishop knew he should keep his mouth shut, the Chief would ask all the questions when he got there. He asked anyway. "The FBI are on their way?"

"Of course. When I called my insurance company they insisted the FBI be called in."

"You've already talked to your insurance company?"

"As soon as I realized there had been a robbery. And considering the amount of money taken." His hand shook, swaying the liquid in his mug so that Bishop wondered if it would slosh over and spoil his expensive suit. Before it did, Outtmann lowered the cup. "Bishop?" The bank manger knit his brow as if trying to remember a science equation he learned long ago. "Didn't you play ball with the Rock?"

As if there was only one.

Jackie's lips thinned. "Gregg is a big fan." Her voice held an edge of annoyance.

Was she always annoyed at her boss or was it his talking football when they should be talking robbery.

Outtmann stood and pointed to a photo. The big quarterback was shaking hands with a star-struck teenager in full uniform. "Helped me get a scholarship, then I blow out my knee. Had to study after that." He laughed, a self-deprecating laugh. "Not that it matters when your grandfather owns a bank."

The last person Bishop ever wanted to talk about was Rock. After an awkward silence they stopped looking at the photos. "About the robbery ..."

"You want to know how much?" Outtmann filled in for him.

Bishop didn't really care. The amount didn't matter, be it ten dollars or ten million dollars, a bank robbery wasn't the same as robbing a convenience store. It was big time, with big prison sentences, and the FBI had jurisdiction – if they bothered to come.

"I'm not certain."

They never were, at least that's what they said. Bishop didn't doubt the man could have opened his ledger and told him to the penny.

Outtmann avoided Bishop's gaze and looked wistfully back at the photos. "You see we were a distribution point for several of the small banks.

"What's that? A distribution point? You mean the money's sent here and then you send it on?"

Outtmann opened his mouth to explain when Jackie gave her head a light shake and he stopped. Seemingly satisfied that her boss wasn't going to spill any banking secrets, she flashed a smile Bishop's direction, the kind of smile a teacher gives a student for good effort but clearly says you're wrong, and annoying me. "It's all banking stuff, you won't understand." As if to soften that she'd backhandedly inferred he was stupid, she added on, "Unless you want to take a few classes in accounting."

Bishop let it drop. The last thing he wanted to do was look at a ledger book with lists of dollars and dates. Let the Chief sort it out. He fought his growing impatience for the Chief to arrive. There was nothing for him to do here. Watch Outtmann drink coffee? The pull of the young witch lying on the cold ground strengthened the longer he ignored her, like trying not to think of pink elephants. And waiting to be dismissed wasn't finding her killer, or improving the mood that had settled on him like a dark cloud of smoke.

CHAPTER SIX

You could feel the atmosphere change when the Chief arrived. He came barreling through the door all lanky muscle and attitude. The artificial lights gave his pale skin a slightly yellow cast and the top of his closely shaved head, where the hair had gone from thin to non-existent, picked up a shine.

"Honey." As if she were a rag doll, he wrapped his wife into his bear arms, crushing her starched linen jacket as he lifted her. Her carefully managed mass of wiry curls bounced and her shoes nearly fell off her feet. Then he let her drop. "You're fine?" He ran his hand down her shoulders and back in jerky movements full of energy, reassuring both her and himself. Perhaps because she was in front of her boss she didn't nestle into him the way Bishop expected a frightened wife would.

She stood a little apart, patting her curls back into place, not at all upset. "Yes. It's all your fault."

She pursed her lips. "If I hadn't been thinking about our trip I'd have seen him." She lightly leaned against the desk, her hands gripping the slick mahogany wood. "I was daydreaming about being together," she turned her head toward the Chief, "on those hot, sandy beaches." Her eyes were bright. They stared at each other. "I should have been paying attention, especially today, but I wasn't, I just kept thinking of all those pesky details that needed wrapping up."

"You should have let me worry about them."

"Yes, well, what's done is done." Jackie nodded, a flash of something crossed her face? Bishop wasn't sure. She held the Chief's gaze, the way old married couples do in a kind of private code. The way he and Claire once had. Uncomfortable, as if he'd caught the Chief with his pants down, Bishop looked away.

Jackie finally broke the gaze, her eyes less intense, and spoke to the air. "I'm sorry, honey, I'm going to have to cancel the trip, I can't leave right now. The insurance company is sure to ask a lot of questions. It could turn into a nightmare of paperwork."

"No, no, you go." Outtmann stood and Bishop noticed that he spoke to the Chief rather than Jackie, the way men in power talk only to other men in power. "We can handle this without your wife."

Bishop reached for the office door. They could handle it without him as well.

"You two have been planning your vacation for a long time. Virna can take care of everything." The bank president glanced at Jackie. "A robbery can happen at any time. You didn't know the special shipment was coming in today."

Bishop paused, his hand on the doorknob. Special shipment didn't mean ledger books. You didn't have to know accounting to know a special shipment to a distribution point meant money, more money than usual. Before he could form a question there was a light knock on the door. The pretty teller Sam had left with came in carrying a square, white, pastry box. Her face finally bumped a memory to the surface and Bishop connected her with the judgmental woman that would call to let him know he had overdrafted and needed to put money into his account, like he could find money lying around between paydays. He hoped she and Sam hadn't sparked anything between them.

The Chief's attention, diverted by the promise of breakfast, focused on the pastry box. He released his gorilla grip from around Jackie's waist and made a beeline for the donuts and sweet rolls. Always the flirt, he grinned at the girl, letting his hand brush hers as he took the offered food. The teller jerked her hand back, glancing at Jackie, before swiftly retreating. Putting the box on the desk, the Chief opened the pristine white lid. After a swift inspection, he picked out the gooiest sticky roll there, and eagerly bit into it as if he hadn't eaten for days.

"We'll let the FBI decide what we should do, honey. If they say it's okay for us to go on our trip we'll go, if not, we won't." The Chief's tongue caught a dribble of caramel sauce that was sliding down his chin and helped it into his mouth. "No reason to jump before the explosion. You know how hard it is for us to get time off together. Maybe a year or more before it happens again."

Bishop seemed to remember they'd had a vacation together just last fall, and with Jackie and the Chief both being pilots they often disappeared for a day of flying, or a long weekend to their cabin in the mountains. But he kept his mouth shut.

Outtmann came around the desk and peered into the pastry box. He helped himself to a donut with a glaze of what passed as chocolate frosting. Everyone except Bishop seemed to have forgotten that they were there to learn about the robbery, not munch donuts and discuss the weather.

"Who knew about the special delivery?" Bishop asked and all eyes stared silently at him as if he had made some social faux pas.

Finally, Outtmann remembered that they were there to solve a crime not have a donut and coffee party. "I never let anyone know when a special shipment is being delivered. Too big a chance someone will let something slip and invite a robbery." He smiled at his own cleverness. "I even get up early and come in myself to meet the truck."

"So you were here when the robbery occurred?"

"No. God, no. The shipment came in about five. When they left I locked the bags in the vault and went home. Took the kid's to school. Came back about seven-thirty. I must have missed the robber by minutes."

"So who set off the alarm?" Bishop knew Muttley had said it was Outtmann.

"Well, I'm not sure. Jackie's always the first one here. I just assumed that she'd turned them off when she came in. Especially after two false alarms last week. If it wasn't for the Chief here intervening we'd have a hell of a fine." The men exchanged that good-old-boy you scratch my back I'll scratch yours smile. "Never thought a thing about it, just went into my office. The phone rings and there's Jackie. 'I'm in the vault,' she says. Calm as a balance sheet. My wife would have been hysterical locked in the vault."

Jackie touched Outtmann's shoulder. "It was only for a few minutes." Was her voice reassuring the way one would a child? Or a lover? Bishop glanced at the Chief who didn't notice, busy instead looking around for the source of the coffee.

"You called Outtmann? From the vault?"

Before she'd called the Chief?

Jackie pulled her cell phone out of her neatly pleated, white skirt pocket. "Never go anywhere without it."

"And the first thing you do is call the bank president?" Bishop didn't care if he appeared obtuse, this wasn't making sense.

"Well, the Chief here didn't pick up." She gave her husband a good-natured jab to the ribs.

"I was busy, darling. Had a mess to clean up." His pale blue eyes looked into her dark brown ones, held an instant, then looked away finding Bishop. Suddenly he was all business. "You got work to do, boy, other cases. Tell you what, you leave Sam here to coordinate with the FBI. Take that new guy with you if you need any help."

The new guy? Sergio? Bishop hadn't met him yet. Knew he'd come from downstairs, knew he'd spent some time in the hospital after being outed during an undercover bust, knew he had family connections to the mayor. Feeling dismissed after a headmaster's reprove, Bishop took Sam's memo pad, the names and addresses of the witches clearly legible in Sam's careful block letters and left everyone to his donuts.

CHAPTER SEVEN

Although he'd told Sam family first, Bishop swung south to the heart of the city. One address had jumped out at him. One address he knew by heart. One place he needed to stop at without anyone tagging along.

Downtown was changing. Where elegant three-story pseudo gothic houses had stood for a hundred years there were now three story office buildings. Except for one. Sandwiched between the glass and brick offices sat an old family dwelling clinging to her dignity. A bit of grass on each side separated her from the bustle of commerce, and the last bit of lawn for a mile any direction gave comfort to inner city souls.

He took the back alley to a gravel turn-off that served as a parking lot, nosing the Subaru against a high wooden fence he'd help build around the house's large backyard and tiny garden. It'd been an attempt to protect the house's occupants from wandering eyes and trespassers of other sorts. Several boards were missing leaving Bishop to doubt the fence's effectiveness. He forced himself to walk past. Not his problem.

Parked parallel in the street, blocking anyone from passing, was an old, beat-up pick-up with scaffolding jutting out the back. The gate stood open, a short man with a large straw hat covering his thick, wavy, black hair came out carrying an armload of broken shingles. Although it wasn't hot, the man's face was shiny with sweat and oil. He noticed Bishop, but didn't make eye contact, shifting his gaze as he passed. He hefted the debris he was carrying into a dumpster that the city had to have put there for the construction waste, then returned to the yard for more. Several men were on the three story shelter house's roof. Like dark spiders they scrambled across the steep incline, some pulling off old shingles, some hammering down new. Two men stood precariously by the chimney, one nodding as the other talked and gestured with his hammer.

Hannah must have found a new benefactor, someone generous enough to donate a new roof. His first instinct was to ask for a few days off, supervise the work. They certainly didn't know what they were doing. Better to pull all the old shingles down before putting on the new. He could show them how to flash a chimney, and how to lay shingles around the cupola, but he stopped himself before his thoughts went too far. It was just that kind of cowboy to the rescue that kept getting him into trouble. He reached into his pocket and ran his finger over the teeth of a key hanging on his key ring, the one to the nine-pin dead bolt on the open gate. He should return it, that one and the one to the side door, the door that led to an inside stair straight down into Hannah's little basement sitting area and bedroom.

Inside the backyard two children, too young to be in school, played keep-away with a yellow mongrel dog. All three stopped to stare at him, watching as he stayed on the uneven concrete sidewalk and went to the back door. Unlike the front with its wide veranda, the back had a little concrete step. He knocked even though he had the key to that door in his pocket as well.

Hannah opened the door, but left the screen between them. She was just as he remembered. Tall, lush, well-rounded in the way that made a man want to cradle her softness in his hands. Her thick, wavy hair was pulled back in a fancy braided bun but loose strands fell in wisps around her face inviting you to gaze into her large, dark eyes, and lean into those full lips.

"Vincent." Her voice was cold, formal, each syllable of his name sounded flat and even as if they were two words.

He answered back in the same formal tone, like a cowboy tipping his hat. "Hannah."

She craned her neck to look behind him.

"Where's Sam?"

"On another case." He waited for her to look at him. When she finally did, when her eyes finally looked into his, he saw the anger, cold and hard as winter ice.

"So this is business."

They both knew it was business. He hadn't talked to her about anything except business since he'd found the closet door open and that beautiful, white, beaded wedding dress hanging there. The dress he instantly knew she intended to wear at their wedding. The wedding he didn't know about. The one he'd never hinted at. That she had just assumed would happen after he'd spent so many nights there.

He wondered what the magic number had been. Twenty? Thirty?

He'd stayed more than that.

Hannah had made it easy to stay with little jobs to do around the place, home-cooked meals, her arms inviting, her bed soft. His house had been a long drive away, empty, with cold memories waiting at the end.

It would have been easy to drift into marriage.

Maybe he should have. He didn't need much room, all his memories in a cigar box. They could have continued to live at the shelter house. Yet somehow it had felt wrong. How many years would they have drifted, neither in love, just taking the easy path for both of them? What if someone else had come along? He snipped the thought before it could bud, and then blossom into full blown guilt. He'd dug in that garden before.

He hoped Hannah had been able to get her money back on the dress.

"I need to talk to Keisha Michaels. She lists this as

her address."

Hannah stepped back and let him into the large kitchen. A woman sat at a massive table that could seat twelve if all the insets were in place. Today it would seat eight. Unusual not to have a full house.

"Go ask Keisha to come down."

"I could go up." He moved toward the stairs. He liked seeing where a suspect lived. It told him more than a laundry list of questions could.

But Hannah was right there, blocking him. "No, better that you stay out of the bedrooms, won't want anyone saying you'd taken advantage of them."

That hurt like a knife between the ribs. He'd never gotten the impression that Hannah had been unwilling. Everything had been fine between them until that damn dress had appeared.

But Bishop backed-off letting Hannah corral him in the kitchen and send the woman for Keisha. While he waited to noticed that Hannah's favorite mug, creamy-white, the last of an old set of stoneware sat on the table, a newspaper folded open to the society page next to it. Although the words were upside-down he read the bold type. Financier weds in surprise Vegas ceremony. The photo had been folded back so all he could see was the edge of a lacy veil. Since when had Hannah cared about the society page? His gaze trailed down to the smaller type. Nick Jordon weds writer ...

Hannah scooped up the paper and thrust a mug of coffee into his hands. A donation with the business logo Bishop & Bishop Architects decaled on the side.

Not his old mug, not the heavy one the ladies didn't like, but that seemed to fit in his hand. That one was gone. Not in the cupboard, not in the sink to be washed.

CHAPTER EIGHT

Keisha Michaels came down the stairs. He didn't remember her from that morning, but then he hadn't talked to any of the witnesses. He wasn't sure how he'd expected a witch to look, someone either young and beautiful, or old and haggard. This woman was neither. She had to be close to his age, early forties. Neatly dressed, like any other professional woman, in dark slacks, creamy blouse and a bold scarf. When she reached for the herbal tea Hannah handed her, the sparkle of too many rings flashed at him.

"So you're Vincent?"

Bishop cursed himself. He shouldn't have come alone. It looked as if he was checking on Hannah instead of following through on a case. If he'd wanted to see where he and Hannah stood, wanted to kiss and make-up, he would have come weeks, no, months ago.

He corrected Keisha hoping that would put an end to either woman's speculations. "Detective

Bishop. I'd like to ask you a few questions about this morning."

Keisha made bold eye contact. "I'm a witch. I have been one for years. There are no laws against it. We have a right to gather together and celebrate the Goddess."

Like he cared. He had a dead girl who shouldn't be dead. He'd like to know why.

"Please sit down." He kept his voice flat, impartial.

In annoyance she glared at him then at Hannah. Bishop turned to Hannah as well, planting his feet, giving her his formal police voice with its strong even tones. "If you could give us a few moments."

She didn't like that, the flash of displeasure across her eyes would have been hidden to most people, but he knew all her looks, from the scowl of irritation to the sigh of satisfaction. "No, I'll stay."

Now she was being contrary like a tired child – or a jilted lover. He couldn't make her leave any more than he could stop the irritation building within himself. She sat. Except for the muffled hammering two stories above them the room fell into silence. For a moment Keisha swayed indecisively, finally sitting across from Hannah.

Bishop remained standing. "Tell me about Blossom Jones."

Keisha took a sip of tea. "What do you want to know?"

He always liked the truth, no embellishing, no editorializing, just the truth, plain and simple.

"How long have you known her?"

"A few years."

He looked for the connection. "You were members of the same coven?"

"Yes."

"You were meeting with other witches to celebrate..." Sam had told him this, "...Beltane"

"Yes. May Day. The fertility of the land. Asking the goddess to join with the earth and the sky to bring bounty to the sown seeds and blessings to her followers."

He didn't understand. "Like a spell?"

"No. Not a spell." She shot back as if he were stupid.

That made the second time this morning a woman had implied he was stupid.

"Witchcraft isn't like that, all old Hollywood, chanting and candles and frantic dancing."

"Then what's it like?"

"We're not supposed to talk about it. The blessings won't work if you dissipate the power by talking about the rituals to non-believers."

She said it with piqued force and he accepted her defensive rebuttal. Like telling an atheist your prayers, at best they would mock you. "So, no chanting, no dancing, no candles." Except there had been candles, and Blossom had been dancing.

"Tell him when you got there." Hannah directed the woman.

"I got there? Oh, it must have been around four-thirty."

Hannah nodded encouragingly. "You left around three-thirty, so that's right."

Bishop mentally calculated the distance. Without traffic, and how much traffic was there after the bars closed down and before the laborers had to leave for work, she could have been to the field by four.

"Yes. I left here about three-thirty. I took the gravel road and parked behind the grove. I was already in my robe. Who was going to see me? So I usually drive in my robe and take clothes for later."

Hannah gave the woman the kind of pleased smile you give a four year old that's mastered some petty skill. "Then what did you do?"

Keisha gave the barest of nods, slightly dipping her chin. "I started getting things out of the back, things for the celebration. Flowers and candles and a fire-extinguisher. I always bring a fire-extinguisher, just in case. Then I heard a scream. I asked what was wrong."

Asked who?

Bishop touched his coffee mug to his lips but never actually took a sip. His gaze never wavered from Keisha's face. They had rehearsed this.

He waited, no prompts, letting the silence grow into a presence.

Hannah gave his line, cuing Keisha. "What did you do after you heard the scream?"

"I ran down to the circle."

"What did you see?" Hannah kept going.

"Blossom was on the ground. Amanda was kneeling over her and pushing on her chest. Then I screamed."

The woman's words were flat and without feeling as she watched Hannah's face to be sure she was telling the story right.

"Then I ran back to the car and got my phone. I called 911. Amanda ran past me. I told her to stop. To wait." She finally looked at Bishop. Her eyes clouded with horror. "I told her to wait. But she got in her car and drove away."

That part was true.

"I heard the sirens, so I went down to the road and directed them to the circle."

He finally spoke. "Just you?"

Her body tensed. "Just me."

"Everyone else was late?"

"I was early."

"But Amanda and Blossom were earlier."

Hannah turned and scowled at him, her face clearly saying he was playing semantics just so he could win.

He changed tacks. "Who else is in the coven? We'll need to speak to all of them."

"She just told you what happened."

He wanted to growl that the woman had told him nothing except a carefully rehearsed script she and Hannah had concocted. Why they had concocted it he couldn't fathom. Unless Keisha had something to hide.

Keisha leaned away from him, her feet suddenly turning toward the door. "We're a small group. We only get together for special feast days. I don't know them that well." She gestured with her hands, the motion drawing Bishop's gaze to the array of rings on her fingers. Every finger had a ring, some even had two. Her right thumb had a thick silver band with large etchings of vines or maybe they were branches.

"How many?"

"What?"

"In your group – coven?" He wanted out of there. He'd come back with Sam if he needed to talk to Keisha again.

"Sssix."

Suddenly alert he tried not to show his interest. Had she been about to say seven, or had she stumbled over the beginning of the word?

"Their names?"

"That nice officer," Keisha emphasized nice, "took all our names."

"He's on another case."

Pursing her lips, she listed off the coven members, tapping the tip of a finger with each name. "Blossom, Laura, Joann,"

She faltered.

"Mimi, Amanda and myself."

"Amanda's new. How long has she been with the group?"

Keisha's shoulders flicked back in disapproval. "She came with Blossom a few months ago. They met at the University. No one liked her. She didn't understand what witchcraft was truly about. She claimed she could do... spells. You know, force people to do things against their will. That's not witchcraft, that's voodoo, or black magic, or something. NOT witchcraft."

He got it.

"So Blossom and Amanda arrived early." It was his turn to ask the questions. "They'd already placed candles around the firepit. They were holding candles."

She flinched as if he'd pricked her with a needle.

"What were they doing?"

"I don't know."

Bishop feigned exasperation, letting his presence dominate the room. "They lit a red candle and began chanting and dancing."

Love or money Frank always said. Bishop had a fifty-fifty chance of being right. Money was green. Red must be love. "They were casting a love spell."

Keisha's eyes shot anger at Hannah, but Hannah shook her head denying any betrayal and reached out to touch the woman's hand.

No, Hannah hadn't told him.

"Who was she casting the spell on?"

"I don't know."

He didn't believe her.

"I have his sock. Part of his sock. It'll have his DNA all over it. You're telling me who will just save time and taxpayer dollars." The lies rolled off his tongue like spring rain fell from the sky. Even if they could get DNA off the sock they needed something to compare it to. And as far as he knew burning someone's sock wasn't a criminal offense.

The silence ticked. She looked everywhere but at Bishop.

Hannah stood, coming between Bishop and the woman. "If she knew anything she'd tell you." But he side-stepped Hannah and leaned over the table suddenly taller than his six-feet, no inches.

"It was Amanda's idea, wasn't it?"

Keisha took a deep breath, her chest lifting and falling, finally the anger erupting. "Of course it was. That girl was no good. She had an old book. Claimed it was her great-great-grandmother's and that it had special spells. Spells for love, and money, and, and anything you'd want."

"And Blossom wanted a love spell?"

"Yes."

"Why?"

"There was someone she met at the university. Someone married."

"Who?"

"I don't know. After she met Amanda, things changed. They turned against me. Everyone whispered about spells that would make them happy. It wasn't right. That's not how it works."

"Who was there with Blossom and Amanda?"

Keisha opened her mouth, then closed it. "No one."

"No one else wanted a love spell?"

"No."

Her eyes flashed to Hannah. Bishop turned, but not quick enough to see what might have been written on her face. Could Hannah have been there? Is that what they were hiding? Hannah resorting to witchcraft to bring him back? That made him as angry as the dress had. In defiance, Hannah folded her arms across her chest. You can't make me tell you her stance declared.

He banked his anger, as he had several months ago, lying in bed, staring at the virginal white dress. He'd gotten up, gotten dressed, leaving the anger to starve, knowing if he didn't feed it, it would lose its heat and turn to ash.

"If I have more questions I'll come back." Bisýÿÿÿ hop placed his untouched mug of coffee in the sink. When he reached the door he heard Hannah hiss at Keisha.

"Tell him."

Bishop paused.

"He'll get a letter."

He turned.

"No, tell him." A smug smile grew in triumph on Hannah's face. Keisha stared at the tea in her cup, talking to the rim of the mug instead of him. "The rent's been raised."

For an instant he didn't understand. "Who's rent?"

Hannah lifted her eyebrows in self-satisfaction. "Everyone's rent."

He knew the shelter house owned properties all over town. Rent more than contributions kept them open. Still he felt the betrayal of not owning Teonna's house. Her will had left the property to the Big Sister's Shelter, not to him. Another week and they would have been wed. Another week and everything that was hers would have been theirs. As was, nothing was his. Her family came in taking everything, her jewelry, her clothes, her perfume. Everything except the memories.

Only Jackie had stood up for him. Fought for him when he couldn't fight for himself. While he was in the hospital she had made sure they hadn't emptied the house of his things. She'd demanded they return the furniture, claiming it was his. Using her influence at the bank she'd gotten deposits waived and his name on the lease so that he had a place to go to after he was released. If not for Jackie all that he would have had left from his brief time with Teonna would have been two pillows.

Keisha must have sensed his pain. "When I moved in ... I'm a realtor." Her pride straightened her spine. Although Bishop hadn't questioned it, she justified being at the shelter house among the homeless.

"My husband took off, left me all the debt. I hadn't sold anything in three years when Hannah found me and the kids sleeping in the car." She paused, there was more, but she stopped herself. "I didn't have a choice." Her posture relaxed and she let a sigh escape. "It was a blessing in disguise. For both of us. Hannah helped me, I've been helping Hannah."

"We're incorporated now." Hannah informed him, a note of gloat in her voice, pushing it into his face that she hadn't consulted him first, like she once had about everything from changing a lock to re-shingling a roof. "It's for tax purposes. Nothing you'd understand."

"How much?"

She smiled like one of those smug girls his mother would pair him with, the ones who knew he had to make nice because their fathers were important and paying full tuition. "One hundred ..."

Bishop winced.

"... and fifty."

Things were too tight already. Rather than lay-off any officers, the city had frozen salaries, except no one had told the gas station, or the grocery store, to stop raising prices.

"It's just good business." Keisha defended the action. "Hannah hasn't raised rents in years. Not just at your house, but any of them."

Now he understood, it didn't matter that everyone's rent was increased, that was just a smoke screen, Hannah had struck at him the only way she could.

"There are expenses," she informed him.

Like a new roof. He couldn't begrudge her a new roof. Still, wishing Hannah would find a new person to hate, he closed the door behind him.

CHAPTER NINE

Bishop glanced at his watch. It was that tween time. He was tired and hungry, but the case was too young to leave. He'd wasted his hours, first at the bank then at Hannah's thinking... thinking what? That she'd go back to where they were? That she'd missed him as much as he'd missed her. But he hadn't missed her. Rarely even thought of her. He'd missed sleeping in her clean sheets after easy sex. He'd missed eating food that hadn't come out of a box. He missed puttering around the shelter house playing handyman.

Backing the Subaru down the alley, he left all thoughts of Hannah behind. It was too early for the lab to have any results. He needed to talk to the other women in the coven. He needed about eight hours of sleep just to catch up from the four he'd missed the night before. And a beer. A beer would taste good right about now. Bishop scratched between his fingers and called the station.

"Dispatch." It was Shirley. He could tell by the clip of her voice.

"Bishop. Where's Sergio?"

"Said he was tired of waiting for you and went to the firing range."

Not a good start. A rookie waited, he didn't go off to the firing range, even if he already had a few years in another department.

"Did he find an address for Blossom' father?"

"He said, to tell you, it was on your desk."

From the way she told him, those little hesitations, Sergio had said a whole lot more. Bishop knew better than to get angry with the messenger. He let his voice drop into a deeper register. The women in dispatch knew him and he knew them, at least they knew each other's voices. He let his voice rumble with testosterone. "He wouldn't have left that address with you, now would he?"

He could hear her smile at his flirting. "You do remember I'm married?"

He never knew.

Papers rustled. "Father's out of the country. Has been for weeks. Won't be back until June."

Bishop shook his head. Maybe Sergio should have called him with that information.

"I'm headed to ..." Bishop stared down at the address Sam had given him for the mother and relayed it to dispatch. "Maybe Sergio has the time to meet me there."

Taking the main road north, Bishop felt a wave of

nostalgia as he drove. He knew the address. Maybe not that house exactly, but that part of town. It had been part of his first patrol, 7 p.m. to 4 a.m., Thursday through Sunday. The neighborhood had consisted of clusters of small one-family homes, and a handful of owner-operator businesses, surrounding an original pioneer church, its thin, white steeple standing the test of time and sins. Back then the area had been a thriving business center, the still vibrant core of a small town before it was swallowed up by one of Garfield Falls many expansions.

He turned right and right again. Everything was different now. Large earth moving equipment roared through the yards like a wild boar in the Black Forest, toppling trees and tearing up driveways. He watched as little houses shuddered, then fell, disappearing beneath the onslaught of a bulldozer brigade. Everywhere he looked deconstruction greeted him. A crane swung its heavy ball at the old mechanic's bay sending dirt and decade's old debris crumbling into the pit beneath the repair hoist. The two-story clapboard house behind the once busy gas station fell and a metal swing-set twisted beneath the wheels of the unfaltering machinery.

Half a mile away you could still hear the noise and see the dust. Bishop pulled into the driveway of a charming World War II tract house. The solid little home bought on low interest offered to veterans only, and built from limited pre-approved floor plans. Two pear trees balanced the lawn and flowerbeds flanked the front walkway, a profusion of tulips replacing the already spent daffodils. Bishop knocked, but no one answered. He went around to the back. A large garden had been laid out, the tiny seedlings trying to flourish in the early spring chill, a huge oak tree with wide branches embraced the corner of the yard where someone had put a fire pit near a white plank fence making a cozy hide-away. If he had expected occult symbols to be painted on the fence, he was disappointed.

Back in the front, he stopped and surveyed the neighboring houses. Two stood empty, no evidence of cars, no drapes at the windows. At a third, a moving van had been pulled onto the lawn, the heavy vehicle making ruts in ground still soft from spring rains. A lone man kept coming in and out, carrying boxes sealed with colorful tape. Probably a recent college graduate, his body still lean from youth instead of workouts, his coarse, thick, red hair short in that I'm looking for a job haircut. There was an easy confidence about him that said he knew he'd find employment soon. Bishop crossed the street, stopping next to the moving van.

The man put his box in the back, shoved it a little further, then turned his attention to Bishop. "Are you looking for Mrs. Jones?"

Bishop waited.

"I don't think she's there. I think she's at the funeral home. You know her daughter died?"

Bishop still waited.

"So sad."

"You knew Blossom?" It was a reasonable guess,

the man being only a few years older than her, but the young man shook his head with a sad smile.

"No. I'm not into all that pagan stuff. We talked once in a while. I'd invite her to Singing Gospels, but she would always refuse." He shrugged it off, saving his ego. "Besides, I think she liked older guys. Looking for a father figure kind of thing."

In the distance, a piece of heavy equipment clanged reverse, and they could hear the muffled roar as it went to full power trampling someone's tattered and abandoned home.

"I'd better keep moving. I want to be out by six."

"Why the hurry?"

"Yesterday a man came by and said we got an extra five hundred for every day we were out before the fifteenth. Everything's been waiting for the gas station owner to sell. Guess it finally happened."

Bishop remembered the man who had owned the gas station back when it had been his neighborhood to protect. Fresh out of the military, gave you the uneasy feeling that he could kill you before you knew to reach for your gun. Then remembered the man had been killed, along with his two sons, in a tragic train accident. Someone had said the widow had gone crazy when she'd been told. He wondered how she was doing. If she'd moved on. He knew how hard it was to move on.

"Is this where they're putting the new mall?" He scanned the horizon, now a line of dirt and rubble. Didn't seem like a good place to him. Too close, and yet too far, from downtown. Even with the edgy

Jordan Tower changing the city skyline and enticing high-energy enterprises back uptown, it wasn't going to keep the inner city from decaying. Rent and taxes were cheaper further out. That's where the businesses went and that's where the people followed.

"Yeah, I think so."

The youth went back to his loading and Bishop went back to his car. Maybe he should move. Maybe he could find something cheaper. Flexing his shoulder, he tried to work some of the stiffness out, tried not to feel the ache deep in the bone that came with the changing of the season. No, he won't move. Moving meant leaving Teonna's house, their house. Instead he called dispatch. "ETA on Sergio." There was no way to keep the annoyance out of his voice.

"Clocked out on a personal." The reply was quick and detached, not like Shirley's cool efficiency. She didn't want to take the heat for Sergio's tardiness. She shouldn't have to.

He shifted, again trying to release the ache in his shoulder. "Tell him I'm headed for ..." He flipped a page on the notepad and gave the address to the next witch on the list. "If he gets there first have him wait." Something told Bishop that wasn't likely to happen. Although he'd missed lunch and passed a fast food establishment Bishop remembered the rent increase, and kept going. Maybe he would stop for a loaf of bread and some bologna on his way home.

As he expected, Bishop got to the witch's house first. The neighborhood wasn't that good, nor was it that bad. A long row of rentals on an older side street, close enough to the bus lines to motivate the landlord to keep things maintained. The address he wanted was in the middle of the block. It looked like every other house. Nothing about it screamed witch, or evil, or crazy. When he rang the bell a normal middle-aged woman, best described as plump, with long hair, styled back in a fancy, interwoven bun, threads of gray becoming pronounced, promptly answered. She must have been baking, her plaid shirt had the sleeves rolled up and a linen towel had been folded and tucked into itself to form an apron around her stout middle covering the front of her faded blue jeans.

"JoAnn Dole?"

She nodded, drying her hands on a soft terry cloth towel she was holding, then not offering to shake hands, just making a sharp pivot on her heel and leading him inside the house. After a moment's hesitation, checking down the street to see if Sergio's fast car was arriving, Bishop followed.

"I'm baking." Without another word she led him past the cozy living room, with braided rug, overstuffed chairs, and two cats. Nothing unusual. Nothing that screamed I'm a witch. There were candles and crystal bobbles hanging at the windows reflecting rainbows of light into the room. But his younger sister had even more candles, giving her house that chemical, floral smell. This house had more of an herbal scent. Sage, maybe. A quaint stylized broom leaned in the corner, the kind you find in home decorating stores, with a twisted branch for a handle, and brittle straw tied with thick twine. Maybe it declared her as a witch, maybe it was a decorating statement.

"I've got bread in the oven."

As if that explained everything she continued down a hallway to the kitchen. A timer went off and she went straight to the oven, opening it. No little children roasting away. No Hansel or Gretel. Flicking her finger off her thumb, she thumped the nearest loaf getting a satisfying echo from beneath the golden crust. With a nod, she removed the bread and the fresh, hot aroma of yeast and baked flour possessed the kitchen.

Bishop couldn't keep his mouth from salivating. Focus, he reminded himself, focus.

"What can you tell me about this morning?"

"I was late. But I knew something was wrong the moment I got there. Keisha had me wait in the trees." She worked with mechanical efficacy, gingerly transferring the loaves of bread out of their pans and onto cooling racks. "Some officer took my name, then that nice young man came over with coffee and asked me again." She stopped and gazed at the loaves, their golden brown welcoming perfection. "These are for the gathering. For Blossom. When they let us ..." Her voice trailed off into sadness. She forced her shoulders back, adjusting the weight of her sorrow before dropping brown sugar and butter into a large bowl and beating the ingredients into a creamy base. Bishop knew what she was doing. His mother did the same thing when she was upset. Like when she'd found out he and Claire were getting divorced. When she found out the reason why. Bread, cookies, pie, the process of baking comforting her, not the food, she never ate what she baked.

"What do you know about the love spell?"

JoAnn's eyes momentarily widened in dismay.

Was she surprised about the spell or surprised that he knew?

"Is that what happened? I warned her. Keisha warned her. You can't just willy-nilly make the universe answer to your whims."

"Did you know the man? The one she wanted to cast the love spell on?"

JoAnn broke the eggs, one, two, into a small bowl then added a large splash of rum and a small splash of vanilla, their aroma marrying together in an unexpected union of sweet and sharp. She finally added it to the creamed butter and sugar.

"No. She never told anyone. Maybe Amanda. But I knew her mother didn't approve."

"Why do you say that?"

"We work together, me and Laura. We're aides out at the school. Sometimes we talk." JoAnn scooped flour, a dark, coarse whole wheat, into the creamed butter mixture, its nutty undertones adding more depth to the already rich smells in the kitchen.

"I know that Blossom was obsessed with him. I never understood it. He was a jerk." She sprinkled baking soda over the flour. "Married. Sneaking around with a sixteen-year-old. What kind of a man does that?"

But Blossom was eighteen.

With a stout wooden spoon, JoAnn blended the dry ingredients into the wet, her arms straining to turn the thick batter. The wooden spoon bent, the thin neck twisted, then broke. The loud crack echoing in the kitchen. The woman stopped. She stared at the broken spoon, the ragged end sticking straight up in the heavy dough.

His grandmother would have made the sign of the cross. It was a bad omen. Even to Bishop it felt like a sign. But the thing about signs from the heavens, or the universe, or the goddess, or wherever they came from, is that they didn't come tied in neat little bows. They came with hindsight and reflection.

JoAnn held her hand to her throat. "I was thinking that I needed to go to the bank."

Nothing ominous about going to the bank.

She removed the broken spoon, scraping off the dough onto the side of the bowl.

One of the cats entered the kitchen. It looked toward JoAnn, then turned its head toward Bishop, its unblinking green eyes boring into him. Bishop didn't dislike cats, but then he didn't like them either. They were just one more thing to feed.

JoAnn pulled open a drawer and rummaged through the utensils, finally removing a large, sharp bladed knife. The cat's tail flicked as Bishop shifted to a better position if he needed to access to his gun. But neither of them should have worried. JoAnn unwrapped a block of dark chocolate and with practiced strokes coarsely chopped it into small pieces before adding the bitter to the sweet batter.

"Blossom loved chocolate."

A sob caught in her throat, and the woman scooped up the cat, hugging it to herself. But the cat never stopped watching Bishop even as JoAnne nestled her face up against it, and it rubbed its cheek against hers.

"Tell me about the other members of the coven."

"I can tell you about Amanda." JoAnn gave a soft, disapproving exhale of breath. "She came to the last celebration of the full moon. Blossom brought her. But she didn't seem interested in being part of the community. She just kept asking about spells and rituals. – If we had a horned-god." The last was said in a whisper, to the cat more than Bishop. The cat pushed its nose against the witch's and they gazed into each other's eyes for a long instant.

Like the snap of the spoon Bishop understood. "You're all Hannah's girls." He hadn't meant to say it out loud. "I mean, you met through the shelter house."

The cat pushed off the woman's shoulder and leapt toward Bishop. Without thought he caught the animal midair and turned it, cradling it in his arm and against his body like one would a small child. The cat squirmed. Bishop scratched the top of its head. A ripple went through the animal, then a slow purr emanated, the rumble vibrating through Bishop's shirt and jacket.

"He doesn't like strangers."

Apparently the animal didn't find him strange.

Flexing, the cat smoothly left Bishop's arm and

climbed to his shoulders, the sharp claws pricking his coat sleeve. It wrapped around his neck. He felt the heat of the paws on his shoulder as if a hand had slipped beneath his shirt and lay hot on his skin, touching the deep scars that lay hidden there. The purring stopped. The animal kneaded its claws in and out of his jacket and Bishop flinched as if needles were pulling to the surface. The hot kitchen seemed suddenly suffocating. He was hungry, he needed to eat, the odor of the oversweet food suddenly nauseating.

"I should be going."

He unwrapped the cat and placed it on the floor. There were more questions, that needed more answers, but he would come back. He would call. Right now he needed air. Cold, crisp, spring air. When he opened the door, he stopped, sucking in the coolness of an early spring breeze. It seemed to clear his head. Hadn't it been a feast day? Like Christmas? Everyone went to church on Christmas. "Was anyone missing?"

JoAnne looked at him without understanding.

"Everyone was there?" He recited the names Keisha had told him. "Blossom, Amanda, Keisha, you, Blossom's mother, Mimi and," he had to know, "... Hannah."

"Hannah? Is that her real name? Her witch name is Venus. That's all I knew her by. She must have left before I got there."

If she was one of Hannah's girls she would know Hannah.

"So Hannah, from the shelter house, she wasn't

involved?"

"That Hannah? No, oh, no, she understood, but she never practiced."

"Can you give me Venus's address?"

The cat came and weaved through their legs, a purr rumbling loud and aggressively.

"I don't know. We don't share that kind of information. I only know Laura's last name because we work together. But I know Venus works at a bank."

Bishop moved off the steps, away from the cat. "Do you know which bank?"

"Somewhere downtown."

That left a lot of banks.

"Near the police station. She talked about the police coming by."

Jackie's bank was near the station, some officer's banked there to curry favor with the Chief. He'd banked there since he was a child, never left, even gotten his last loan for Sonny's tuition there.

"There was this police officer that she liked, but I don't think he noticed her. She might have been the third."

"Third?"

"The spell, the one they were talking about doing, it needed three." A timer dinged in the kitchen, and JoAnn anxiously glanced into the house.

Bishop nodded dismissing JoAnn back to her baking. Of course, three patches of trampled grass, there would have been a third. She would be the one who screamed and left. Left even before Amanda. But no one liked Amanda, and everyone was ready to point a finger at her. Bishop got into his car and drove away. In the rearview mirror he noticed the cat sitting on the porch step seeming to watch him.

CHAPTER TEN

Down the road, well away from the witch and the cat, Bishop shook off the odd sensations being in the house had covered him with. Good thing it wasn't Halloween. This time he got Sergio's cell number from dispatch and called only to have it go straight to voice mail. He snapped the phone closed without leaving a message. A few moments later the phone buzzed, a text message appeared: shift over. Bishop held back his flare of temper. A homicide investigation was different from other police work, sometimes you stayed with a case all night.

The dispatch radio crackled. "A Mrs. Penni Turner has been trying to reach you."

Bishop clenched his teeth in no mood for the woman's foolishness. He'd been nice to her once. Fixed her door and replaced the lock after her husband had kicked it in on his way out of her life. That had been over ten years ago. Since then she'd acted as if they were the best of friends, calling him whenever she needed something. So much for being a Good Samaritan. Rather than delay and be hounded by her, Bishop dialed the number.

"Detective Bishop?" Age joined with booze and cigarettes made her voice rough, not in a sexy Lauren Bacall way, but a nail across a chalkboard, repulsive wheeze. "You have to find my boy."

Her boy had just turned eighteen and been dancing in and out of trouble since his dad had disappeared.

"He didn't come home last night. I got a bad feeling. Something's wrong."

"Maybe he found someplace else to stay?"

"No, no, not my boy. He knows I need him." She fought to suck air into her lungs, the steady click of her oxygen apparatus helping her along. "He has my car, and he knew I had to go to the doctor today." Her breath exhausted, she fell into a coughing fit.

Not wanting to appear too friendly, not wanting to encourage her, Bishop silently waited, watching the sun creeping along its curve, the edges of its hot orb beginning to touch the tops of building. It hung there, dallying between day and night, promising summer when it would hang on the horizon for hours.

The coughing momentarily under control, Mrs. Turner gasped into the phone. "Something's wrong." Another wheezy suck of air, another sharp click of machinery. "He's been in an accident. I just know it. A mother knows these things." She started coughing again, taking longer to get her breathing back under control. "I've called the hospital. They say he ain't there. But I know. I feel it in my bones He's laying in a ditch somewhere. He'd come home to his mama if he could." She started to cry, that helpless, pitiful cry of a lost child. "He's dead. I just know he's dead somewhere."

What could Bishop say? "I'll tell the patrols to watch for him."

The sobbing stopped. "You go look for him. You'll find him. You're the only honest cop in this town." Her voice turned hard with an edge of anger.

Bishop took a corner and looked for an out.

"The Chief kept him out of jail." Bishop reminded her. Her boy had been caught, gun in hand, shooting out his ex-girlfriend's car tires. If the Chief hadn't intervened, posted the kid's bail, and gotten him into a first offender program, Turner would still be sitting in lock-up.

"Introduced him to that floozy. That Spanish woman."

From her inflection Bishop knew Mrs. Turner wasn't believing the Chief's aid had been helpful.

"That's why he took my car, to drive his floozy around. She's bewitched him. Put a love spell on him. It'll come to no good. No good at all. She'll use him and lose him, and there will be my boy, his heart broke. When I find that boy, I'm going box his ears. He'll know not to leave his mama waiting."

So this was about a woman. "I have to go." Bishop took a corner too sharp, trying to hold the phone and turn at the same time he momentarily lost control.

"I'll do what I can." He snapped the phone closed, straightened the vehicle, and sped on. After a heartbeat's worth of guilt, he called dispatch. This time Shirley's efficient voice answered and he knew for sure that the shift had changed.

"Could you put out a call to Jefferson and Muttley? Have them watch for Elmo Turner. Male, late teens, thin, dark hair," he hesitated, "… green cowboy boots. Might be driving a late model Chevy. They know him."

"And if they find him?"

"Have them tell him to call home. His mother's worried."

Phone closed, Bishop realized he was passing the bank. Jackie's bank. After five, it was closed. No point in stopping. And what would he say? A witch had a psychic revelation about the bank. Not even a revelation, a feeling, a bad feeling. He kept going.

A block down was the city library, its lights were on competing with the fading daylight of early evening, sending a beacon to those sitting in front of a television or computer screen with as little success as the glow from the window had challenging with the sun. He stopped and let the librarian pull a dozen books on witchcraft, everything from the history of, to turning your enemies into frogs.

He dropped the books on the passenger's seat and stared at the fading sun. The lighting would be the same as when the robbery had occurred, the shadows would just be pointed the other direction. He doubled back, taking an alley instead of the street. It was one car and a dumpster wide. If he was robbing a bank and didn't want his license plate on the video cameras this is where he would have parked, behind the huge, smelly garbage receptacle where the businesses brought their trash. He walked to the next side street. A mound of landscaping with flower beds separated the street from the bank employee parking lot. An easy walk. Even carrying a duffle bag of money.

Bishop approached the building, turning the clock backwards and envisioning that it was early morning instead of early evening. At the corner near the door, a trio of scraggly shrubs hugged the wall, their leaves open, but scant. Even in the fading light, he could see the wall behind. Maybe if the robber had been dressed in dark colors. He studied the tight space between the wall and the bush. Maybe if the man had been fashion model thin. But no matter how he played it in his mind, it would have been hard for Jackie to have missed someone standing there.

Not his case.

No motive. She and the Chief were doing well. They had a new home. They both drove big Mercedes. Flew their own airplane. An early spring mosquito landed on his neck. Bishop automatically smacked the pest, coming away with blood on his hand. What was he doing? Why was he standing there being a grocery store for bloodsuckers?

The phone rang.

Sam.

"Yeah."

"Hey, you free? We're at the diner on Third."

It was only a few blocks away. When he arrived, Sam and the two FBI agents were already seated. Bishop slid into the booth next to Sam. He shook his head at the menu and ordered the special, with a water. The two FBI agents sat next to each other, their bodies stiff as Marines, carefully not touching. One was female, sitting she seemed tall, one never knew, but her head reached above the man's shoulder. Sam kept looking at her, all moon-eyed, an I'm-interested-smile on his lips. Glad the bank teller was more interested in Sam than Sam had been in her and he wouldn't be placed in the awkward situation of Sam knowing every time he overdrew his account, but feeling the tension between the two agents, Bishop crossed his legs deliberately kicking Sam in the shin.

Sam looked over and gave him that what? look.

"So how long you two worked together?" Bishop asked, trying to clue Sam in.

The man flashed the barest flicker of discomfort, but the woman concealed any unease the question had touched on.

"Three years. And you and Sam?" She threw the question back letting him know she knew that it was inappropriate.

Bishop smiled. "A year," giving Sam several extra months as a detective.

"They got a description of the car." Sam eagerly filled in, the tension at the table obviously lost on him. He leaned forward resting on his forearms. "It was parked on a side alley that had a surveillance camera. Black Chevy, older model, you can see someone get in with a big duffle bag and then head south."

The food came, two steaks, rare for the male FBI agent, and uncharacteristically rare for Sam as well, a salad for the woman, a plate of spaghetti with garlic bread for Bishop. He bit into the bread, may as well, he wouldn't be kissing anyone tonight.

Bishop uncrossed his legs, kicking Sam again. "Sounds like Turner's car." He hadn't meant to say that. Turner must have still been on his mind.

"Turner?" The woman's fork stopped just above the leafy salad sans dressing.

Bishop wished he hadn't said anything. "Local teenager. Gets himself into trouble now and then."

"You didn't mention earlier that you knew the car."

Sam gave Bishop a scowl. "Yeah, well, you can't be sure about these things. Lots of black, late Chevys."

"But this Turner drives one. And you know him?"

Sam shifted and glanced at Bishop not sure what he should or shouldn't say. Bishop chewed the soggy noodles, the beef sauce was flavored with yesterday's leftover hamburgers. He'd had better. He put his fork down and took a drink of tap water. He couldn't remember having had worse.

"Did you put out an APB?" It would kill two birds with one stone. If they hauled in Turner, he would call his mother for bail.

Sam shook his head. "The tape was too fuzzy to get a number off the license. And the robber had a mask, so the inside tapes didn't show much. I guess it could have been Turner. Skinny, wiry kid, held his hand in his pocket like he might have had a gun."

"Doesn't matter." The female agent flaunted her knowledge of the law. "According to Mrs. Johnson, he said that he had a gun." Everyone at the table knew implying that you had a weapon in a bank robbery was the same as having a weapon.

The words were out before Bishop could stop himself. "Cowboy boots?"

The male FBI who had held himself aloof finally joined in, dipping his head in what might have been a nod that there had been cowboy boots, or it might have been a suppressed burp.

Realization flashed across Sam's face. "Yeah, those stupid, green, pointed-toed boots he wears. Why would he leave them on?"

Why? Because they were so much a part of him that he could have easier left his hand at home and worn someone else's.

"Because all criminals are stupid." The woman expounded.

Bishop didn't believe her but kept silent. A lot of criminals were smarter than him, they just couldn't control all the variables, no one could. And Bishop's job was to find that one variable that had slipped past them.

"You got an address?"

All the officers in Garfield Falls knew the Turner address. Without hesitation the FBI left their food and started out. The woman veered to the bathroom as the man paid. Sam pushed against Bishop, trapped on the inside of the booth. "We're going, aren't we?"

"You won't find anything."

"Sure we will, Turner's a dick. He'll discover how much he got and party till there's no tomorrow."

Bishop shook his head. "His mother called me looking for him. Said he was hanging with a Spanish woman." He didn't add floozy.

Sam hesitated.

"You go, you're the liaison. Just," there was no delicate way to say it. "Sam, they're sleeping together." Bishop stood and Sam slid past him.

"Who?"

Bishop hoped Sam hadn't thought he meant Turner and his mother. Sam's face went from puzzled to obstinate.

"No, they're not, I've been with them all day, they don't even look at each other."

"That's because he's married."

"Neither has a ring."

No, but Bishop knew the shadow of a ring when he saw one. Without thinking he glanced down at his fingers. Even without a ring he felt the lock Teonna held on him.

He forgot about it the minute the female FBI agent came out of the bathroom. She wore flat shoes now, and the bulge of a gun under her jacket was larger. Sam followed out the door, his shoulders a little slumped, his steps not so cocky. Bishop sat back down. He pulled Sam's half-eaten steak over. As the waitress cruised by Bishop flagged her down.

"Too late to add a beer to the tab?"

"No, the guy left it open so you could have desert."

That sounded good, he hadn't had desert in months. "And how about some salad dressing? Blue cheese?"

After finishing Sam's steak, the woman's untouched salad, a slice of chocolate cake, and two Bud Lites, Bishop added a generous tip to the charge. The FBI could afford it.

CHAPTER ELEVEN

Bishop woke to the thud of a book falling to the floor. He sat in the recliner in the living room, his muscles stiff, an open book on his lap. Other books, their dark covers like black stepping stones, lay scattered across the floor. But stepping to stones to where?

A loon called from across the lake. It would be dawn soon. Bishop glanced down at the page the book had fallen open to. A picture of a moon with crescents on each side glowed up at him. He picked up the book and closed it. He should get some sleep, real sleep, in a bed, one with pillows and lace, one that smelled like a woman's perfume. He shook the fantasy away. It was so far past late that it approached early. There was no point in even going to bed.

Instead of heading upstairs Bishop changed to his jogging clothes and shoes. He secured his 9mm in his back holster, and went outside. It had rained in the night leaving the grass slick. The air hung heavy and moist bringing a fog up off the lake. Bringing the first stench of the rotten water to the surface. Frank had been certain they'd clean up the lake. Frank had been certain the short row of houses would be worth millions when he retired. Teonna had agreed. So they'd put everything they'd had into a dream that had never happened.

The house next door, Frank's house, sat in a shroud of darkness, silent and abandoned. Broken toys and empty carry-out debris lay scattered about the lawn adding to the forsaken mood surrounding the building. No one stayed there long. It had an aura of bad luck about it. Or maybe he was getting superstitious from all the witchcraft encircling him. It was just a house, a tiny, dark house, two stories, but no basement, which meant no storage. The furnace, the water heater, even the washer/dryer had to be designed into space that should have been used as closets. That meant the rent was bound to be cheaper. Perhaps he should move next door. A knot formed in his stomach at the thought and he knew he couldn't. No, leaving the house meant leaving Teonna and forgetting the memories that he clung to like the mist clung to the lake. No, he wasn't ready for the sun to burn away the past.

He turned away from the empty rental and his usual route east toward the rising sun, instead going west toward the old factory. There had been complaints of lights and cars coming and going at odd hours. No one had checked them out. With budget cutbacks, officers were spread too thin, or maybe no one cared. Either way, he stretched his legs and ran, pushing himself to the edge of his endurance. The brush was thicker this direction, spring foliage filling in the crooked path. Winter debris, once buried under the snow, made the ground uneven and forced him to run on light feet. The water from the lake had already started to stink as the warmth of the sun cooked whatever little microbes lay latent all winter.

A swarm of insects hovered like a black cloud just off the crude path. He slowed, then stopped. Beneath the cloud of black, the brown and dusty coat of a dead deer blended into earth and fallen foliage. A fly buzzed past and landed on the animal's nostril. Bishop moved a branch and stared down at the carcass. The hindquarter had a long gash, the rear leg lay at an awkward angle. Likely hit by a car, a day ago, maybe two.

Behind the deer, poison ivy, its bright red leaves, small and new, climbed a tree. Bishop looked down at his hand where red blotches tattooed his fingertips. Could he have brushed against the plant yesterday, or the day before? He hadn't gone that way, but where there was one plant there would be dozens more. Not much that could be done, the land was too wild, and he was the only one who ran this way. He shrugged it off and continued down the path until he reached the end where a chain link fence stopped people from entering the factory grounds. A huge sign proclaimed, no trespassing, another sign a hundred yards down warned him to stay out or be prosecuted, he wondered who would charge him. Maybe Sam would drag him off in handcuffs? Then Bishop shook off the morbid humor. It wasn't funny when a cop had to arrest another cop.

The factory had been closed longer than Bishop could remember, certainly before Frank had bought up the surrounding land. When the owner had been ordered to clean up the factory's pollution he'd skipped town with all his bank accounts. While the city fought with the county over who was going to pay for what, the homeowners fled the stench, wisely abandoning their investments. Only Frank had bought what he could at public auction, believing in the potential value of the land. Him and Teonna. Now renters came, and come summer, renters left. While Bishop waited for the clean-up promised every election, and forgotten the day after.

Not forgotten were the memories of him, Frank and Teonna, dreaming about their big score when the lake was finally cleaned up. About how much the land would be worth. Laughing in Frank's kitchen over beer and late night pizza, until he and Teonna would leave Frank drunk asleep on his couch. They would walk the short distance next door to her house and make love until dawn in her big bed with the white, lacy sheets. He reached up to pull her face down to his lips. Instead of Teonna's soft, long blonde hair, his hands found a low hanging branch. Slowly, he lifted himself off the ground forcing himself to leave the memory. He focused on the pull of muscles injured too often not to ache in the winter. Lifting, lowering, warming the stiffness out of damaged tissue. Sweat beaded on his forehead and still he pushed against the pain.

At the top of his lift, a flash of light came from the factory, nearly blinding him. Bishop squinted into the brilliance and tried to see the source. Had to be a broken beer bottle catching the reflection of the sun. That would explain the lights coming from the abandoned factory.

No. It was a mirror. Bishop released the tree branch and let himself drop back to the ground. A mirror? Where would a mirror come from? He wiped the tree bark from his hands and walked to the security fence. A post had been knocked down by the snow and wind dragging the chain-link with it so that Bishop could merely step over the barrier and into the abandoned parking lot. Half hidden beneath a stand of bushes, only the mirror sticking out, was a late model Chevy. By summer, when the leaves filled out, it would have been entirely hidden.

Cautiously, gun steady in both hands, ready to switch to either, Bishop approached the vehicle, and peered inside the back window. Empty. A mound of cigarettes in the ash tray. Candy wrappers strewn across the floor. Flies buzzed in and out of a rusted out hollow over the back wheel well. The light breeze brought a distinct odor from the rear of the vehicle, an odor Bishop was too familiar with, the sweet-sour smell of rotting flesh.

Bishop reached for his cell, then remembered it was on the kitchen table. After a moment's hesitation he turned back home. The factory sat at the end of a long lane with two locked gates, no one was just going to happen by while he was gone. And since it was at the very end of Garfield Falls' jurisdiction, it would take a while before anyone could get there, even after he called it in. His jog back to the house took less time than the jog out had. The phone sat on the kitchen table, next to his keys.

The first number on the list was dispatch, the second, Sam.

"Yeah." Was Sam's muffled response making Bishop wonder if Sam was at home or spent the night somewhere else.

"I've found Turner's car."

"Give me –"

The bed squeaked.

"Forty."

Bishop smiled as he disconnected and headed up the stairs, stripping clothes as he went. That gave him time for a shower, or more of a rinse. He splashed water on himself, then dried with a threadbare towel, the lace trim faded and re-sewn on. He dressed in dark pants and one of the dozen light colored shirts hanging on the left side of the closet. Teonna's side was the right, still empty, just as it had been when he got out of the hospital, her uniforms gone, her dresses and blouses gone. He shrugged into his shoulder holster, tight against the scars, and finally a dark jacket, its pockets holding his notepad and pen, evidence bags and thin plastic gloves to protect his hands.

Outside, he paused by the garage, keys in hand. No, by now the lane would be a traffic jam of squad cars, instead he jogged back to the west. Jefferson had arrived and taped off most of the unused parking lot.

"The FBI here yet?"

It was their jurisdiction, he should wait.

Morning birds called to each other and a soft breeze of cool air rippled off the lake. A swarm of flies buzzed around one of the factory's side windows drawing Bishop's attention to the abandoned building. He missed stepping in a squishy pile of vomit near the side door when he pushed through a bramble of bushes to peer inside. Through the dirt and grime encrusted on the cracked and chipped glass, he could see several steel rubbish barrels, rusted and charred. They had been moved to one side, an air mattress nestled between them. The shiny sheets tousled. Someone had made a love nest complete with a dozen candles arranged on top of the barrels. But it was the swarm of insects in the center of the emptiness that drew his attention.

There would be another body there.

He was done waiting.

Turner first.

Sam got there as Bishop opened the front car door. He punched the latch release and the trunk popped open. Jefferson gagged and stumbled backwards. Although decay had started around the mouth, nose and tips of the ears, you could tell that it was Turner, still in his unique green cowboy boots, so young that his cheeks had a fuzz to them rather than a real beard. Three shots: chest, chest, middle of the forehead. The kid was dead before he hit the ground. Very professional. But who? Who had Turner gotten tangled-up with?

A smell zone away from the body Sam watched Bishop. "Someone surprise him?"

"Not that close." It was disbelief on Turner's face, not fear. Bishop could almost hear the scream of betrayal strangling out with Turner's last breath.

"So you think it was someone involved in the robbery?" Sam asked.

"Mostly likely."

Muttley grinned. "Someone turned on Turner. That's a good one."

Sam gave the chuckling officer a sour look. "Then he knew his killer."

Good conclusion, or he was the trusting sort who let just anybody walk right up to him. Another squad car arrived. It pulled off the lane and into the bushes.

"Hey, you can't park there. That's for the Chief." Jefferson called out to the newcomer.

Bishop set his jaw in annoyance. He should have checked out the bodies before he called them in. Every officer in the city seemed to be arriving, milling around and making noise. He shook his head, he couldn't concentrate. Forensics would take photos, he'd have to work from there, still he didn't like to rely on them too heavily, there was the chance the photos didn't develop, or were lost. He locked the scene into his memory. Then he remembered that it wasn't his case. Not Turner anyway. But he could hear death's call from inside the factory.

"Got a warrant for the building?"

"Not yet. The Chief's still in bed."

Bishop looked at Sam. "You didn't call the FBI team?"

Sam studied the dust at his feet. "Nobody picked up, so I left a message. Then I called the Chief."

Sam understood, so did Bishop. Hard to get untangled after a forbidden night of pleasure. That was that, no reason to make an issue of it. Sam only had his ego bruised. Seemed someone had already softened the blow for him.

Bishop again stared down at Turner's body unable to shake off that whoever had killed him had been a pro. Quick, clean, bang, bang, bang, dropped him right into the trunk, slammed the lid, put the car into neutral and gave it a little shove into the bushes. If Bishop hadn't decided to jog that way, if he hadn't stopped to do pull-ups, if the light hadn't been just right to flash back into his eyes, the bushes would have grown around the car. It might have been months, maybe years, before the body would have been found.

Finally, Bishop turned away, answering the siren song calling to him. Maybe the body inside would give him answers. The side door had been jerry-rigged with a sturdy bracket and set up for a hanging padlock. Except the padlock was gone. Bishop examined the bushes avoiding the remnants of vomit. Forensics would ID the spew as Turner's. Likely Turner had gone into the building, saw the body and came out running, up-chucked in the bushes, then gone to the car to wait. Bishop looked across the pavement for affirmation in the dust. Only there wasn't any dust. Last night's rain had cleansed the area, erasing any footprints. He didn't need them. A court might, but he didn't. Logic dictated the scenario. What he needed was to find where the logic broke down. That's where he'd find the killer's mistake.

Bishop eased the door open. Light played through the skylights and windows making a lattice of shadows. Dirt and debris forced through cracks and holes by the winter winds covered most of the floor. He motioned Sam and Muttley to stay, while he entered the building. Wind shifted and echoed in the flat rafters. A nest, the young birds already chirping to be fed, balanced preciously on a crossbeam. They fell silent as he passed beneath them. He took the widest path to the makeshift bedroom. The scent of a dozen candles, a sharp, cheap rose and vanilla, competed with the stink of machine oil and ancient grease. Closer to the bed the musky order of sex lingered. A blotch of brown, dried, and crusted blood, stained the shiny red sheets. Evidence not of stealing someone's virginity, but evidence of stealing someone's life.

For some reason he thought of Blossom. Was this what she'd wanted with her witch's spell, that exhilarating sexual moment? The bedroom dance mistaken for love ever after? Did she think she could steal her unnamed lover from his wife, then bind him to her with her youth and charms? Bishop shook off her intrusion into his thoughts. Blossom had nothing to do with Turner.

A wide swath had been made in the thick layer of dust on the floor. Someone had dragged something, making a trail in the debris leading to the black pit in the center of the room. Another swarm of flies lifted from the floor. Bishop followed them, followed his nose to a hole, ten feet wide, twenty feet long. He peered over the edge. And about ten feet deep. A deep, black abyss left from when they'd removed some piece of machinery. Probably the only thing of value after the EPA had shut the place down. "Anybody got a flashlight?" He turned to look at Muttley and Jefferson still standing in the doorway, their silhouettes a comedy of short and tall.

Before either could respond, the Chief pushed between them. He stopped, letting his eyes adjust to the thin light before stomping in. "What are you doing here, Bishop?" The Chief paused at the love nest and lifted a candle. He sniffed it, shook his head, and put it back, knocking over several other candles, and then setting them upright. "One case ain't enough for you?"

Although not big in size, the Chief was big in presence. He swept through seeming to fill the entire space as he took the most direct path to the pit. Bishop cringed. He'd been careful to make a wide berth of the most logical path to the room's center. Maybe they could have gotten a shoe print from the dust, instead anything that might have been there was destroyed or compromised. The Chief had been sitting at a desk too long. He'd taught Morris, and Morris had taught Bishop. A well-maintained crime scene made for a good solid case.

Muttley followed the Chief, handing him a flashlight. The Chief flicked it on and illuminated the bottom of the pit. In mass, flies rose up, soaring into their faces, forcing the men to move back, covering their noses with their sleeves to keep from inhaling the insects.

Bishop stepped forward first, staring into the pit. A shiny red comforter, that matched the red sheets, lay at the bottom. A hand extended from beneath it.

"Somebody get a ladder." The chief bellowed. But he didn't wait, instead he scrambled over the side. Sam lowered him a few extra feet before letting go of his wrist and allowing the chief to drop. He approached the body slowly. Bishop wondered why the caution, did he think that the body was going to jump up and shout boo at him. Finally the Chief reached down and flipped the blanket aside revealing the corpse.

No surprise that it was a woman. She wore tight jeans and a colorful blouse with a bold floral pattern that offset her black hair and nearly hid the bloom of blood over her heart. In the cool of the pit not much decomposition had occurred. Her features remained mostly intact. A Spanish beauty.

Only one shot. Two different MO's. Two different shooters.

Impatient, Bishop scrambled over the side. Without Sam's help he dropped into the pit feeling the jar of the landing shoot through his leg and rip into his bad shoulder. Something about the dead woman was familiar. Bishop tried to remember if he'd seen her before. Maybe next door. In that chaotic mass of bodies that had arrived late last winter waiting for spring and the demand for menial labor that came with it. She could have met Turner here in the factory, stolen a few moments now and then.

Until someone found them. Or found out about the planned robbery.

But Turner? A low-life, skimming through on his mother's disability checks and petty theft? No, a woman like her, even past her prime, could have done better.

The Chief shook his head. "Not your case, Bishop." He turned the flashlight away from the corpse and into Bishop's face. "I can feel you itching to listen to her whispers. But this is not our case. It's connected to the FBI's robbery."

"I know her. I think she lived next door."

The Chief grunted in warning. "You think? You talk to her? She tell you she was meeting up with Turner to do the midnight Samba?"

"No. But I..."

He put his arm around Bishop's shoulder and turned him away from the body of the dead woman. "All them Mex's ... you don't know anything for sure."

The spindly legs of a metal ladder appeared at the end of the pit away from the body and the face of the male FBI agent, his eyes tired from too little rest, and too much guilt, peered over the edge.

"Here, now, here's the Calvary." The Chief pushed Bishop to go up first.

He stood waiting at the top when the silhouette of the female FBI agent filled the door. "Thanks, we'll take it from here." She looked fresh, like a well fed cat. Sam trailed behind watching the footprints her heels left in the dust rather than her Pilates tight buttocks.

With the Feds, support personnel came like a swarm of flies. They brought cameras, fingerprinting equipment, infrared lights, every toy and detecting aid you might want. More than you'd need for a small bank robbery. Bishop bit back that the more people the more likely the scene would be compromised.

Tossing an amiable arm around Bishop's shoulder the Chief guided them away toward the door. "You let them do their job."

"She was living with some migrant farm workers." He didn't say illegals even though he had his suspicions. ICE and murder were the only two reasons people left town in a hurry. "They left town yesterday."

"Well, I'll let them know that. You got another case to work on. Get out there and find whoever killed that sweet little witch."

CHAPTER TWELVE

Bishop left the building and found Sergio standing outside, leaning against the hood of his bright orange Camaro like James Dean, a rebel without a cause want-to-be, posing tough yet as far away from the smell as he could get. His square jaw and swarthy good looks irritated Bishop. He tried to fight the dislike and scratched at his hand. Maybe it was just the weather. His shoulder ached telling him it would rain again in spite of the clear sky and warming spring breeze.

The Chief came out of the building and waved toward Sergio. "Guess you two missed each other yesterday."

The men nodded, appraising each other, neither speaking.

"You tag along with Bishop, here. He'll teach you everything you need to know about catching a killer." The Chief slapped Bishop on the back. "If Bishop doesn't catch you, you won't get caught." Bishop got into the passenger side of Sergio's car. He'd rather have gone back for his Subaru but this car was there.

Bishop's personal phone rang and he dug it out of his pocket.

Shirley.

"Have an urgent message for you to call a JoAnn Dole."

Sergio drummed his fingers on the steering wheel while Bishop dialed. Before a second ring JoAnn picked up. "Officer Bishop. Are you alright?"

He ignored her question even though it made him uncomfortable. Why wouldn't he be alright? "You were trying to get ahold of me."

"Yes! Yes, I had a dream."

Deep inside a groan erupted, but Bishop caught it before it escaped his lips.

"There was a deer standing on a road, and this big, black car comes and hits it. And the deer runs away, but its ghost stands there and watches the car drive off."

"Ghost?" Why was he listening to this?

"Yes, a white shadow, it leads you through a doorway. Then this older police officer – he had brown hair, and piercing blue eyes, and was in a light colored, long trench coat, you know the kind they wear in the movies. He was standing and looking down at the body of a beautiful Spanish woman. And you came, and you stood beside him. And you said: 'Love or money?' And he said, 'Sometimes it's both.' Then he faded away, and I woke up."

JoAnn stopped. The silence grew. What could Bishop say? She could have been describing Frank with his tattered long, tan trench coat. "Makes me look like a TV cop," he would say, and then laugh. And it did. That's probably why JoAnn had dreamed of a cop in a long, tan, trench coat, she'd seen cops on TV wear them. But the scene she just described, the deer leading him, that made the hairs on the back of his neck stand on end.

Her voice, low as if afraid to draw the evil she had seen in her dream to herself, she continued. "I think you're in grave danger."

He wished she hadn't put it that way.

"When's your birthday? I'll do a chart."

"There's no need, but thank you for your concern." Bishop closed the phone before she could say anything else.

Sergio stared at him impatiently, "Where to?"

Bishop gave him the address to Laura Jones's new house. They rode in silence. Finally Sergio spoke. "About yesterday.... Met the Chief's wife while I was at the target range. Didn't think it'd be polite to just leave."

"Jackie was at the range?" Why did that surprise him? She was a crack shot, her and the Chief spent a lot of time on the range.

"Yeah, was showing me what she'd do the next time some low life entered her bank."

Working out her feelings of helplessness. Some victims did that.

"Fine shooter. Quite a looker." There was the

heartbeat of a pause. "Don't get me wrong, but it surprised me, the Chief being white and her being..."

Bishop didn't respond. It surprised a lot of people, less today than ten years ago when she and the Chief had wed. Another ten years and no one would even notice.

Morning traffic filled the main artery through town. Sergio aggressively switched lanes and cut in between two other vehicles. After a long silence, he glanced at Bishop. "So, you always worked homicide?"

Garfield Falls didn't have an official homicide department, but since most homicides happened at night, when emotions ran the highest, and he had no family to leave, it was Bishop who caught most of the unattended death calls. He shifted so the seatbelt didn't cut as severely across his shoulder and tried to make nice. "No. I worked a beat, then second floor." Something inside winced as the words came out. "Before moving to Special Cases."

"How long ago was that? That you worked second floor?"

Bishop didn't want to talk about it. Second floor was a place onto itself. They worked prostitution, gangs, drugs. The SWAT unit was housed there, along with undercover, and stings. Adrenaline junkies is what Sam called them. Sam was right. And Bishop had been right there among them. Him, Frank, Teonna. Again, he tried to shift away from the deep ache in his shoulder. It was going to rain. Broken bones never truly healed, they could always sense the rain coming.

Sergio slid through a yellow light, but Bishop

didn't say anything about his bending of the traffic laws. "See any action? I mean real action?" When Bishop didn't respond Sergio lifted his shirt, exposing a section of a hundred sit-ups a day abdomen and the scar across the side of his lower rib cage. "Took a bullet. Drug deal gone wrong."

Bishop let his gaze flick to the scar, a thin, red puckering of skin that would someday be hidden in the fold of fat old men got around their middles. He shouldn't judge. It was just as terrifying to have a bullet come at you and burn your skin like an unwanted suitor ripping at your clothes as it was to have it burrow with teeth and claws into your flesh until the crack of bone, breaking and splintering, stopped its rampage through your soul. He winced, feeling the drip, drip, drip, before forcibly cutting off the flood of memories waiting to pull him under and drown him. "Yeah, nice scar." He hadn't meant it to come out sarcastically, but it must have.

Sergio dropped his shirt down with a little too much vigor. "Anyway that's why they booted me upstairs. Have to stay low until they forget my face."

Sergio looked at him defiantly. Bishop pointed left. "Turn there."

After several rounds of phone tag Bishop had reached Laura Jones at her new address north of town in an upscale neighborhood planted far enough away from the congestion of the city to avoid the crime, but still close enough to enjoy the shopping, and to receive city services. The houses were quaint with a storybook feel. His father called them Cotswold cottages, a style that had come and gone quickly at the turn of the century and was now returning as a symbol of a kinder, gentler time. Except these weren't exactly cottages, the square footage was six times Bishop's house, and what was saved in going green was lost in going large.

They parked in the three lane wide driveway, in front of the three stall garage that had two of the doors open. Without speaking, Sergio headed straight for the front entrance and rang the bell, but Bishop paused. A lone BMW was parked against the far wall, while boxes and furniture huddled against the side closest to the house. A quilt, once bright yellow and white, now faded, discolored by the sun so that the two colors blended together, was folded and placed on top of an antique dresser. He knew the design. His grandmother had one just like it, from a kit called Summer Sun, only his grandmother's stayed in a box in her closet, while this one was worn and well-loved. Next to the dresser was a six-pack of Blue Moon beer, one of the bottles missing.

When the door opened, Bishop followed Sergio inside. Laura Jones didn't look like a witch, more like a woman you'd bump into at the grocery store. Her middle-aged figure held back from time by either good genes or regular exercise. Her hair, the same reddish brown of Blossom's, only shot through with white, was held back in a long ponytail, tied low and draped down her back. Even though she had known he was coming she hadn't made an effort with her clothing, she wore old jeans and a t-shirt that featured a tree with a Save the Planet slogan beneath.

She led them through the living area and its stack of boxes. The light scent of herbs, heavy on the sage, hung in the air. A couch and end table had been placed haphazardly in the middle of the room, with little tables at the compass points, a candle on each, starting with pink in the East, just like the candles around the firepit. A mock broom, the old-fashioned kind with twigs for bristles and a crooked branch for a handle, leaned in a corner. Unhung pictures of night skies, leaned against the walls. In one, two intertwined lovers kissed in front of a huge blue moon. Sergio studied the picture, a smirk crossing his face.

Laura gestured toward the boxes. "Mr. Jordan moved me." She stared at the cubes of cardboard as if they had appeared by magic and she wasn't sure what to do with them. Apparently they had. "He hired a crew to come in, and pack everything, and move it all here." Her life, taped-up and waiting, staring back at her. After a moment, she gathered herself and slammed her emotions down, retreating from them to the kitchen. Bishop didn't have to be told what it was like to see your world shoved into a suitcase and be booted out the door. The guilt came with you whether you packed it or not.

The kitchen was large, inviting, with white cabinets and yellow walls. The counter and work island strained with containers of food. He recognized the fresh bread from JoAnne's kitchen, a plate of dark chocolate chip cookies next to it, and wondered if the two women had talked about JoAnn's dream. Of course they would have. They were friends, probably twittered back and forth. An open box, half-unpacked, sat on a chair near the dishwasher.

Bishop began. "We're sorry to have to ask you these questions. It's just routine."

Or would be if the examiner's report said accidental death

"Yes, of course." Laura stared into the box. Without feeling, she pulled out a bundle of brown packing paper, carefully unwrapping a cartoon character glass that was the prize inside. Bishop remembered them. They had been a give-away from a fast food chain, he couldn't remember which one, Claire had made him drive all over town looking for the last, missing one, while Sonny cried inconsolably in the back seat. It hadn't been about the glass. It had been about being an absent father. He tried to relax his shoulder, forcing the muscles not to lock up on him. He understood. Laura was going through the motions, touching the objects of her life without any feeling of joy, or hope, moving forward while looking back.

"Hard time to move."

She nodded, her eyes were dry but her hands shaking as she put the glass into the open dishwasher and dropped the wrapping paper into a trash can at her side.

"Did Blossom have any problems with anyone? At school maybe? A boyfriend?"

"No. She was a good girl. A little shy, but

everyone liked her. She had friends."

"Like Amanda?" Sergio interjected.

Laura didn't look up just nodded her head and reached into the box for another bundle of paper. She took a deep breath. "Amanda. Yes, I thought Amanda would be good for her. Get Blossom out of her shell. But – "

Sergio pushed forward. "This Amanda. She was a bad influence. Blossom started doing things she shouldn't. Staying out late. Smoking. Drinking. Drugs. You started arguing."

Laura's back stiffened. Her chin lifted in angry defiance.

"You think I was a bad mother? That marrying young and divorcing when Blossom was still a baby was wrong?"

No one had said anything about being a bad mother.

She took a step toward Sergio, but the officer held his ground so that they stood within striking distance. "Well, I was devoted to my daughter. Unlike her father who thought he could come and go as he pleased. Who used his family's money as bait to attract young girls and then, when he was bored, he tossed them aside, and went after someone even younger."

This wasn't getting the investigation anywhere.

Bishop pushed between them. "No one's implying anything." The men's eyes locked. Bishop picked up a random plate off the counter and shoved it at Sergio. "Why don't you have a cookie?"

And shut up.

"You don't mind if he has a cookie?" Bishop turned his head to glance at Laura. Tears filled her eyes. A desire to wrap his arms around her and comfort her took him by surprise. He normally didn't react to a woman's tears, certainly not a suspect's. Annoyed with himself, Bishop pushed the impulse aside.

Laura shook her head as if to dispel any doubt Sergio had created in her mind. "Blossom wasn't like he said. She didn't drink, or swear, or do drugs. She was a good girl." Her eyes pleaded with Bishop to understand. His voice dropped to a deeper tone and a sensual rumble slipped in, soothing her. "We're just looking at all the possibilities. Maybe if I could see some of her things?" He resisted the urge to reach out and touch Laura's arm.

After a hesitant glance toward Sergio, who stood, plate in hand, a scowl frozen on his face, she led Bishop to the garage. "These are all hers." Laura stopped short, she reached out and touched the quilt. The stitches large and clumsy as if done by a child.

"Her dresser?"

Laura nodded.

He turned his back to Laura and focused on listening for Blossom's whispers. Anything would help. A clue as to her life before her death. She had a story to tell if he would just get out of the way and let her tell him. Gently, he opened the top drawer, the thin one where woman always store their underclothes, and lace nighties, and things dear to their hearts. Blossom's checkbook rested on top of the fabric jumble. "Things were ok – financially?"

Just because you lived in a big house didn't mean you had money.

"Yes, well, now." She gazed around the big garage. "All those years struggling on late child support checks..."

Bishop winced.

"...and working two jobs ... Mr. Jordan traded us this house for ... for ... the one I got in the divorce settlement."

Yes, she would have kept the house. Women did that, after all they were the ones who hung the drapes, who hung the pictures, who hung onto the memories.

"Keisha says it's a good deal. That this is a show place."

Keisha was right.

"Blossom's father, he's in Europe?"

"Yes. Took his new girlfriend there for her sixteenth birthday." There was no mistaking the bitterness, then the tears came back to her eyes. "I'm not sure he even knows."

"You don't stay in touch?" He didn't add for the child's sake.

"He's, his family's, quite well off. They always thought I wanted his money, their money." She lifted the quilt off the dresser, and carefully refolded it before hugging the memory soaked fabric to herself, touching a corner against her cheek. "They saw Blossom as a trap and wanted nothing to do with her, us."

Bishop nodded, some women laid traps, back when having, or not having, a father mattered to society, mattered to the father. He casually opened the checkbook. The top check was 1005. A new account at the Garfield Falls Bank and Trust. As he handed the checkbook to Laura, he let the register open and glanced at the balance. It was more than he made in a year.

Laura seemed embarrassed by the amount and quickly closed the cover. "When she turned eighteen she came into a trust set up by her grandfather."

"It by-passed you. Now what?"

"There's no will. What eighteen-year-old has a will? We'll fight in court – again."

Possible motive. Money was always a possible motive.

Laura reached into the open dresser drawer, and lifted a faded blue nightie with frogs and willow pads and magic swirls. "She said they made her dream of her prince charming."

Careful not to touch the rumpled stack of silky panties, Bishop reached to the back of the drawer, his fingers finding more fabric. Only it wasn't silky, it was rough and knit. With a push, a sock rolled forward. A man's sock. Brown. The kind you can buy anywhere. The mate to the one he'd found in the fire?

"That's not hers."

The mother, Laura, her name was Laura, shook her head, her hand to her throat, confusion brewing in her eyes.

"May I take it?"

"Yes, of course."

He tucked it into the open evidence bag in his pocket. Then reached back into the drawer, feeling along the top. Something was taped there. With a gentle tug it fell into his palm and he pulled it into the light. A little, round, white case. Birth control pills.

Laura pulled in a sharp breath. A sob fought to come out.

Bishop checked. Eleven refills left.

"She ever talk about anyone?"

Either not trusting her voice, or unable to speak, Laura shook her head.

Bishop mentally noted the doctor, not that he'd speak to him, Blossom was unlikely to have told the doctor her lover's name, but Bishop knew the doctor volunteered at the free clinic near the University, the one Hannah always took her girls to.

The next drawer down held the usual, plain t-shirts and soft sweaters. He reached to the bottom and came up with a book. The cover was stiff, dark leather. A cheap lock of pot metal formed a clasp. "A diary."

Laura shook her head. "Her book of spells."

His face asked for further explanation.

"A spell isn't a cake recipe." Laura defended without his attacking. "It's more like predicting the weather. You write down what things were like before the rain began. As many details as you can, the clouds, the temperature, and then try to reproduce them. Some witches are better at noticing what details are the most important. And their spells are more universal. But it's all trial and error."

He fanned through the pages. Little drawings along the edges, words, some in lines like poems. The light scent of rose cologne. Looked like a diary to him. He'd peeked into his sisters' often enough to know one when he saw one.

"May I take this?"

"No." She took the book from his hands, her cold fingers brushing against his warm ones. He had to let her keep it. If the ME came back with suspicious death he could make a stronger request. When the ME declared suspicious death, he corrected himself. Something had made the county boys think murder and call him.

He opened the bottom drawer. Hidden under the neatly folded t-shirts and sweaters he found a snapshot of Blossom in the mountains, her back to a waterfall. She was young, not eighteen, more sweet sixteen. It must have been spring, the plants had that over-bright green they always have when they're growing like weeds. Behind her the bright red leaves of a vine wrapped around a tree.

"I didn't know she'd kept that."

"Vacation?"

"No. Yes. She'd gone to the mountains with a friend. There was poison oak." Laura pointed to the red foliage in the picture. "Blossom got some on her and had a horrible reaction. The girl she was with left her there. I had to go out and bring her home."

Sixteen, it was a magic age. "What was her

name?"

Laura looked puzzled for a moment. "Who?"

"The girl that Blossom went with?" Not that he cared. She just seemed to need to talk.

Laura shook her head. A few wisps of curls slipped free of the harsh rubber band holding back her hair, they framed her face and seemed to soften the grief for an instant. "I don't know. She never said. I think she was afraid of getting the girl into trouble." Laura stared a moment longer at the joyous smile on her daughter's face before she returned the picture to the deeps of the past and closed the drawer.

As Bishop stepped back to give her more room, to keep from crowding her, his foot brushed the carton of beer bottles and they clinked like church bells calling the believers.

"Blue Moon." Nice beer, smooth, too expensive for his wallet.

"I think one of the moving crew left that by mistake. I don't drink."

They both stared at the empty space where a bottle was missing. No one accidently left good beer.

"She might have used it in her spell."

Bishop stood and looked down at Laura. She was just the right height, the height he liked women to be for easy kissing. She smiled, that let-me-be-helpful smile women have. It made her attractive. Her eyes honey brown and her skin softly tanned. For an instant the worry lines disappeared, and he saw her as she must have been twenty years ago. More than attractive.

"A blue moon brings lovers together." She told him, a bit of witch trivia.

He nodded as if he understood. The big garage felt small and uncomfortably hot. Teonna would have made a joke, something about witches and love spells. About how she was going to bewitch him and bind him to her forever. Maybe Teonna had.

CHAPTER THIRTEEN

After miles in silence, leaving the quiet neighborhoods for the main thruway that cut the town in half, Sergio still slammed the brakes and punched the gas, weaving through traffic like a man who knew he'd missed a life's opportunity. "I had her, she was ready to confess." His words were as hard and angry as his driving.

Just as annoyed, Bishop shot back. "To what? We don't even know if there's been a murder." Except Bishop knew. If he strained he could hear Blossom whispering: Give me peace. He'd seen accidental death, this wasn't one of them.

"You were handling her with kid gloves."

He knew that accusatory tone, that glare, that avoidance of eye contact, and tried a different tack, softening his voice instead of matching Sergio's hard clip. "She'd just lost her child. We needed her on our side. We need to know about the love spell and the man Blossom was seeing."

"What love spell? What man?"

Bishop swallowed a snort of frustration. Had he been that stupid when he'd joined the special cases unit? No, he remembered following the Chief around, silent, watching, hurting inside so that even the most gruesome crimes washed over him. And when the Chief had been promoted to shift leader, and Bishop had been teamed with Morris, he'd been seasoned. The two of them had worked as a unit. Morris liked the paperwork, leaving Bishop the footwork. Slowly Bishop had learned to read a crime scene, to see the un-seeable clues, to listen as the dead whispered to him.

Again the Chief had been promoted, this time to assistant police commissioner, pushing Morris to shift leader. Since then Bishop had worked alone. Or with whoever he could get to crawl out of bed to look at a dead body. Last Christmas Sam had been bumped upstairs. The Chief had picked him before Sam had even taken his detective exams. It was a good call. That's why Johnson was one step down from police commissioner. And would be commissioner if it wasn't an elected position, the Chef liked to run things without politics interfering. Yes, the Chief made good calls. Sam was getting it. He was letting go of his preconceived notions and looking, listening, learning. But this one. Sergio wasn't ready to convict criminals, he only wanted to catch them and prove that he was bigger, better, stronger. A grunting, growling, alpha male.

"They're just a bunch of old women who couldn't get a man and are now getting their rocks off playing magic."

They had followed a turn-off past a strip mall and on into another middle class neighborhood. Row after row of identical houses like silent soldiers at parade rest greeted them. Lost, Sergio hunted the house numbers. Bishop pointed to the third house on the left. The mailbox had a sexy witch decaled to the side. Along the walk were gazing balls scattered among the new bloom of spring flowers, an occasional fairy figurine lawn ornament peeking at them from behind the petals.

When Bishop rang the bell a high pitched, mechanical voice cackled in maniacal laughter. He expected an overly tall butler with a long, sad face to open the door, instead an elderly woman with white hair and a spry attitude appeared. "Mimi Yreka?" He stumbled over the pronunciation but she didn't correct him.

"Are you the police officers?"

Bishop only nodded while Sergio took out his badge and let the woman examine it.

"Well, come in. I have a few minutes. My granddaughter's home sick from school, or I'd offer you coffee."

Sergio paused. But Bishop continued in. He'd been exposed to sick kids before, first Sonny, then his ex-wife's daughter Lexi. Now his neighborhood seemed to attract every young female with a fatherless child, and the children seemed to find him like iron fragments find a magnet. A half flight of stairs took them up to the living room, at the other end another half flight of stairs went to the kitchen. They could see a young girl, maybe five, sitting hunched over a large white sheet of paper on the kitchen table, an array of colored pencils scattered around her.

Mimi's gaze followed Bishop's to the little girl. "What do you do?" She shrugged her shoulders in resignation. "Her mother has to work." A spontaneous smile eased the wrinkles on her face. "We were drawing fairies."

"And dragons." The girl corrected her grandmother without even looking up.

"Yes, dragons." Finally, Mimi turned her attention to Bishop. Without preamble, or even a question being asked, she started. "I didn't know anyone from the coven that well. I just needed details for my latest book series. I write online."

Both Bishop and Sergio must have given her a blank stare.

"Emma, honey, will you get Grandma a business card from the desk?"

The young girl disappeared to the side of the room Bishop couldn't see.

"They were a lot of help. I based my last book on Blossom. A young witch trying to break free of her mother's influence. Of course, I jazzed it up a bit. Put in a handsome warlock, they don't actually call male witches warlocks, but that's what the public knows them as, so I thought I'd better as well."

The girl came down the stairs, her bare feet silent on the carpet. When she passed Sergio he pulled back as if the germs would leap off the child and onto him. But the girl didn't seem to notice. She handed the card to her grandmother and wrapped herself around Mimi's leg, shyly staring up at Bishop. No fever flush, no cranky set to her mouth, her eyes interested, but not overly bright. From experience Bishop guessed she'd gotten the I-need-some-adult-attention flu. Mimi handed the card to Bishop. It wasn't actually a business card, more a baseball card in size, on one side was a book blurb with website and buying information, on the other a shadowy woman, her head tipped back in the thralls of passion, and a book title, Savage something, blazed across her throat in deep red.

"That's good for ten percent off."

Bishop doubted that he would need the discount, westerns were savage enough for him, but put the card in his pocket anyway.

"So Blossom and her mother weren't on good terms?"

"Oh, no, I wouldn't say that. Blossom just wanted love. Romance. You know. Girls do at her age." Mimi lowered her voice as if revealing a secret. "But she found the wrong man."

Finding the wrong man, that could happen at any age. Bishop didn't know why he thought of Hannah.

Still without a prompt, Mimi kept going. "I didn't know him. He was married. And she met him at the University."

A lot of men went to the University. "Do you know what courses she was taking?"

"Ah," Mimi wrinkled her already wrinkled forehead. "Oh, my, Criminal Justice. The professor is a young hottie. Real stud. I used him as a cover model. He was happy to get some undeclared income. Educators don't make as much money as you'd think."

Did anybody?

"You've got to get cheap artwork where you can." She paused and appraised their appearance. "You boys ever ...?"

"Ever?" Sergio asked lost in the zigzag of the conversation.

"Pose, you know, for books covers."

Bishop expression must have said don't even go there, and she let the subject drop.

"All the girls flock to the class before he flunks them out."

"Flunks them out?" Sergio repeated like an idiot parrot.

"Of course, they aren't there to study, just swoon over him. I used the set-up a few years ago when mysteries and college professors where all the rage. A teacher and a young student get together and murder his wife. Never sold very well."

Bishop could see why, one was bound to turn on the other. "Married?"

"Yes, and has two of the most darling little boys."

"Got a number?"

She was organized. Had to be. She gave Bishop the number, and another card, this one with a photographer's information. "If you ever need to make a few bucks. I'm coming out with a more mature hero next year. Do you have any tattoos? No? We can Photo Shop those. Scars?"

He politely put the card in his pocket with the other one. You didn't get to his age without scars.

She handed another card to Sergio. "The ethnic look is in. Hispanic?"

"Italian." His voice held that edge of irritation that clearly said the mistake had been made before.

Bishop turned the conversation back to the dead witch. "What do you know about Amanda?"

"Oh? Her." Mimi stroked the top of her granddaughter's head, smoothing the curls. "She didn't come to many meetings. But when she did she'd try to push her way to the front. You know the kind – I just arrived but obviously, I know more than you and everyone should listen to me. Anyway, she had an old book of spells. Her great-great-something grandmother's." Mimi's hand paused and the curls on the child's head bounced back. "I have to give her, it was quite a book."

"Why do you say that?"

"Oh, the spells that were in it. I used a few in Witch Way Do I Turn, Blossom's story. Lots of nasty spells to hurt people, and then the love spells. Keisha said such things never worked. But I think that's why they were there."

"Who was where?" Sergio barked at her, his voice loud in the small house.

The child buried her face in her grandmother's

leg. Mimi shifted her gaze from Bishop toward Sergio and stared as if she were memorizing his features. Her hand slid down her granddaughter's back reassuring the child. "Why Blossom, Amanda, and Venus." She spoke slow and carefully. "They were casting a love spell."

Bishop kept his interest out of his voice. "What do you know about Venus?"

"Not much, Venus wasn't her real name. It was a made-up name. She didn't want us to know who she was. Very mysterious. Would park her big Lincoln down the road. Arrive in a heavy veil. Think we couldn't see her. But you can. Very attractive, like a Hollywood witch, high cheek bones, a pouty mouth, vampire pale skin. I tried to get her to pose for one of my covers, but she wouldn't come near me after that. Blossom knew her from somewhere else."

A big Lincoln, didn't want to be seen, ran from the scene. "From the bank?"

Mimi blinked in surprise. "I'd never thought of that, but you could be right. They laughed at the money spells. That they had plenty of money – it just wasn't theirs."

Sergio drove south, back toward the center of town. As he wove through the traffic, he read the cards Mimi had given him, before finally stuffing them into his pocket. "You think that's legit?"

Bishop didn't care. His shoulder ached. Throbbed would be a better word. But the sky was clear. Not a rain cloud in sight. It was as if the old wound had been pierced, and the festering pain, so long kept in check, threatened to overwhelm him.

Sergio gave Bishop a disdainful look. "Is this all you guys do? Talk, talk, talk?"

Bishop forced the pain to the back of his mind and stared over at Sergio. No, they listened, to what was said, and more importantly, to what wasn't said.

"If we'd stayed much longer she'd have pulled out the tea and cookies."

Without telling his intent, Sergio turned away from the station house and parked in front of the diner, taking the only free spot as a car pulled out. Bishop had a bologna sandwich and a handful of limp carrot sticks back at the station.

"Early for lunch." He could hear the annoyance in his voice.

Sergio tapped the clock on the dashboard. It read eleven-forty-five. "Seems about right to me."

Inside the lunch crowd filled the lobby waiting area, a crude line had formed waiting for the hostess to seat them. When a booth emptied, Sergio didn't wait, jumping the line and budging out two women in heels that weren't paying attention. A third woman had gone to the bathroom and they'd been busy sharpening their claws on her flaws. Noticing, one of the women scowling at him when she'd realized what had happened, Sergio smiled back, his high cheekbones and brooding eyes saving the day.

They didn't wait long before a waitress appeared, two water glasses in one hand, menus in the other. Mindlessly she repeated the menu board as she cleared the plates left by the last diner, a glazed look on her face and around her eyes. Mandy, the name tag read, her face over made-up with foundation, like a teenager covering a bad case of acne. Only she wasn't a teenager, she was older, mid-twenties.

"The special's corned beef on rye with a side of slaw." She didn't look at them, didn't give them that give me a big tip smile.

Bishop reached backward, thumbing through the faces stored in his memory. Nothing. Maybe the relative of a crime victim? Something about her was familiar. Whatever, she was having a hard day. Deliberately dropping his voice to that lower, soothing rumble that he knew women responded to, he nodded. "Sounds good. Water to drink. No hurry."

Bishop let his hand brush the woman's when she took the menu and she finally made eye contact. For an instant they stared. She pulled in her bottom lip sinking her teeth into the soft fleshiness before looking away and touching the silver chain around her neck, briefly exposing the ornament it held. A silver circle with a crescent shape attached to each side.

"Yeah, same, except I'll have a Bud."

When she removed Sergio's menu, Bishop noticed that she was careful to keep her fingers on the edge of the stiff laminated sheet and well away from where Sergio's hand might be. Although she didn't respond, Sergio maintained an aggressive flirt with her throughout the meal.

As they finished Sam called.

"They found some of the bait money."

"That was fast." Bishop wasn't sure he'd ever known bait money to get found, tellers didn't have time to check serial numbers on the money coming through their drawers.

"I guess it had some red stain on it and was easy to spot. So the FBI is getting warrants to look at tapes." Sam didn't sound too happy.

"Done with Turner and the Jane Doe already?"

"No, they're holding the bodies until they can arrange transport. Oh, and the ME wanted to talk to you."

Bishop closed the phone. While he was talking, the waitress had come by with the check. Sergio finally picked it up, but neglected to leave a tip. Bishop opened his wallet. Only a few bills held the thin leather apart. Picking out two ones he dropped them on the table.

When Sergio parked in a no parking zone at the hospital Bishop didn't say anything, just as he hadn't said anything on the short drive from the hospital. It was Sergio's ticket. He lead the way through the maze of hallways, ignoring the posted signs, taking an emergency-only stair down to the basement and coming out directly in front of the double doors labeled no admittance, hospital personnel only. After fifteen years whispering to the dead, he could have found his way in the dark. Sergio hung back; his hands thrust into his pockets, scowling like a teenager while Bishop shoved open the door to the morgue. Without warning the odor of cleaning agents, formaldehyde, and death swirled out.

The ME leaned over a table giving them both an eye full of her soft round breasts that filled her tight lab coat to over flowing. Sergio shuffled, an unmistakable tension of interest emanating from him. Bishop stared at the dead girl rather than the ME's chest.

"You're too fast, Bishop, I'm not ready."

He doubted that.

Sergio's interest drew the ME's interest and she straightened. Her tiny pink tongue touched her top lip, then disappeared.

"Sam said you called me."

"I thought he'd come with you."

"He's on another case." Done with the foreplay, Bishop looked down at the body. "Cause of death?"

"In layman's terms..." She stared at Sergio. "...suffocation." Her eyes ran up, then down, his body like little mice chasing a bit of cheese. "The victim inhaled something that caused her membranes to swell..." She gave the last word a push and paused before continuing.

Sergio caught the innuendo and exhaled through his nose in response.

"...blocked out all the oxygen, trapped in all the carbon-monoxide." The ME moved around the table to stand closer to Sergio.

"Do we know what caused the reaction?" Bishop asked without looking over at the two of them sizing each other up.

The ME reached for the chart, bending so Sergio got a full view of not just her creamy white bosom but the edge of the pink tips as well, then flipped over a couple of pages. "I've sent tissue to the lab. Give it a few days."

"Speculate for me. Something off the street?"

She shifted and bumped her leg against Sergio's thigh

"If I find anything, it'll be in the report."

Sergio stood his ground and took the offered opportunity to again stare down her cleavage while she sucked in his scent. They shifted in unison so that Sergio's leg was between hers. The ME moistened her lips and tipped her head up.

"So, where is Sam?" Her voice didn't lift in interest and her gaze never left Sergio's face.

Bishop guessed she asked out of habit, forgetting that she'd asked before, or maybe she wanted to be sure she wouldn't be interrupted later. Without bothering to answer, Bishop took the chart from her then turned his back on the pair. A soft movement told him Sergio was following her dance. There was a long pause where Bishop could hear breathing – heavy, lustful breathing.

"I have this ... thing, I can't seem to reach." Her voice aspirated a soft growl. "Do you think you could help me with it?"

Footsteps headed toward the back storage room, Bishop doubted it was to get something off a top shelf. He didn't have to hear the rustle of clothing pushed aside, the rhythmic whisper of flesh to flesh, or the escalating breathing to know what was going on.

He concentrated on the report. Swelling of the

lining of the lungs indicating a severe reaction to inhalant. Possibly smoke from open wood fire. Smoke residue and ash were found in lungs and on exposed body and hair. Sample sent to lab for identification. No reason to think homicide.

Bishop begrudged that the paramedics had been right. Blossom had been overcome by the smoke created by her own spell. He stared down at her face, the death scream still trapped in her throat. She lay silent and cold refusing to talk to him.

Finished before Sergio and the ME, Bishop flipped the page. Beneath was a fresh form, only the name filled out. Elmo Xavier Turner. The FBI hadn't wasted any time getting the bodies to the morgue. Their people would be here shortly to do the formalities.

The sounds from the back ramped up in volume making them harder to ignore. Bishop went to the bank of refrigerator vaults along the wall and opened Turner's. He pulled out the corpse, laying silently on its silver bed and stared down at a face not yet old, the growth on Turner's chin more down than beard. His fingers itched to brush a wayward strand of the corpse's hair back behind his ear, the way he'd seen Mrs. Turner do time and time again. Instead, he forced himself to crawl into Turner's skin.

Why? Why?

Bishop recalled the dead body shoved into the trunk of the car. The armpits of the shirt heavily stained. Sweating in the cold spring air. Two duffle bags full of money in the trunk. Two? He didn't question it. That's a lot of money for a kid that's grown up on government checks and church lady charity.

The ashtray had been full of cigarette butts.

You wait, smoking endless cigarettes. Outside in your car. Why not wait inside away from the sharp, wet wind coming off the lake? Because you'd been inside, you'd seen her lying on the bed. Gasping, choking, you'd run outside, vomiting into the bushes. That's what everyone did with their first dead body. The stomach knots and churns and heaves. It was almost as if by offering up whatever nourishment you had in you, you could appease their soul and keep the evil away from you. Were you the one who moved her, tried to hide her in the pit? No. No, you'd run. Run outside and vomited. You're scared. You sit shivering, the music off, afraid of dying.

You're waiting. Waiting for someone.

You're not a big thinker. Getting from A to C is a struggle. You were supposed to give the woman the money. But she's dead. You wait. Outside. Afraid. Why not run? Who else are you waiting for?

All that money. A minor leaguer pitching with the pros. Sweating in the cold. Stomach churning. Why can't things be like they were?

Someone arrives. You want out. You argue.

Then he smiles, he puts his arm around you, and walks you to your car. Hands you money. You look at the wad of bills. Blood money. Not what you'd agreed on. Not the killing. You're sick, and afraid, and want to go home. Too late you realize that you will be blamed. When you look up you see the gun pointed at you.

Not enough time to run. Not enough time to scream.

Chest, chest, head. Like a doll you fall into the open car trunk. Into the darkness.

Heavy breathing and grunting came from the other room overshadowing Bishop's slow, steady inhaling and exhaling of the cold air escaping the body vaults. After a moment's hesitation, punctuated by a deep moan from the storeroom, Bishop closed Turner's vault, letting the adult-in-years-only whispers fall silent. He should wait in the hall. After one step, he stopped. A silent scream seemed to reach through the steel door of the vault next to Turner's. Like a sailor headed toward the rocks Bishop opened the vault.

The woman from the warehouse. Even in death, her face no longer animated, he could tell she'd been a dusky beauty, an Esmeralda.

Who is your Quasimodo?

He couldn't envision her with Turner.

No, she was above the bad boy's pay grade. He chided himself, sometimes women saw see things in a man other than his paycheck. Well, some women, not the ones he knew, not his ex-wife. Bishop paused. He hadn't put the child support check in the mail. Then he cringed. It wouldn't clear anyway.

Focus on me, focus on my pain, she seemed to scream at him. Look at my heart.

Not broken. One shot at close range. Two MO's. Two killers. Someone had shot her, and left her there, lying on the bed. Logic said Turner shot her, someone else shot Turner.

Her dark hair curled into ringlets around her face. No, not Turner. As far as Bishop knew Turner had never hurt anyone. He'd thrown rocks through windows, shot out car tires, shop lifted. If Turner had been mean, if he'd been able to do more than whine, the gangs would have sucked him in. No, if Turner had shot her, he wouldn't have been sitting outside in the cold. He'd have lit a fire in one of those empty barrels. He'd have been smoking a cigar and counting his money.

So, not Turner, someone else. Someone Esmeralda wasn't expecting. Who she knew but didn't know. Why would he think that? Bishop didn't question. Answers came later, for now he listened, and Esmeralda whispered.

Take the money and run. Forget the love nest, that was over, had never been more than one using the other.

But she'd never seen the money. Turner had arrived with the money after she'd been shot.

So much money. More than enough to share.

Maybe she wanted out as well. Maybe the amount of money, at first intoxicating, but in the cold light of the morning, looking more and more like a Vegas marriage.

Bishop pushed the table back into the wall unit, slamming the door to cover the gasping final moan of the ME. A few moments later, Sergio emerged tucking his shirt into his pants and carrying his jacket. Not bothering to wait until the ME came out of the backroom Bishop placed the clipboard on the desk and left without saying a word. Sergio followed, a satisfied grin on his face.

CHAPTER FOURTEEN

Sam would have known to drive a little, to head out of town and back, let Bishop clear his head and puzzle on the whisperings of the dead bodies, instead Sergio turned the radio to top volume and rocked to the decisive beat of an angry song with garbled words. When they pulled into the police parking lot, Bishop's head pounded as hard as the music and his shoulder throbbed. He stood, half in and half out of the car, scanning the sky. Not a cloud in sight and yet his shoulder ached as if the heavens were about to burst. Consciously he forced himself to put the pain away, thinking about it didn't help, never had, never would.

Not his case anyway. His case was a young witch whose dream of love had exploded in her face. Only she didn't trust him. He'd never solve the case if she didn't trust him.

Inside, the elevator doors stood wide-open, waiting. Bishop turned left toward the stairwell while

Sergio got on the elevator. As he took the steps alone, Bishop listened to the faint echo of his footsteps on the metal stairs, but they weren't loud enough to overshadow the whispers from Turner and Esmeralda, their early deaths overpowering the young witch's gasping silence. What had they expected? A quick score? Then a run for the border? Had Sam talked to Turner's mother? Or had the FBI? They'd have gotten more information if Sam had talked to her alone. No, Bishop should have talked to her. She knew him. She would have trusted him enough to tell him what was going on. Too late now, what was done was done, once you cross some lines there was no going back.

At the third floor, Sergio was already there, the grin the ME had put on his face unmistakable. Beat you old man, Sergio seemed to say without opening his mouth. Ignoring the taunt, and the call to muscle flexing, Bishop went to his desk. After glancing around and finding only Morris deep in schedule sheets, a bottle of antacids at his elbow, Sergio sat at the middle desk where they always put new officers.

"Where is everyone?"

Bishop thought of the bank. Was anyone there, asking questions? No one had mentioned a dye pack so how had the bait money gotten red stains? Was it the courier's bait money or the bank's? Had they looked at old surveillance tapes? When had Turner come in and looked around? Or had that been Esmeralda's job? Who else did Turner hang out with? This had to be someone new, someone who played hardball. Her friends? Her family? Maybe the Chief would know, he'd gotten Turner into the rehab program.

If he went to the bank he could put his finger on why things didn't feel right. A special shipment. A distribution point. An inside job. Bishop glanced at Sergio adjusting the set-up of his computer, moving pens and pencils out of one drawer and into the next. He couldn't take Sergio to the bank. They both knew it wasn't his case. Sam would have gone anyway, understood, or at least hung back and not commented.

Not his case. He had a case. Putting away his curiosity about the bank job, forcing the whispers of the dead to quiet, Bishop focused on his case. The ME said Blossom had reacted to something in the smoke. What was in the smoke? Only things she put in her spell. What did witches put in their spells?

He tapped his pencil on the desk. Detective Torres stomped in, her heavy shoes hitting the floor like a drunken trucker. Even though she'd been there a month Bishop didn't know her. He wanted to think it was because he was busy, but he knew it was because he wasn't interested. Today he was. Today he noticed that she was a woman. Tall, toned, the full magnum under her jacket only half concealed. But she wasn't Teonna. The only way they were alike was the air of confidence. He tried to pull up the image of Teonna. He'd never had to try before, she'd always been right there. A smoky picture of intense eyes and blonde hair tangling in the wind came, burned, and was gone.

Sam arrived breaking his thoughts. When Sam passed Sergio's desk the new officer leaned back, his hands locked behind his head. "Just met the ME, if you know what I mean." With a wink, Sergio clicked his tongue and grinned. Bishop could tell Sam knew what Sergio meant. It would have taken an idiot not to know what he meant.

Sam glumly nodded and sat at his desk without comment. When had Sam gotten tangled with the ME? The woman flirted with him, hell, she came on to everyone, but Sam had always been too smart to take her up on her offers. Silently, Sam stared at the phone and Bishop understood – wrong set of initials.

"Why aren't you with the FBI?"

"They took off."

"They're done processing the crime scene already?"

Sam shook his head. "Don't think so. Another bank south of here found more of the bait money in with their business deposits."

"Really? They didn't throw the bait money?" Hard to believe. The criminals were both very lucky and very stupid. The biggest score a small time delinquent on his first big-bad could ever hope for, and after killing him in a double cross the murderers run, spending money like drunken sailors and waving behind a trail as noticeable as a flag in the wind.

"Yeah. The FBI think the robbers didn't know what it was." Sam's gaze returned to the un-ringing phone.

He had to ask. "You talk to Turner's mother?"

Sam shifted in his chair the resulting squeak making Sergio look up. "She had this jumbled story about him doing somebody a favor. That he was mesmerized by this Mexican woman."

Bishop doubted Mrs. Turner had said mesmerized.

"That she used voodoo on her baby. Put him under a love spell. That her boy would never rob a bank. Bawled her eyes out."

"Yeah, sounds like a great mom, catch the kid with his hand in the cookie jar and she says my kid didn't do it."

Neither Bishop nor Sam responded to Sergio's comment and after a moment Sergio went back to personalizing his desk. Bishop rummaged through the bottom drawer of his desk and retrieved a magazine of Sudoku puzzles, tossing the booklet at Sam. "Here."

The slick cover paper skittered across the desk table and Sam caught it before it fell over the edge. He picked up a pen and Bishop shook his head tossing him the pencil he'd been tapping and annoying Sergio with. Sam arranged himself within easy reach of the phone and opened the booklet.

Sergio watched. "So what am I supposed to do?"

"Reports." They replied in unison.

Without a pencil to tap, Bishop reread his notes. He'd put Blossom's red candle into evidence but never really looked at it, that meant a trip downstairs. Like most buildings in the upper-Midwest the station had a basement. May as well, since you had to put footings below the frost line. Throw up a few walls and a floor, call it a basement and count it in the square footage of the building. Like most basements things collected there. Beside the file room crammed with paper reports, beginning in the days when Garfield Falls was a whistle stop for the trains, was the evidence locker. Boxes and bins of evidence, the remnants of lives destroyed by crime, sat on sturdy shelves behind heavy chicken wire barriers and double locked gates. Bishop avoided the place whenever he could. The persistent damp made his shoulder ache, and no matter how much light you fixed to the ceiling it never came close to the power of the sun.

He couldn't see anyone to let him in, and hesitated a moment staring at the lock. A sub-standard F series that even a rocket scientist could have broken into. Out of courtesy, and because he wanted to stay away from his desk as long as he could, Bishop pushed the buzzer, the sharp, vibrating note piercing the silence. From the back a large sergeant, with the kind of round belly middle-aged men and Santa Claus often acquire, worked his way to the front, squeezing through the tiny aisles. Bishop couldn't remember his name but knew he'd been the keeper of the keys and logs for years. That he had been a decent officer before that, until bad knees and good cooking took him off the streets.

"Hey, Bishop, I was just thinking about you." The big guy chuckled and his belly lifted with the quick inhales and exhales.

Bishop shifted uneasily. If the man knew him that meant he must know the sergeant, but no name came to him. He took Bishop's case number and headed back into the maze of storage. As he passed through the boxes he would reach out and touch certain ones as if touching old friends. From the dark recesses of the storage room, his voice came in muffled spurts. "Remember this one. Man kills his wife, and tries to make it look like a burglary. Took you about ten seconds to see through that ruse. All because he wanted her trust fund, only to find out she'd left it to the shelter house. Never got a dime."

Bishop nodded. Yeah, he remembered that one. The man claimed the thief came through a window that had been broken from the inside.

"What'd he get? Life?"

"Thirty plus." How could he remember that and not remember the sergeant's name?

"Oh, yeah, that's right." He came round from a different route than he'd disappeared down, carrying a small box. "You want everything?"

"Just the red candle."

The sergeant rummaged through the contents of the box, his white gloved hands protecting the contents from being contaminated with his DNA, deftly sorting through the contents. Finally he came up with the candle. "This one?"

"Yeah."

"There's more."

"No, just that one."

He nodded and handed Bishop the transparent evidence bag. Then pointed on the log for Bishop to sign, date, and record a file number. He lifted the box and started back into the catacombs, then paused, touching a huge box on the floor. "This one's from that night. Moving it to inactive cases."

Without asking, Bishop knew what night he was referring to.

"My first week in the field. What a week. The big train wreck, then the warehouse shoot-out." They both stared at the banker's box, the cardboard still bright white, the lid snug, as though the box had never been opened. "What a week. How many did you take down? Ten? Some say it was twenty."

Bishop felt yanked back in time. His hand trembled as he wrote. Ten? Who'd stopped to count? So many shots had been fired that the room had been thick with smoke. Its sharp bite mixed with the metallic tang of blood that was everywhere. On his clothes, his hands, his face – in his mouth.

"When we rolled in I thought Armageddon had arrived. The door to that warehouse kicked in, smoke coming out of it like it was on fire. And the blood. I've never seen so much blood before or since."

He heard Teonna's scream coming from his right, then echoing through the smoke. Gunshots so loud, coming from every direction that he seemed to be standing in the barrel of a pistol. He fired and fired, scrambling to find Teonna in the haze of exploding gunpowder. Sounds muffled through his broken eardrums, but his own heartbeat pounded like the William Tell overture. He'd found her on the floor and pulled her to him. The warmth of her blood soaking through his shirt, and matting the hairs on his chest.

Bullets hit them from every direction. He needed to carry her away from the death closing in on them. But his legs wouldn't work. She kept sliding from his arms. He couldn't stand, couldn't lift her. He should have been able to lift her. He'd carried her before, carried to her bed, laughing, her laugh hot and sultry like a summer wind. But he couldn't lift her. Instead he'd buried his face in her hair and inhaled the cleanness of her shampoo thinking it would be his last breath. Relieved that they would die together.

"Didn't you get a medal or something for that?"

""Yeah, something." It was in a box in the back of his closet. His wedding ring, his medal, Teonna's badge, the shards of his life.

"I thought you were all dead. Officer Erickson, wow, she was quite the looker. You'd wrapped yourself around her, like you were Superman and could stop the bullets." Belatedly, he seemed to recall that Bishop and Teonna had been an item. After a heartbeat, he awkwardly cleared his throat. "You ever see Frank?"

Bishop didn't reply. Standing on the concert floor had given him a chill. He needed out of there.

"Might have been better if he'd died."

Might have been better if they'd all died.

"I stopped going. Had to, made me depressed." He stopped talking. Bishop could feel the sergeant's eyes silently staring at him.

Finished signing, he looked up and met the sergeant's gaze. After a pause, the sergeant finally looked away with a shrug. "Well, old times," he mumbled, lumbering back to his stacks of boxes.

Without removing it from the evidence bag, Bishop sat the candle on his desk and stared at it. Nothing unusual. Neither tall, nor short. Slightly smaller around than a woman's fist. Pillar, not tapered. The kind you bought at a boutique store. He sniffed the bottom. Roses, definitely rose scented. Red. Red roses like a lover might give. He held the candle closer to the window, the sunlight making shadows where random lines had been etched into it. Or were they random? With the precision of a draftsman he sketched the lines onto clean, white computer paper. The ache in his shoulder crept down his arm. He flexed his fingers and pushed through the pain, copying every twist, turn, and swirl until he had an accurate representation of the design. Leaving a long blank space where the candle had melted against the hot rocks.

An unusual quiet settled on the squad room. Sam filled in several squares of the math puzzle, then switched the pencil to his other hand and scratched between his fingers. Bishop folded the paper to make a tube and turned the resulting shape, comparing it to the candle. Across the room, Sergio stared at the white screen and whined. "There's nothing to report. We talked to a woman. Big deal."

The large electronic clock on the squad room wall whirred.

Sergio hunt-and-pecked at the keys. "What was that woman's name?"

Without looking up from the now flattened

paper, Bishop absently answered. "Which woman?" The design meant nothing to him, just a collection of swirls, some forming hearts, some flowers, some stars.

"Not the mother, the other one. The grandma that wrote smut."

"Mimi Yreka." He turned the sheet upside down.

"How the hell do you spell that?"

"Y-r-e-k-a." If he tipped the paper sideways one of the flower petals seemed to make a Y.

Sergio looked up from typing in the name and stared at Bishop. "How do you know that?"

"It was on the mailbox. You should get into the habit of looking at your environment, making note of things that don't seem important at the time and writing them down." Not that he ever did, odd things just seemed to etch themselves into his memory. Bishop pushed the paper away and tried not to stare at it.

"Yeah, yeah." Sergio bent back over the computer keyboard. His stiff back told Bishop to shut up and stop lecturing. After a flurry of typing, a relative silence engulfed the room.

Sam scratched at the fingers of his other hand.

Sergio scowled at him. "What is your problem? Dry skin? Need a little lotion?"

Sam put down the pencil, vigorously clawing at his fingers and wrist. Bishop glanced over. Red blotches blossomed on the backs of Sam's hands.

As Bishop stood to get a closer look, the Chief exited the elevator and looked at everyone looking at Sam. He stopped at the desk and motioned for Sam to show him his hands, then motioned for Sam to turn them over. "Poison oak. You been tumbling in the woods there, Sam?"

"I haven't." Sam lifted his head and looked up into the faces surrounding him. Finding Bishop's, he amended his denial. "I was in the woods on the Blossom Jones case."

Bishop nodded. Sam had gone into the trees and talked to the women.

"But that was two days ago." Sam told the cluster of officers surrounding him, gazing from one face to another.

"Some people react faster than others. I saw a girl brush against a plant and not two minutes later she was covered in hives. Big nasty hives." The Chief informed the by-standers as much as Sam. "Well, get to the emergency room there, boy. You need some allergy meds to stop the swelling." The Chief looked around the room. "What have you been touching? Wash down everything that he touched."

Sam shook his head. "Bishop's pencil." He looked at the offending pencil sitting next to the Sudoku magazine. Bishop stared down at his own hands. They had nothing more than a blotchy redness while Sam's hands seemed to become more inflamed by the instant, tiny blisters lifting the skin, making translucent bubbles.

Sergio bent his neck to get a better look, but didn't budge from his desk across the room. The Chief backed away from Sam. "Get going, and keep your hands away from your face. You don't want any getting into your throat."

Using an evidence bag, Bishop scooped up the pencil before grabbing Sam by the arm and hustling him to the stairs. Behind them he could hear the Chief. "Get some dish soap to break down the oils. Plain water won't do. Scrub down, and I do mean scrub, anything they might have touched. Sergio, get a move. Throw away that magazine."

CHAPTER FIFTEEN

Sam sat on the examining room table. With his shirt off his clean skin glistened under the harsh hospital lights, the well-toned muscles rippling across the hairless chest. Bishop noted that there wasn't a single visible scar. The doctor entered, a silent nurse with clipboard followed, pulling the drape-screen closed behind her. The doctor gave Bishop a nod, and although everyone in the room knew she was married with three kids she gave Sam's physique an appreciative once over. She could have looked at his hands with his shirt on.

"I'm impressed, blood pressure, heart rate, everything's perfect." She stopped and looked up from the chart. Bishop got the feeling she had been talking more about Sam's body than his vitals. "I've prescribed a topical lotion and an antihistamine." Her gaze lingered a moment longer on Sam's sleek torso. "That'll make you drowsy. Take the afternoon off, don't want you shooting anyone."

She turned toward Bishop and motioned for him to show her his hands.

He had refused to get undressed, or get on the table.

"You have a much milder reaction. Try some hydrocortisone cream if it bothers you. Should be gone in a couple of days."

"He went into the woods two days ago and I didn't, why'd he react now?"

"Not likely he was exposed two days ago. Not with the intensity of that reaction. Must have touched something that touched something."

She tried to concentrate on Bishop, but her eyes kept flicking back to Sam's naked chest. The pretty nurse who had followed her into the room handed Sam his shirt, and Sam shrugged into it, rippling more muscles. The light scent of his body wash, like smoke covering a love spell, hid the pheromone explosion happening between them.

"Everyone's different. Fifteen percent of the population never reacts to poison ivy at all. The more you're exposed to it the faster you react the next time you're exposed."

"Ever had poison ivy before, Sam?" she asked, turning to look full at him and his romance novel muscles.

Sam missed a button on his shirt, realized it, and started to unbutton them. "Yeah. Got into it at camp. Some kids thought it would be funny to put it in my sleeping bag."

Torment the tall kid, yeah, sounded like camp. Bishop took the evidence bag out of his pocket and stared at the yellow number 2 wooden pencil inside. "So Sam might have gotten it from the pencil? There's some poison ivy near where I jog, but I wouldn't have taken a pencil with me."

"No, but you might have touched the plant, then the pencil, probably a dozen other things around your house. It's the oil in the plant that people react to. I'd do a thorough cleaning when you get home. Not just water. Dish soap is the best, breaks down the oils."

Silently, Bishop rolled the bagged pencil between his fingers. Hadn't he stirred the foliage at the bottom of the firepit with the pencil? What had the Chief said? Don't get it in your throat. "What if he'd inhaled it? The oils?"

The doctor was watching the nurse help Sam with the buttons on his shirt. The two of them playing look into my eyes – don't look into my eyes – like flirty teenagers. "Could swell the inner lining of the throat, close off the airways."

"And you could die from that?"

"If the reaction was severe enough."

Bishop hated to break up the fun, but Sam needed to keep his hands medicated and he wasn't going to if someone didn't put a stop to the overflow of estrogen and responding rise of testosterone.

Once in the car Bishop pulled out his phone and called the ME.

"Bishop?"

"When you said Blossom Jones's lungs had

swollen shut with an irritant could it have been poison ivy? In the smoke?"

He gave her time to think. "I've heard of that. Those big forest fires can hit on a patch of poison oak and urushiol will release into the air causing lung irritations. If someone is highly sensitive –"

"So you're ruling it a homicide?"

"Don't you have enough work, Bishop? It's only murder if the person who added the poison ivy to the fire knew the victim would be standing in the smoke, and knew that she was more sensitive than the general population. Whoever built the fire probably grabbed whatever branches were lying around and tossed in some poison ivy by mistake. I'm leaning toward accidental death."

"Have you already filed the report?"

"No." She sounded annoyed. "But the Chief called and asked me to expedite it." Her voice got that little lift of exasperation at the end.

Bishop tried to think of a reason to delay the report so he could keep investigating. "I haven't interviewed everyone yet."

"You want to bring that nice ass down here and we could talk about it." Now she was purring and he could almost feel her top heavy body rubbing up against his.

Bishop closed his phone. He needed to find the girl who had talked Blossom into casting the spell in the first place.

Sam's apartment complex sat on the west edge of inner city. A modern, three story monster with too much glass and not enough character. Cheap to build, expensive to maintain. "Get some rest. I'll call the Chief."

After a quick call, mostly filled with grunts and nods the Chief told Bishop to clock out as well. "You're heavy on the overtime there, boy. Call it a night. The ME is sending the paperwork. Blossom Jones's death was accidental."

"I don't think so. I think someone knew she was allergic to poison ivy, knew she'd be out there casting a spell, and deliberately added it to the ingredients in her spell."

For a moment the phone seemed to go dead. Finally the Chief came back on the line. "That so? Well, what you got to go on there, boy?"

Nothing. He knew he had nothing but a feeling.

"That's what I thought. It'll keep until morning."

Bishop kept going south, finally turning toward his cluster of houses. A light mist turned into rain. The terrain dipped down toward the lake and Bishop noticed how dark the area was. A single streetlight remained lit over the two block length, the rest broken or burnt out. Not a single light in his house was on to welcome him home. The windows of the now empty house next door reflected his car headlights back at him. Without stopping he drove out to the highway. The car took him north into the gentle rain. Maybe now his shoulder would stop aching.

CHAPTER SIXTEEN

With a flash of lightening and a clap of thunder, rain exploded from the heavens. Where moments before the wipers had squeaked a steady rhythm, they now frantically danced to clear the windshield. The cold of the rain hit the heat of the car fogging all the glass. From nowhere a figure appeared on the road. Bishop had just enough time to register a pale face with large eyes and long dark hair before reacting. He cranked the steering wheel putting the car into a spin. Like a dancer on ice, man and machine spun-out. After a lifetime of driving on winter slick roads Bishop understood the physics and didn't fight the spin, knowing he'd travel down the road in a circular pattern instead of a straight line. Finally, as the car slowed, losing its momentum, he turned the front wheels into the skid and coasted to a stop. He hadn't felt a slam of flesh against metal so he knew that he'd missed her. The girl should be only a few yards back.

Bishop put the car in reverse and eased backwards. Nothing. No one.

As quickly as it had come, the rain stopped. He stared across the open field and blamed the chill that went down his spine on the sudden burst of adrenaline going into a spin had given him. The grove of trees stood dark against the black night sky, all the stars and the moon obscured by the low hanging clouds. Without realizing it, he had driven to the witch's meeting place. After searching the ditches and roadside for a full twenty minutes he eased back onto the highway. Then took a gravel turn-off, approaching the grove of trees from the back. Coasting the last hundred yards with his lights off, he parked under a huge oak. The grass crunched under his feet, dry, as if it had never rained. When he reached the witch's circle, the clouds scattered bathing him in moonlight. He stood where Blossom would have stood, the fire flickering in front of her, her candle held to the sky. As if pulling magic from his heart, he lifted his hands and threw the spell into the flames where it grew and strengthened. Tipping his head back, he inhaled the magic.

Nothing happened. The clouds closed together. The wind lifted the lapels of his jacket and ruffled his hair. But no goddess appeared. No voice from the heavens gave him an answer. In spite of the hydrocortisone cream, his hands itched. He looked down at the dead fire. Someone had scattered the charred, black sticks.

Behind him a branch snapped. Bishop spun

around. A deer stood staring at him from the shelter of the foliage. No wood sprite. No will-o-wisp. A young doe with soft brown eyes. Is that what he'd seen and mistaken for a person? A deer, not a ghost.

Glad that he'd come alone, and didn't appear foolish anywhere but in his mind, Bishop got back into his car. He drove home slowly, obeying all the speed laws. It took two beers before sleep would crawl into bed with him. Still he woke before dawn. A cold, spring breeze fluttered the curtains. The light of the moon cast odd reflections into the room. Again he thought that he saw Teonna standing at the window, a sheet wrapped around her shoulders, her long hair bed-tousled. But it was just shadows mixed with sorrow.

He sat, shaking off the ache. More ghosts.

Without thinking he dressed, old sweatshirt, sweat pants, jogging shoes, gun in a back holster. The door slammed shut behind him, and he ran. East toward the not yet rising sun. East through the bramble of trees and undergrowth. East to the winding creek that spilled into the lake. He dropped and did push-ups until his shoulder popped and he couldn't lift himself. Then he went back. Sweat dripped into his eyes and he rubbed the wet away with his sleeve. He slowed at the knoll to his house, their house, walking the last few yards to cool his muscles. As he went inside the wind caught in the tree branches, tickling their trunks, making them laugh. He missed her laugh the most and hung unto the sound, but it faded just as her memory seemed to be fading.

When Bishop entered the detective floor, he knew something was happening. Morris had already started the morning staff meeting. Sitting at his desk, Bishop motioned to Sam's hands. The younger officer held them up. The blisters were gone, even the redness was faded. The young healed fast.

"The FBI followed a trail of bait money south." Sam informed him in a whisper.

Morris shot them a look of impatience then continued reading the day report. "Last evening the FBI were able to identify several individuals off a store surveillance tape who may have knowledge of the Garfield Falls Bank and Trust robbery. They are setting up road blocks to apprehend and question." Morris paused, again looking up from the paper. This time speaking to the general group of detectives clustered together, clinging to their coffee mugs. "Please remember to offer any and all assistance. Sam is the contact person so pass questions, or information, on to him." Bishop noticed Sam watching the Chief's closed door. He caught the tall officer's eye, and lifted an eyebrow.

Sam inched his chair closer, leaning toward Bishop. "Jackie's here." He whispered.

Jackie never visited the police station, not since Teonna had died. She said it was too hard. That she always expected her friend to appear around a corner. Bishop understood. Every time he got on the elevator he expected Teonna to appear behind him. Expected her to grab a quick kiss when the doors closed, then step back, that pleased cat smile on her lips, the taste of her on his, the doors opening to find them standing as if nothing had happened.

"How long has she been in there?" Bishop whispered back.

"She came in with me half an hour ago."

Finished, Morris sent another scowl their direction, but didn't call them on their inattention.

Nothing unusual about a wife visiting a husband. Some officers would never see their wives if they didn't drop by the station. Bishop forced himself not to watch the Chief's door, instead shuffling through the papers in his top desk drawer, the thin one where men kept important things, and found a palm-sized leather address book. Black. A gift from Frank after Bishop's first case had resulted in a conviction. No good arresting them if you can't convict them, Frank had always said. He fumbled through the jumble of names, some of the numbers crossed off and new ones entered, little slips of paper with more names and numbers sliding free. Finding what he needed, he called Hank directly instead of having dispatch put him through.

"Just updating you on the Jones case." Bishop doodled down the edge of his blotter pad, trying to sound nonchalant. "No report from the ME yet." He reached the bottom of the paper and started filling in the loops. "Just wondering if you have much of a problem with poison ivy out your way?"

"Not so much. DNR did a big hunter awareness program a few years back. There's patches here and there. Why?"

Bishop didn't really know why. "Looks like the girl had a reaction to poison ivy."

"You can die of that?"

"If you have a bad allergy and you inhale it."

The county sheriff seemed to relax. "People around here are whispering the Lord took offense, and her spell killed her. Guess they were right." They both chuckled. "At least dividends are coming out on Friday, and everyone will have something else to talk about."

"Dividends?"

Bishop could almost hear Hank shake his head and smile. "The local co-op issues dividend checks to all its stockholders at the same time as the filter factory gives out bonuses. Everybody gets drunk. You should come up, it's a wild weekend. Could get ugly though, if the banks don't get their cash in."

"What do you mean?"

"Aren't you in on that big robbery there? Guess you have too much crime to be in the know on everything. All the little banks around here had their extra cash in that shipment, now they've all had to re-order and hope it comes before the checks are issued."

"Why was their money at the Garfield Falls Bank?"

"Those armored guard companies charge a fee according to dollars and mileage. So the smaller banks pay a bigger bank to act as their drop-off point then send someone with an off-duty officer to pick the money up. Costs less than they would have had to pay to the armored guard company to go the extra miles."

Worked until someone got robbed.

"How often they do that?" Would be an easy way to pick up a few extra bucks.

"Not that often."

"Who would know about these drop-offs? Jackie?" Why did he think of Jackie? She couldn't have anything to do with the robbery. Maybe she'd said the wrong thing at the wrong time, and been overheard. Maybe she'd let slip how much money would be in the special shipment?

"No, no. We deal directly with Mr. Outtmann. He'll call about a week before and we'll arrange for an officer to ride along."

Bishop hung up the phone. The Garfield Bank and Trust had been the distribution point. Esmeralda could have overheard something when she'd been in the bank cashing her paycheck. Did she get a paycheck? Where had she worked? She might have told Turner. Maybe even encouraged him to rob the bank. Won't be the first time a man had foolishly proven his love by breaking the law.

While he'd been talking Bishop had made a trail of doodles down the side of his desk calendar. The loops and squiggle's that had been nothing more than random lines shuffled themselves as he stared. Teonna. After so many years he thought that he'd compartmentalized her into a place in his mind that he tried not to go to. Not at work. Only at night. Only when he was alone. Hastily, he tried to disguise her name by adding vines, twisty- twirly vines, and then stylized, pointy leaves. When Jackie came out of the Chief's office he was still staring at the paper. With several quick, vigorous strokes of his pen he blacked out the design before she saw it.

But her focus was elsewhere. She gave Bishop a quick, absent smile before getting on the elevator. As the doors closed the smile dropped, a scowl formed on her forehead making a V between her eyebrows. Had to have been a lot of money. She must have felt the brunt of pointing fingers. Bishop hoped she didn't have to cancel her vacation because of it. Bishop hadn't been on vacation in... he stretched his mind backwards hunting for a memory.

Not since he and Claire had taken Sonny to a water park for two days. Sonny had been three. Did that count? Claire had been, he fought at the memory, he wanted her to be a shrew, to justify cheating on her, but lost. She'd been beautiful. Her long blonde hair wet and clinging to her back. Little tendrils drying around her face. Her serviceable one-piece swimsuit revealing just enough to keep him wanting her all day. Exhausted, Sonny had slept hard, and he and Claire... For two days they'd been happy with each other. And then her period had been late. She'd been angry and blamed him. And when it turned out that she wasn't pregnant – she'd been relieved and Bishop, Bishop had been oddly disappointed.

Throwing his doodle into the trash, Bishop pulled up the internet. He could check the sports scores while waiting for Sergio, but Rock was in all the headlines. Even after retiring the football legend made the news with his antics. Rock and Claire, what a pair they had been. Beauty and the Beast. Claire had been right to break-up with him. But had her heart ever left him? Irritated that Rock still got to him, Bishop emptied his pockets looking for Mimi's card. Finding it, with a few quick strokes of the keys, he was on her website. The cover of her latest book greeted him. Under a full moon, a delectable witch in a weightless garment that flowed around her and hugged her in all the right places seemed to leap from the monitor. Between her ample breasts a moon-shaped necklace with crescents on both sides amplified the glow of the moon.

Bishop had seen that necklace before. Where? A library book? He searched several websites on moon lore, and found the imagery the necklace had to have been based on. Three moons: waxing, full, waning; representing the phases of life. He flipped through his memory and smiled to himself. The waitress at the diner on Third. The one that had been upset. The one with the thick make-up. But the name wouldn't come to him. Not Amanda, he was sure of that. Having a moon necklace didn't mean the waitress was a witch, maybe she'd just bought a pretty necklace not knowing, or caring what it represented. It only meant something if she knew it meant something. Could be a lot of witches in Garfield Falls, they didn't sign up in a registry. There was no Sunday morning church he could sit in front of to see who went in, or who came out.

The next elevator up had Sergio, a manila envelope dangling from his fingertips. He yanked a flash of pink off the packet, tossing the heart shaped sticky-note into the trash can where it caught on the side, a tender pink heart in a cold darkness. Then dropped the envelope on Bishop's desk. "Here." Sergio headed for the bathroom.

It was from the ME. Bishop opened the clasp expecting to see Blossom. Instead Esmeralda's death photo whispered hello. Even in death, even on the wrong side of forty, she was beautiful. Her face a prefect heart shape. Her skin a rich mocha. Her thick-lashed eyes seemed to open, staring at him. Why hadn't he found her killer? Her full, red lips curled in a haughty display of sensuality. Too much woman for a child like Turner. Too worldly wise. Bishop scanned the report. Death between four am and six am. If he'd been out on his morning jog he would have heard the gunshot. If he'd gone that way he might even have encountered the killer. 35mm at close range. One bullet through the heart. Body moved approximately one to two hours after death.

Sergio came out of the bathroom complaining loudly of suffering the ill effects of bad carry-out even though Bishop noted a spring in his step. Everyone looked up waiting for the I-just-got-laid story Sergio was bound to tell. The Chief still hadn't stuck his head out of his office. The higher-ups must have been chewing his ass for the robbery. It was bad news, made the force look bungling. But it was good news for him. The Chief hadn't told him to stop investigating Blossom's death.

"Come on." Bishop picked up his sports jacket.

He wanted to talk to that waitress.

"I just got here."

But not with Sergio in tow.

"And you're just leaving."

Yet he was stuck with the young officer tagging along. When they passed the diner there was no red car in the employee lot so Bishop directed Sergio north.

The drive to the university lengthened to an eternity. Bishop tried to tune out Sergio's detailed revisiting of his previous night's escapade. Not with the ME, as far as Bishop knew she never left the morgue, but someone Sergio had met in a bar. Perhaps Sergio should get together with Mimi and they could exchange notes.

Between the sunshine and the motion of the car rocking him, Bishop fell into a light doze. When the car stopped with a sharp bump against the curb, he woke.

"Late night, old man? Stay up and watch the news?"

Bishop ignored the taunting and shook off his fatigue. The campus swelled with activity. Students overflowed the dorms, he-ing and she-ing on the patios and walkways. For a moment he thought that he saw Sonny, the tall lanky kid the image of himself at that age. Except for the self-important football swagger, and other students didn't separate so Sonny could go through. The kid veered to the right and into a building. Sergio stopped in front of a sidewalk kiosk as if that was where they had been headed in the first place. The younger officer idly studied the flyers and posters.

"Now there's some sweet tea."

Bishop pulled his gaze away from the far building. No point in going after Sonny if the kid was ducking him. He'd only ask for money. And payday always seemed a long ways away.

It wasn't hard to see which poster Sergio was looking at. Beneath the homemade signs looking for roommates, a flyer for community outreach tooting the thrills of doing a ride-along with a real police officer, and the pronouncements of exciting summer courses, including exploring everything from London to local caves, was a mass-produced flyer with the picture of a young oriental female, beautiful in her exoticness. The caption read: Have you seen Tiffany Foss? Her eyes seemed to focus on him. He hated missing person cases. They were lose-lose. If you found them and they wanted to be lost, everyone blamed you. Loved ones just didn't understand, adults could go anywhere they wanted anytime they wanted. They didn't have to tell you they were sick of the relationship and leaving. Made for hard feelings. Made for wasted man hours. Sam could go on and on about that.

And then there were the other cases. The cases he got out of bed in the middle of the night for. When the body was found and he had to put a name to it. They all had a name. Some he found quickly, some ....

Bishop moved away from the kiosk. He had a professor to talk to. He had a girl whose name he knew to put to rest. Still he felt the eyes of the lost girl silently follow him, boring into his back.

"Hey," He made eye contact with a passing student. "Professor Bedford's office?"

The boy pointed left and Bishop turned them that direction, away from what was becoming a busy intersection of pedestrians. They found the professor's office door at the front of a line of young females, books clutched against their chests, arms crossed over the books in a vain attempt to protect their already melodramatic hearts. Bishop lifted his hand to knock and noticed a computer generated sign giving office hours. A quick glance at his watch told him they had a few minutes to wait. One of those plastic file holders had been attached to the door beneath the makeshift sign. Bishop took out one of the papers in the file and scanned the neatly typed sheet.

Syllabus – Criminal Justice 101. It gave assignments, and times and dates of guest speakers, with a bold notation that attendance would be taken on the nights when there were speakers. Of the eight presenters Bishop knew three: the ME, the Chief, and Jefferson. Should have had Muttley come in to speak, the man could have talked an hour without taking a breath. Then corrected himself, he knew four if you counted Claire's husband. Juniorcowski, the tongue twisting Slavic name shorted by everyone, even Claire, into Junior. It was an impossible name to miss on any list. Bishop had only met him on those odd comings and goings of exchanging offspring. Those awkward minutes when both stood in doorways or on porches waiting for the scurry of children gathering backpacks and essential handheld electronics, while fathers sized each other up and said as little as possible. Bishop vaguely recalled that his ex-wife's new husband worked closely with the mayor's office, in administration, or perhaps internal affairs.

A male, early thirties finally approached, keys jangling in his hand, Bishop could see why Mimi would put him on the cover of her book. He had clean good looks with an edge of bad boy command.

"Professor Bedford?"

The man stopped, his eyes narrowed slightly, the tension of uncertainty across his shoulders. Neither Bishop, nor Sergio looked like a student.

"If we could have a minute."

The professor unlocked his office door. No one said anything when Bishop and Sergio budged in line, entering before any of the waiting females.

"If this is about one of your daughters ..."

Not sons.

"... getting a bad grade, I must tell you that I'm not at liberty to discuss any of my students without their written consent – even if you are the parents."

Sergio caught that the professor had assumed they were a couple and jumped away from Bishop. "We're not – ."

Bishop flashed his badge. "Garfield Falls police. Officer Sergio," He motioned toward the younger investigator. "I'm Detective Bishop. What could you tell us about Blossom Jones?" Bishop watched closely for his reaction. But the prof genuinely looked bewildered before a flash of memory crossed his face.

"Blossom. Wrote an excellent paper on Subcults and the Law as Pertains to Unconventional Religious Believes. Other than that she didn't seem interested in the class. Skipped most of the lectures. Came for the speakers." The prof paused. "Didn't she just die? An accident or something?"

"That's yet to be determined." Sergio made bold eye contact with the educator. "Maybe it was murder."

"Murder? Really? What would have been the motive? Are you here looking for who she associated with?"

"You didn't know her on a ... personal level?" Sergio hit the end of his sentence hard leaving no doubt as to his implication.

Now it was a tugging match, each dog had his bone.

"What makes you think I did?"

"Oh, I don't know. The way you pose for the covers of dirty books might imply that you're open to _"

"I did that cover to pay on my student loans. I have two kids. College professors don't make as much as you think."

No one did.

Bishop stepped between the two dogs. First he glared at Sergio. "No one's implying any improprieties occurred." Then nodded sternly at the professor. "She took your class. We're just wondering if you could help us out."

The professor's tense glare remained on Sergio. "Motive, means, opportunity." He held his hand up for Sergio to see. "I have no motive. Didn't know her personally. She was just another student." He folded a finger down. "As for means – I don't even know how she died. The papers didn't say." He folded another finger down. "And for opportunity – early morning I would have been in bed – with my wife." He gave Sergio the bird. Bishop had seen that one coming.

Satisfied that he had won the day, the professor went to his desk, sitting down in a large wooden chair, the rollers not even squeaking as he pulled forward and rested his elbows on the armrests and steepled his fingers. "No gentlemen, I'm not your man. The criminal you're looking for would be a psychopath. Someone with an escalating history of criminal activity." Abruptly he straightened. "Perhaps another student."

Another cop-want-to-be who thought he knew more about police work than the police. Only this one had all the theories coupled with an academic degree.

Professor Bedford warmed to the idea. "Now let's see, who did Blossom hang out with?"

As if they hadn't asked that question when they'd walked in the door.

"Blossom always sat in the back on the left. I pride myself on noticing these things." He tapped his fingers against each other in rapid descending order.

"Never next to the same person twice." He paused in his finger gymnastics. "Except when Chief Johnson came to speak. That night she ended up in front." He waved the thought away. "But it was a full house, as the Criminal Deviants class joined us. Rusty is a great speaker. Have you ever heard him? Very dynamic."

The professor stopped, staring for a long moment at Bishop. "Did you say that your name was Bishop? The Bishop? He talked about one of your cases. Called you the ghost whisperer."

His stomach knotted. He'd never liked the Chief calling him that. They did the whispering, he just listened. It was his job. Carefully, Bishop refocused the conversation. "About Blossom, did you know she was a practicing witch?"

The professor gave him an are-you-stupid look that Bishop was used to getting from women. "Of course. I told you that was what she wrote her paper on."

"So she was quite open about it?"

"Oh, I see, you're wondering if she might have offended one of the other students. An in-your-face to their Christianity. Not as far as I know." He leaned back, rocking his chair in the tiniest of motions, fingertips again straight-up, touching, tapping rhythmically. "It would provide a motive. Being fellow students they only had to meet somewhere. She was killed in a woods just outside of town? A romantic rendezvous, perhaps? But the means..." He straightened and assumed his I-am-the-teacher role. "How did you say she was killed?"

Sergio opened his mouth, but Bishop cut him off. "We didn't say. Just asking a few questions."

"Of course. Keeping things back. Only the killer will know the details."

"No one said it was murder."

"Unusual for someone so young, without medical issues, to die so suddenly." He stopped tapping his fingers. "Or did she have medical issues?"

Bishop didn't reply. Obviously the man had studied police work, and the criminal mind - from a distance, case studies and reports. But Bishop had looked into the eyes of murderers and knew it wasn't that simple. What made one man kill, while another, with the same provocation, walked away?

Suddenly, Sergio was the prof's best friend, smiling and nodding. "If you could suggest someone for us to look into."

"As I said before, I didn't know Blossom very well. She was only a marginal student. Other than one notable paper she was failing."

The professor stood, his interest fixed on Bishop. "You know, I have guest speakers. Perhaps, sometime, you might ..."

"No."

"How long have you been a policeman?"

Bishop was beginning to think too long. "Thank you for your time. We won't keep you from your work."

The line outside the door had grown while they'd been inside. Sergio followed him, eyeing several of the co-eds before trotting behind. "Well, that was a waste."

Folding the syllabus and stuffing it into his inside jacket pocket, Bishop didn't think so.

CHAPTER SEVENTEEN

Sergio pulled his cell phone out and checked the messages. A scowl formed on his forehead and he snapped the phone shut. "You should have warned me about the ME." The ride back to the station was tense as Sergio continued to whine. "She keeps calling. Wanting to know when I'll be bringing by another hard body. That's creepy."

What could Bishop say? If he spent the day cutting apart cold, dead flesh he might become obsessed with the feel of hot, pulsating life. But warn Sergio? No, he never told a man who not to sleep with. You had to learn that the hard way.

At the police station the front steps were a scene out of a movie. The local television station had a van parked, two wheels over the curb, blocking the sidewalk. A pretty, young reporter with flat-ironed brown hair and a determined stance stood in front of the main doors. The wind carried her words in bits and pieces to them.

"... heinous double murder ... over a million dollars in small bills ... How could this happen here in Garfield Falls? ... FBI ... Johnson refuses to comment ... no leads as yet ..."

They went round the back. Sergio parked in the closest spot to the door. "Can you believe that?"

Bishop could, it wasn't the first time the press had pushed for answers. They were in the fast-business, old news was the same as no news. Bishop wanted to think he was in the get-it-right business.

On the third floor everyone had hunkered down, the Chief's door again closed. Only computers whirred, and keys clacked. Sergio looked around and spoke to the room in general. "Can you believe what's going on downstairs? It makes us look bad. Can't she find anything else to report on?"

A few eyes glanced up. The phone on every desk rang simultaneously and everyone became intensely busy, ignoring the ringing as if it hadn't happened. Without sitting down, Sergio grabbed the receiver. Bishop, like everyone else in the office, knew it would be dispatch. If a call went to all the desks instead of specifically to you it was a hot potato. But Sergio didn't know that, not yet.

His face already taut and tense, he snipped into the phone. "Stop calling me." He paused. "Sorry, madam, I thought you were someone else." Everyone looked up as Sergio backtracked and watched him intently listening to the caller. "Your daughter is missing?"

Frantically, Sergio began scribbling notes onto his desk blotter. Sam continued staring, but Bishop took off his jacket and draped it over the back of his chair, sitting down. Orlando would take this one, Orlando had made finding missing girls his specialty, he knew every pervert in town, and all the places they hung out.

"We'll have an officer right there."

Tearing free the address he'd just jotted down, Sergio sprinted into the Chief's office, not even bothering to knock on the door. A few moments later the Chief came out his arm around Sergio's shoulder, instead of an angry at the lack of respect glare, the Chief had a half swallowed smile.

"We have a little incident here, boys. Missing teenager. Sergio is going to issue an Amber Alert. Orlando, you go pick up the mother, and bring her to my office."

Bishop looked at the Chief in dismay. An Amber Alert? On one phone call? They hadn't even verified any information. And why was he smiling?

"Bishop, you go down to the high school. Talk to her friends. They told the mother they saw a dark van cruising the area earlier. See what you can find out."

Sam hesitated, half standing.

"That's right, you go along. I'll let you know if the FBI call."

Bishop shrugged back into his jacket. What was the Chief doing? Taking Sergio down a notch? Everyone would look the fool if they called an Amber only to have the girl show up as a run-away. Or the mother turned out to be an alarmist and the kid was at the neighbor's watching television. Then it hit him, better to look the fool doing something then the fool doing nothing.

If it had been a sirens blaring, lights flashing emergency he would have let Sam enjoy the thrill of driving, but most of the time he drove. It kept the seatbelt strap off his bad shoulder. For the hundredth time since Blossom Jones' death he checked the sky. Robin's egg blue without a speckle of white. Not even a soft breeze to stir-up some moisture into a cloud.

Finally he noticed that Sam was unusually silent and glanced at him.

"Just say it."

"Say what?" Bishop asked.

"I told you so. They were involved. She slapped me down faster than a frog smacks a fly."

Interesting metaphor, now if only Bishop knew which woman Sam was referring to.

"There are other women." Hopefully Sam had gotten out before his heart had gotten involved.

"There seem to be a lot of women. But how do you find the right woman?"

Bishop turned into the school parking lot. He thought of Teonna. Of her quick smile and intense eyes. He wanted to think he hadn't been attracted to her from the start, but he had been.

Only she'd been the wrong woman at the wrong time and things had ended all wrong. Things had worked out better for the Chief. He'd left his wife for Jackie, and they'd found their happily-ever-after.

After this long everyone had forgotten that Jackie had once been the other woman, even he had until just now.

"Sorry, guess I shouldn't be asking you, things didn't work out for you and Claire."

He'd never told Sam about Teonna. Never mentioned her to anyone. No one asked. Either you knew, and knew better than to talk about her, or you had heard rumors that kept you from asking.

"Maybe there's no such thing as the right woman."

But for that little time he'd been with Teonna, nestled in their big bed, hiding from the world's judgment, everything had been so right. He'd give his good arm to hold her again, yet she seemed to be slipping away. He couldn't feel her presence the way he normally could. Couldn't feel the warmth of her skin almost touching him as they stood, blue uniform to blue uniform.

Bishop stopped at the school office and the principal led them to a classroom close-by. "The students are quite upset. The counselor has been with them. He went to get some grief brochures, but will be right back. Perhaps you should wait."

Bishop peeked through the door's large glass window into the classroom. A cluster of girls in too tight clothes, with too much make-up, sat near the front, two next to each other, one behind them, and another a little further back. He wondered if the one further back had isolated herself, or if the others had ostracized her. Several males in low-hung jeans and

too much hair, their arms dangling over girls'
shoulders like modern day epaulets, stood along the
back wall. He recognized one of the girls in her
pseudo-Goth attire and fake nose ring. He hoped it
was a fake nose-ring. Her silky blonde hair in Lolita
pig tails standing straight up from either side of her
head like an excited puppy's ears. He doubted Claire
had let her daughter leave the house dressed like that.
But he knew kids, likely Lexi had changed after
getting to school the way Claire often had.

No one looked like they were grieving. Opening
the door, he didn't wait for the counselor to return.
"Thanks for staying late. I've just got a few questions.
It will help us find ..." He paused, no one had told him
the girl's name.

"Jennifer." One of the pair in the front told him.
The girl who spoke was strikingly attractive in a very
grown-up way, her mahogany skin glowing with
youth and scented oil, but her face had too much
make-up, and her already bloomed physique too little
clothing. She stared at him, her eyes unblinking, and
dry as a desert storm. She knew she was the queen.

And he was dirt under her feet.

Like the court jester, Bishop fumbled taking his
little notepad out of his inside jacket pocket, then
patted his jacket looking for the pencil, before pulling
it out from right where he'd left it. With a weak smile
of apology, he started.

"So who saw Jennifer get pushed into the van?"

No one said anything. He let his gaze bounce over
the girls. The one who had supplied the name had to

be the leader, the one on her right was her BFF, the one directly behind the mascot, and the one in back ... Bishop made eye contact with the one in the back.

"Did you see what happened?"

The one in front twisted in her chair and glared a warning that was obeyed. The girl shook her head. For the moment Bishop let it slide, concentrating on the front row. "So ... I'm sorry, I'm bad with names ... so ..." He waited. She waited. Finally she gave him her name.

"Ruby."

"Ruby." Bishop tapped his pencil on the pad, the graphite point leaving little dash marks. "So no one saw anything?"

"No." Her pointed chin tipped-up and her over-glossed lips, bright crimson and succulent, froze in an immovable line that was neither a smile nor a frown, just haughty.

Bishop nodded, bouncing his shoulders as he did.

"Who discovered that she was missing?" He shot his gaze to the back, to the weak link. She froze and he thought that he'd overshot when she finally answered.

"Her mom. Her mom came early to pick her up, and take her out for her birthday."

"Her birthday?" Bishop tried to sound surprised. "How old? Eighteen?"

Ruby preened, jutting her well-endowed chest forward and shifting her shoulders in vanity. Definitely fifteen, and going too far. "Sixteen."

"Did she know her mom was coming?"

The mascot shook her head.

"So you saw this dark van? Was it following you when you left school?" He looked at his notepad. "No, wait, you hadn't left school yet. So when did you see the dark van?" He looked straight at the girl in the back. "At lunch? Nice spring day, I'd eat lunch outside if I could."

Ruby stood, not even wobbling on her four-inch ribbon-strapped sandals with their spike heels, and sashayed back to lean over her friend and put her arm around her. The friend didn't say anything.

There was no dark van, there was no kidnapper, there was a girl who'd just turned sixteen and left school early while her friends covered for her. And why would a sixteen-year-old girl leave school early and need her friends to cover for her? Bishop knew the answer. The only answer. There was a boy involved in this. He mentally shook his head. But how did he get them to confess to their lies?

He turned his attention to the line-up of kids standing against the back wall. "Which one of you is Jennifer's boyfriend?" If he had a daughter he wouldn't want any of them to be her boyfriend. The two boys, shoulders touching, were likely gay. The tattooed, face-pierced senior with his arm draped around Lexi in studied nonchalance didn't look capable of handling one relationship let alone two. Another two girls, the last of the hanger-on's, too young to be part of the pack stood with two boys who, from the looks of faces starting to lose their teenage sharpness, should have graduated. No. The boyfriend wasn't there.

"None of you? He must be out looking for her. So who called him?"

Everyone shifted uneasily, their bodies unconsciously turning toward the door wanting to run.

"No one wants to be the bearer of bad news." Bishop shook his head. "I understand. I'd hate to call him. Hey, dude ..." He put his hand to his ear, holding out his thumb and pinkie as if talking on a phone.

Two of the girls giggled. Rudy's tower of Babel was cracking.

"... someone's, like, kidnapped your girlfriend." He dropped the false humor. "Some pervert trolling the school yards shoved Jennifer into a van." He made eye contact with everyone standing against the wall, their backs pressed into the bulletin board, little thumbtacks poking at their conscious. Everyone looked away. The silence grew and all eyes went to Ruby.

"Jennifer doesn't have a boyfriend." Ruby informed him with a saccharine smile.

Bishop inhaled sharply. He should have gotten an Oscar for his faked surprise. "I can't believe that. You wouldn't hang out with any losers. Why I bet all the boys follow you ladies." He'd fallen into the Chief's self-depreciating patter. "Oh, that's right. She just turned sixteen. Have to be sixteen to have an older boyfriend. And you like older men."

This time he locked horns with Ruby and pushed. The tension mounted. She was used to confrontation, but an angry parent that wanted you to love them was different than a cop whose life quite often depended on being able to take an I'm-in-charge stance. "But her mother didn't approve."

Ruby broke eye contact, looking away, and making that exaggerated sigh teenagers use to inform adults that they could never understand the difficulties of being a teenager because when they were teenagers life was so much easier.

"So maybe it was the boyfriend who pulls up in his dark van. Maybe he forces her to leave early with him." Bishop kept the pressure on.

"Walter doesn't drive a dark van, he drives a white Toyota." She snipped at him to show him how stupid he was, then realized what she'd let slip.

"And Walter's last name?" More silence. Bishop tapped his pencil, then shrugged, and put it back into his pocket. "I'll call her mom."

From the back Lexi straightened. "McFee, Walter McFee."

Bishop gave Sam a quick, meaningful glance. The door opened and the counselor, a handful of colorful brochures in his hand. Sam stepped around him into the hall, his cell phone already out to his ear.

"What's going on here? Who gave you permission to talk to these students? We have a potentially life altering event going on and they need to be guided through it correctly, or their psyches could be ruined."

"Just taking names. We may have questions later."

Sam came back with a clipboard.

"I believe that is an invasion of privacy. You have no authority here."

Bishop looked around the group. He'd remember them if he needed to.

"I guess that you're free to go then, unless there is anything you want to tell me."

"Which you do not have to do." The annoyed counselor handed each one a brochure as they filed out.

Bishop watched Lexi pick up her backpack, not even looking his direction, inserting her skull shaped ear-candy headphones into her ear lobes. The other students jostled her as they passed. She'd pay a price for telling. He wanted to thank her, but anything he said would just get her deeper into trouble with her friends. Silently, he watched her leave. The tight clothes, the patterned stockings, if he was her father he'd be watching her a little closer. But then he wasn't her father. Sure he'd taken her on outings with Sonny when Claire had wanted to get away, just her and Junior. And once, when he'd helped Lexi worm her fishing hook and filet her catch, Lexi had thought he was the coolest. But seven wasn't fourteen.

CHAPTER EIGHTEEN

Sam watched the last teenager leave. "If you were celebrating your girlfriend's emancipation from jailbait to a good time where would you go?"

Bishop looked up at Sam. Emancipation? Where had Sam found that word?

"Her house." Sam answered himself. "The majority of young girls loss their virginity in their own homes while their parents are at work."

How would Sam know that? Why would he know that?

"Mother came home early, didn't find her."

"His house?"

Bishop considered it. Older boyfriend might have his own place. He thought of himself and Claire on prom night. The cold parking lot, the dark backseat, the tussle with unwanted clothing. Both of them having something to prove. Then he suppressed the past. "No, they've been waiting." Anticipating, planning. "It would be somewhere special."

"Isn't there a cluster of cheap hotels along the old highway?"

Bishop nodded. It was worth a shot, teenagers with overflowing hormones didn't go to the Ritz. Picking up their pace, Sam hit the left outer door as Bishop hit the right, popping them open as if the school bell had just rung on the first day of summer. Sam drove. No siren, but too fast for the law. Bishop radioed dispatch. Shirley answered. "Possible McFee at motel near school. Checking for white Toyota."

She would pass the information along. A few moments later the radio crackled with the plate number. Having reached the old highway, Sam slowed and they scanned the lots of the dejected hotels, the meager lawns no longer maintained, the buildings in need of fresh everything. Only a smattering of vehicles occupied the parking areas.

Sam pointed, seeing the car before Bishop. "White Toyota." They went past the lot as Sam looked for the hotel turn-off. Bishop checked the license. They had a match. He radioed in again. "Found McFee vehicle at Easy Sleep Motel on old highway. Will make inquiries."

Finding the driveway, Sam stopped in front of the registration office. Bishop left him to watch the boyfriend's car while he went inside.

When Bishop flashed his badge the front desk clerk didn't seem surprised just put-out. Without asking, the older man reached under the counter and retrieved a five-inch c-ring filled with keys. "Knew they were trouble. Boy all nervous. She stayed in the car, but she looked old enough."

Bishop bet she had. If she was dressed like the girls at the school, underage and trying to look older would have flashed at any man not fixated with a primal need to get as much of his sperm into the gene pool as possible. The clerk came around the counter, carefully locking drawers, and computers as he went.

Bishop impatiently glanced out the window in time to see Sergio's orange Camaro racing along the highway toward the hotel. Like Sam, he missed the turn, but instead of backtracking he jumped the curb, and flew across the dirt and grass strip into the parking lot. Wheels squealing, the car spun to a stop, blocking the Toyota.

The manger froze, the ring of room keys dangling from his stunned fingers. "What the...?"

Sergio exploded out the driver's door. Torres, in full swat gear, burst out the other side. Within seconds they flanked the motel room door.

What did they think this was a damn movie? "Wait!" Although he ran all out, Bishop knew there was no stopping them.

"Police." Sergio yelled drowning out the wail of protest from the motel manager.

With a quick nod from Sergio, Torres kicked the door right above the lock. At the same moment Sergio rammed the flimsy wood with his shoulder.

The door burst open to a high pitched scream. A man's high pitched scream.

CHAPTER NINETEEN

Sergio and Torres blocked the doorway, staring dumbfounded into the room. Finally reaching them, Bishop pushed through. A young man, tied to the bed, a studded dog collar constricting his voice, screamed again. The girl straddling him wore a hot-pink leather bustier, garters and stockings, and held a matching pink whip above her head. In slow motion she turned toward them. Although her face was obscured by a feathered, vinyl mask Bishop didn't doubt that they'd found Jennifer. No wonder nobody wanted to talk.

"Bishop!" Sam called from the parking lot.

Bishop turned to see the television mobile unit from the police station careen into the parking lot. Cameraman and reporter leapt out as the vehicle slid to a stop. Bright camera lights zoomed through the open motel room door. Using his body as a barricade Bishop prevented the pair from rushing inside. An instant later Sam was there backing him up. Bishop forced the door closed. It hung lopsided, half the hinges gone. Satisfied that no one could get through Sam, Bishop turned to look at the four stunned occupants of the room.

Naked as the day his mother had birthed him, sobbing and shaking like an infant, the hysterical male fought at his bonds. "She's sixteen." He kept informing Sergio. Twisting, he tried to free himself from the handcuffs, only digging the metal deeper into his flesh. "She's sixteen. I swear, nothing happened."

From the sneer on the girl's lips, Bishop believed him. In one motion he grabbed the hotel bedspread off the floor and tossed it over Jennifer, shoving her into Torres arms. Regaining himself, Sergio tossed a sheet over the boyfriend.

Walter, Lexi had said his name was Walter. Just for being saddled with a name so out of fashion, Bishop took pity on him. With one turn of his pin-knife, Bishop popped the lock on the cheap handcuffs, freeing a sobbing Walter.

Every eye turned to Bishop. There was no back way out. He peeked through the room blackening drapes – this wasn't the first time this room had seen lovers playing too rough. Camera in his face, and squinting against the glare of the light, Sam was doing just fine. They had a few minutes.

"Torres, on my mark, you get her out of here." He glanced at Sergio. "You and Sam take him. I'll talk to the reporters." The last thing Bishop wanted to do was talk to reporters. But he was the senior most officer.

He let everyone get a deep breath, waiting, then heard the sirens. He'd guessed right, the manager had called 911. Bishop tapped the door twice, signaling Sam they were coming through. Timing was everything.

"Now."

Muttley and Jefferson made a textbook skid, rocking the police cruiser to a stop close by the door. The camera and lights added to the confusion. The reporter's voice demanded to know what was happening. Like a dance, Bishop moved forward, Sam moved sideways, the occupants of the room dashed out. Jefferson threw open a passenger door, Torres pushed the girl into the patrol car, bounding in after her. Sergio led the boyfriend, a sheet loosely wrapped around his shoulders, the long tail flapping in the breeze, toward his Camaro. Sam ran interference. He slammed the door closed behind Walter. Before he could open the passenger door, Sergio hit the gas leaving Sam standing on the hot asphalt.

In an instant the dance was over.

The reporter dropped her microphone and glared at Bishop, her eyes flashing rage more than confusion. "What just happened here?"

Just because the mike wasn't in his face didn't mean it wasn't on. "No comment."

"We got a tip that the girl from the Amber alert was here. Was that her? Was that her abductor?"

"No comment."

He didn't know the woman, but she must have

known him. "Come on, Bishop, give me something." She whined and pouted with thick ruby lips that he was certain normally got her what she wanted.

"No –"

"Yeah, yeah, no comment." Angry, as only a beautiful woman can be when told no, she locked her jaw and sucked in her cheeks. Her gaze took in Sam. The scowled deepened, and she toggled a button on the microphone. "Let's go." She made a cut gesture with her free hand while storming to the van. The cameraman looked puzzled for a moment, then trotted after her.

Sam joined Bishop at the hotel room door. Shoulder to shoulder they watched the van pull away. So much for keeping a low profile. Bishop studied the damage, the hotel would have to replace the door and most of the frame, but the lock still looked good.

"Wow, did you see that?"

Yeah, and he thought that he'd seen it all.

"She was magnificent."

Bishop looked at Sam in surprise. He didn't know Sam was into that kind of thing – being tied to beds, whips, handcuffs. "She's sixteen."

Sam looked back in confusion. "What? No, not her. I'm not into ... I meant Torres. Did you see the way she kicked in that door? Woo. Like a beautiful, black Amazon."

Guess Sam's broken heart had healed.

CHAPTER TWENTY

After taking Sam home, Bishop went to file his report. Technically special cases didn't have a night shift, not enough crime to keep officers sleeping on taxpayers dollars, if it was important enough the regular officers would call dispatch to send someone out. Usually that someone was Bishop. But in actuality, Bishop and someone else always seemed to be there at night. Tonight that someone seemed to be the Chief. The light shone through the frosted glass window of the door. Bishop knocked and got no answer. He turned the handle and knocked again. A slurred reply granted him admittance.

It wasn't the first time Bishop had encountered the Chief drinking far into the night. Usually it was after some heinous crime, some violence that made even jaded officers stop and question why. Tonight the vodka bottle sat openly on the desk blotter, a shot glass of clear liquid amplifying the Chief's thick fingers like a child's toy magnifying glass. He hadn't turned when Bishop had walked in, just continued staring out the window at the night lights. Past the quiet of the parking lot was the silhouette of the hospital with its red beacon on top and random room lights going on and off. Few stars bothered to appear, let alone twinkle. The new Jordan Tower dominated a major part of the sky line, a red beacon, like a cherry on top, warning passing airplanes of the high structure. Tonight the top two floors were ablaze with lights. Bishop had heard that Jordan had turned the top two floors into his private palace. They must have been having a party.

"That Sergio sure gave us an interesting afternoon." The Chief chuckled. "Quite the diversion."

Bishop heard something else, something more than hazing the new guy, but he couldn't put his finger on what and let the feeling slip away.

"But you saw right through it. What tipped you off?"

Bishop couldn't say. The way the girls were dressed, the way they weren't afraid. That it was her sixteenth birthday and she was no longer jailbait.

"Hate to commit a crime and have you on the case."

"Not likely to happen."

The Chief smiled and poured himself another shot of vodka, the clear odorless liquor only fooling some of the people some of the time.

"Not heading home? Thought you were knocking on that shelter house lady."

Bishop didn't want to answer the unspoken question, but did. "Things got too serious."

"About time you got serious, boy. Teonna's not coming back."

The muscles in Bishop's bad shoulder involuntarily twitched. No, she wasn't, but that didn't mean he had to stop waiting.

"God, we were young. Remember Jackie and Teonna back then? Fire and Ice, Brown Sugar and Hot Spice. What did those wild women see in two married men like you and me?"

Bishop didn't know, never thought about it.

"Just a game to them. Ruined both our marriages." The Chief turned his glass round, and round. "Of course my marriage wasn't much to ruin, but you and Claire. I always thought you'd make it." The glass paused in its turning. "Ever think, what if?"

Suddenly tired, his shoulder throbbing with phantom pain, he didn't care why Teonna had cast her love spell on him. He had resisted her as long as he could and in the end she had loved him, just as he had loved her. It was enough.

"If I could have saved her, I would have."

"I know." Just like Bishop would have saved Jackie in the same situation. But there had been no saving anyone in that room of bullets and death. "I'm going to finish up the report on the Amber Alert." Bishop stared at the half-empty bottle of booze. "I could drive you home first. Jackie will be waiting."

"Oh, she'll see the news, and know that I'm busy."

But the Chief wasn't busy and wasn't moving

except to put glass to lips.

"Find out anything about that sweet, little witch?"

"No." It was the second time the Chief had referred to Blossom as a sweet, little witch. But then he would have read all the reports. Bishop shook his head, he hadn't learned much at all. Blossom was the loser in a love triangle. Happened to everyone at some time. Most of them didn't end up dead because of it. Maybe they felt like they were dead, but their hearts kept beating and their lungs kept breathing. In time it didn't hurt so much. If you could let go of the anger you'd get through it. "Why the interest?"

The Chief spun his chair around, and faced Bishop, giving him that disarming smile that had made him Chief long before he'd achieved the rank, and had left Morris and Orlando working for every advance. "Why, I'm interested in all your cases, boy, yours, and Sam's, and Orlando's. I'll even be interested in Sergio's once he's proven himself not to be an idiot. It's just not right, such a pretty little thing."

A silence grew between them. Bishop had known the Chief a long time. Razzed him when he'd thrown-up after his first dead body. Been there when his first marriage, like so many police marriages, had fallen apart. Taken him home to Jackie after nights of too much numbing the pain of being a cop. "Waiting for the ME's ruling." Bishop finally said.

"Everyone says it was the smoke."

Bishop didn't openly disagree. "It's more than that. Something in the smoke. I think someone knew she was allergic to poison ivy and deliberately added it to the spell she was casting."

"Now you're chasing ..." the Chief grinned, "... smoke." He turned back to the dark sky. "The ME will declare accidental death. Send me your paperwork in the morning. We'll find another case for you to work on. Not Sam's. No, the boy's got to learn on his own. You'd just go solving it for him. Can't have that."

Bishop left the Chief sitting and staring out the window. If Claire had had her way it would have been him sitting in that chair. At least he'd escaped that fate.

On the way home Bishop swung past Claire's. It wasn't really on the way home. It was on the opposite side of town. He wrote out the child support check at a stop sign balancing the checkbook on his knee, but not bothering to enter the check into the registry. No reason to do that unless he was going to subtract it from the account – and bankers hated when you subtracted something from nothing. The car behind hit its horn and flew past rudely saluting.

Bishop turned off the main streets, then down an avenue complete with center tree lined meridian and tulip studded strip. There was stone fencing on either side of the entry of the gated community, with a little sign that said Mayfair, as if warning him that he was entering a British comedy. Each home tried to outshine the next. Bishop recognized several from his father's worktable, French Provincial seemed to dominate, but a few Colonials, and one Prairie style balanced the mix. He passed the Chief's neo-classical revival with its stately Corinthian columns, Claire called it the Gone with the Wind house. A forty foot motor home sat out front with a for sale sign in its side window.

He pulled into Claire's driveway leading to a three car garage with boat shelter. He couldn't stop himself from admiring the beautiful, new two-story Colonial with its manicured lawn and cultivated shrubbery. As he stopped the engine his Subaru popped making a loud noise. Like belching at a funeral. He tried to remember what exactly her husband did. Something at the mayor's office. Something that was police work but wasn't. Internal affairs? Administrative? The academy? At least their paths never crossed. It would be awkward working with the man who had married your ex-wife the moment the divorce had become final.

Bishop went up the walkway to the expansive patio and rang the bell, inside the perfectly pitched chime faintly sounded. Almost immediately a tow-headed boy opened the door a crack and peered up at him. That twinge, that regret, this should have been his house, his child, his wife, exploded in his chest. Claire appeared behind the child, fully opening the door. She glared at Bishop, her eyes narrow with suspicion, and the sudden want went skidding into the past where it had come from.

"To bed, Tobias." The child gave Bishop one last

look before disappearing. Claire waited, finally satisfied that the boy was gone, she turned to Bishop her expression more neutral, but displeasure still turning down her mouth. "What are you doing here, Vinnie?"

Bishop remembered the divorce. Claire had gotten the lawyer. Claire had demanded payment for her pain. He had given her everything. Anything to be with Teonna. Is that how it had been for the Chief? He seemed to remember Jackie and the Chief's ex getting into it. Charges had been pressed. How had that turned out? He'd been in the hospital when the Chief's ex had left town. She'd just up and left from what he'd heard. Claire would know. If he'd ask her. But he wouldn't.

Claire's foot tapped impatiently.

"Brought by the check." He handed it to her, and she reached for it. He pulled it back an instant before her fingers touched the paper.

"It's early. Don't cash it until payday."

Claire's hand shot forward, and she snatched the check from him. She held the compensation for her pain between them. Another woman would have glanced down at the amount, but they both knew he paid to the penny, every month. It was just never enough, would never be enough to repay the lies, and the hurt. She stared up at him, the hurt still there after all the years. Looking away, he tried to bull his way into the house, but she didn't budge.

"Now tell me what you're doing here."

They were face to face, too close , he could smell

her musky perfume and the yogurt she always had before bed.

"I was out at the school. Lexi's ..."

"Not your concern." Claire stepped forward shoving him with one hand and closing the door with the other. But Bishop was ready and blocked the door with his body, grabbing Claire's wrist.

"You need to talk to her. Not this yelling thing you do." Beneath his fingertips her pulse raced. "She's hanging with a fast crowd."

Claire pulled her arm away, and he let her slip from his fingers.

"And what kind of crowd is Sonny hanging with? You don't have a clue. You don't know that he's changed majors – again. He's trying to find himself."

She'd meant that one to hurt, and it did.

"You don't know that this summer he'll be crawling around caves with some college professor."

How much was that going to cost him?

Her brain seemed to stop forming words and hatred shot at him through her eyes. "Why don't you do what you're good at and leave?"

He'd heard that one before. Claire shoved him. Bishop let her. He even took a step back. He felt her anger was just as raw and bleeding as it had been when they'd first parted.

"I'll call Sonny. You talk to Lexi."

"You have a hell of a lot of nerve. She's not your daughter." Claire slammed the door. Bishop stood a moment staring at the steel high-end door painted red in the old German tradition of welcome. Claire had been saying that for thirteen years, yet ten months was all they'd been apart when Lexi was born. He'd been in too much of a fog then to notice. Now it gnawed at him. Ten months. Claire hadn't even waited for the sheets to get cold. He was out, Junior was in. How long had Junior been waiting on the sidelines? Bishop had never asked how she'd met Junior, never questioned Claire's fidelity.

And yet it bothered him. Babies came in their own sweet time. Some babies took ten months. But Lexi was a miniature Claire, like Sonny was a miniature Bishop. He hadn't questioned that Sonny was his. No one questioned that Lexi was Claire's. But did Junior ever stand there wondering, just as Bishop wondered. Bishop turned away from the house. It would take a DNA test. And then what? He didn't need a second child. He couldn't afford a bigger child support check. What did he want to prove anyway?

CHAPTER TWENTY-ONE

When the phone rang, Bishop shot awake like a soldier hearing gun fire. He hand was on the cellphone and it was open before his eyes were. "Yeah."

"I need you to unlock a door for me."

He knew the voice. Hannah. Wasn't she angry at him? Or was he angry at her? Either was he shook the sleep out of his head. "Zeus Locksmithing on Third has an emergency nmber. It's in the book."

Bishop closed the phone and fell back into the tangle of blankets. Before he could settle against the pillow, the phone rang again. He checked the time. Two a.m. Caller ID blocked.

"Damn you, Vincent, this will only take a minute."

"Yeah." A minute to open the lock, but another hour by the time he dressed, drove to wherever the lock was and drove home again. He may as well kiss a night's sleep good-bye.

"You won't go back to sleep anyway. It'll itch at you not knowing if I helped this poor woman." She took a deep breath. "To protect and to serve," she pounded at him with her clipped tones. "I guess those are just words to you. Sweet dreams."

Hannah killed the connection without saying goodbye.

Bishop slammed against the pillows, then grabbed an edge of the blankets and snapped them straight only to have the fabric lose momentum half way and plop against his legs. He closed his eyes and took a deep breath. Damn woman. Tossing the bedding to the floor, he tromped to the bathroom and scowled at the face in the mirror. Not until he was dressed, keys in hand did he call her.

"Where?"

Sappy sweet, she knew he'd come, she gave him the address. It rang a bell. JoAnn Dole's house. "The woman with the cat?"

"Just hurry."

Traffic was light and now that he was awake, Bishop was curious. When he got there he recognized Hannah's old Honda sitting in the drive, with another new Honda alongside. Before he could touch the doorbell Laura Jones opened the door.

"I'm so glad that you came, Officer Bishop."

She wore an old cotton nightgown with a high collar and a tightly tied bathrobe that smelled lightly of lavender. Her long hair fell loosed around her face and down her back. The moonlight softened the lines around her eyes and mouth, hinting back to her youth. She must have been very attractive, back then, back then she was young. After and awkward moment, she turned into the house. He followed through the living area and past the kitchen to a tiny hallway with a door off to the left. Hannah, JoAnn, Keisha, and several cats hovered about the door. From the opposite side a cat howled. All the other cats joined in with a resulting escalation of decibel level any trash band would have been proud of.

Everyone except the cats made room as Bishop sat down his tackle box and studied the lock. One cat climbed on his bent knee. Laura Jones pulled it away and handed the animal to JoAnn only to have another cat take its place.

"Well?"

Bishop looked up at Hannah. She was no more dressed that the others. A jacket thrown over her faded nightgown, the one with the buttonholes so worn that they undid with a touch. He fought the primeval stirring, lust not love made him want to take her into his arms, to get paid for his labors. One look exchanged and she knew what he was thinking. With a self-satisfied smile, she pulled her jacket tighter. It was the smile that extinguished the lust. He'd seen that smile on Claire's lips when she'd won and he'd lost, her mind keeping some punitive tally. Now Hannah was playing the same game. He wouldn't go down that road again.

Bishop gave his full attention to the lock – an antique of pot metal with a crystal knob. The keyhole rusted, heaven only knew what condition the tumblers were in. He wouldn't be able to use the ring of blanks, or the burglary tool he'd brought to bump the cylinders into releasing. The easiest thing to do would be to drill. He didn't carry those kinds of tools around with him.

"This can't wait till morning?"

The cat behind the door started wailing again with a corresponding reply from all the other cats.

"What do you think?"

Convinced that it couldn't, Bishop pushed aside another feline as it tried to come between him and the door. The creatures seemed to be coming out of the woodwork. "Get them out of here."

Everyone grabbed a cat, some took two, and disappeared. He heard a door upstairs open and close, followed by a huffy protest from the animals. Satisfied that the beasts weren't returning, he again stared at the lock. After coming all this way he had better try something. He took one of his business cards, folded it into a 'v', and tapped some graphite into the mechanism. Then he used a thin, tapered blank to work the powder into the tumblers. The women returned making a half-circle around him. Hot, anxious breathing warmed his neck and back. Had they broken into some unlocking locked doors chant he wouldn't have been surprised. Rummaging through the tackle box, he brought out a ring of master keys. One after another he tried the steel keys, each turned, then slipped, none lifting the tumblers.

He rocked back on his heels, looking up to study

the door frame and hinges. Old wood, old hinges. The trim painted and repainted. "I'll have to take off the door."

"Really?" Hannah's voice held more than a little exasperation. "Can't you work any of your magic to get it open?"

"It's not about magic, the tumblers are frozen with rust. How did it ever get locked in the first place?"

The women stared at each other, their gaze finally resting on JoAnn. "I don't know. I never lock that door. I never go into the basement. I woke up and heard Percy meowing."

Bishop stood, dusting off his knees. Making accusations wasn't getting that door open, or letting him get back bed. He noticed that arrogant cat smile on Hannah's face. His own bed. Alone. He wasn't falling victim to her love spell. "Do you have a crowbar?"

The women all looked at each other as if one of them was hiding it under her nightie.

He had a tire-iron in the car that might work. It was just a matter of leverage. Bishop was out and back while the women were still discussing where a crowbar might be found. In the basement seemed to be the consensus. He tapped the hinges with the socket end, loosening the metal, then pushed upward. Muscles strained, his shoulder popped, the hinge screeched, setting all the cats into an off-key accompaniment, before the hinge finally yielded with angry high pitched protests. He handed the bottom bolt to Hannah and repeated the process, freeing the second hinge. Awkwardly the door pulled open a few inches the wrong direction, the lock slipped from its setting, and the whole door dropped into his hands, the weight of the thick oak pulling painfully at his shoulder.

"Percy." JoAnn called.

No cat appeared.

"Percy!" She called again.

Finally the beast strutted through the opening, something dangling between its teeth. JoAnn squealed, retreating from the animal. "A mouse. By the goddess, Percival has a mouse!"

The cat dropped the bit of brown at Bishop's feet and stared up, its green eyes hypnotic. Bishop bent down. Not a mouse. A glove. He picked up the glove and turned it round and round in his hand. A brown, knit, cotton glove, not thick enough for winter, but enough to keep your fingers warm against the cold of a steering wheel on a chilly morning.

"Thank the spirits, it's just a glove."

There was a collective sigh of relief. JoAnn swooped down and lifted her cat. The two rubbed cheek to cheek and a loud purr soothed the room. The air seemed to thicken. Bishop moved away from the opening to the basement with its musty smell and into the kitchen where the women had gathered, laughing and jabbering.

Someone handed him a cup of something hot. Bishop handed it back. "I have to go."

"No, no, we have to do something for you." JoAnn

insisted.

"A reading?" Keisha volunteered.

"What a splendid idea." Laura agreed.

One of the women lit a candle, another tossed a handful of dry leaves into a pot of water simmering on the stove. Sage and lavender. The soothing aroma of herbs soaked into his muscles and, mixed with fatigue, made them leaden.

He needed to sleep. A mist like a dry ice fog swirled cold around him.

"Who has a deck?" Was that Hannah? Or JoAnn who'd spoken?

Bishop couldn't tell the voices apart. With a strong yank, Hannah took the tackle box from him. Keisha's dark hands shoved a stack of cards into the resulting open palms. Through the haze he saw Hannah give him an oversweet smile. Had this been a set-up?

He tried to shake the grogginess from his brain. He had sisters. He knew what was going on. They would tell his fortune and somehow it would be that he should marry a dark haired woman whose name started with an H.

"Shuffle the deck three times."

Swept along, unable to fight the tide of women's voices, he mixed the heavy, thick cards.

"Now cut it three times to the right."

When had they moved to the kitchen table? The lights off. Lit candles everywhere. The herbal scent of sage filling the room. He placed the deck, faces down, onto the table top. He didn't remember the wood being so rough before, the butcher block surface furrowed from use. Without thought, his hand reached down and touched the cards. They seemed to fall into three stacks, the ornate light and dark design on the back of the deck parting then coming together. Keisha scooped the cards up and held the deck against her heart, the rise and fall of her bosom hypnotic beneath her tattered sweatshirt.

The cat jumped from JoAnn's arms to Bishop's back, settling itself on his bad shoulder, its claws finding his scars and rolling in and out of his jacket fabric, watching along with the others. Solemnly, Keisha lay out the cards, five in a cross, and five at the side. Everyone leaned forward, a collective breath drawn in, as the first card was revealed, a sigh let out.

A man, dancing away with an armload of swords.

"I see something being stolen." Keisha told the group.

The bank robbery was all over the news. Nothing surprising there.

Laura shook her head. "Not necessarily money, things other than money are valuable""

The next card was a heart with three swords thrust through it and rain coming down.

"A wound to the heart."

"Betrayal." Laura modified.

Keisha scowled, and hastily flipped the next card. The women pulled back with one simultaneous gasp. "More swords."

"Conflict."

"Death. He's surrounded by death." JoAnn

moaned.

Bishop dealt with death nearly every day, death did not bother him. The dead expected nothing, it was the living who lied, and cheated, and stole.

"No, look, here's a cup."

"The five of cups. Not good, not good."

"And the moon."

"A new beginning?"

Laura shook her head. "Things are not as they seem."

He shook his mind. The fog seemed to thin.

Hastily, her black hand flipped over another card. "A young child."

Laura closed her eyes, breathing deeply, "Female, fourteen with long blonde hair, and jade green eyes."

His senses sharpened. Lexi?

"You can't know that."

"She feels it." JoAnn snipped back in defense of her friend.

"It's my reading." Keisha snapped the next card up.

The women leaned forward in anticipation. "More lies."

"Or truths not recognized."

Keisha's brow wrinkled unbecomingly and she bit her lips. In quick succession, she flipped the remaining cards. "Answers at great cost. A knight who means you harm. A queen that may or may not bring happiness. Locks and secrets." She turned the last card. "Redemption."

"Perhaps at too great a cost." Laura added and

stared at him, questions in her eyes.

Not the reading he had expected the women to use to nudge him and Hannah back together. The fog gone, but the pain in his shoulder like flames licking his flesh, Bishop backed away from the table.

"That's a ridiculous reading. Try it again." JoAnn demanded.

Percy leapt off Bishop's shoulder and landed on the tabletop, scattering the cards with a flurry.

"Look, he's torn the queen. The Queen of Cups! And the Tower! You need to get me a new deck."

"Oh, no, that deck was falling apart. It wasn't Percy's fault."

Bishop retreated out the door. None of the women seemed to notice, except Hannah. She blocked the exit, her long hair tumbling down her back, another button on her nightgown popped open revealing the swell of her breast, rising and falling like the tide against a shore.

"I thought you might be looking for this." She held a watch out to him. His watch. He had wondered where he'd left it. No, he'd known, but hadn't wanted to ask for it back. "Since you hadn't come by for it I thought I'd give it to you." She paused, her voice held a question. "Unless ...?"

Was it an invitation to turn the clock back and return to the way things had been? He took the watch. The steady buzz of the battery. The second hand sweeping across the numbers. No, it was over. She wanted more than he could ever give her. The streetlight reflected off the moisture in her eyes. But she wasn't crying. They both had regrets, but not tears.

Once in the car he remembered the tire iron. None of the women had left, the lights were still on, Hannah stood in the open door watching him. He could go back. Instead he turned the key, one last glance in the rearview mirror. The cat sat on the porch, the glove hanging from its mouth, its green eyes glowing.

CHAPTER TWENTY-TWO

Although his shoulder ached as if the clouds would open, silence instead of rain washed the streets. Maybe he should go see a doctor. As quickly as the thought came, Bishop discarded the idea. He'd had enough of doctors to last a lifetime. What he needed was a cup of coffee. He wouldn't sleep anyway. Without thinking he pulled into a parking spot right in front of the only all night restaurant in town. At least the only one he, and Teonna, and Frank had ever gone to. The over-bright lights poured out onto the sidewalk, the tide of the past pulled him in. It was too late to go home and sleep, just as it was too late for the bar crowd, and too early for the working stiffs.

Out of habit he scanned the diner, someone in a back booth lightly snored, otherwise the place was empty. There seemed to be the only one waitress on duty. She stood by the long counter, a bucket of sudsy water nearby, a cleaning cloth floating between the bubbles and the scum. He sat at the far end. At this hour of the morning, she automatically poured coffee. He didn't stop her. She didn't recognize him until she put down the water glass and handed him the menu. "You're back? I didn't think the special was that good."

It was mindless banter, the kind waitresses use when the face is familiar but you're not a regular. With a glance, he checked her name tag, Mandy, the 'y' ending in an extravagant flourish. He hoped it wasn't one she'd randomly grabbed from the back.

"So, what will it be?"

He scanned the prices, found one that his wallet could cover and still let him leave a tip. "Got any pie left?"

"Apple or pumpkin?"

Like he cared. He handed her back the menu. "Whatever looks good."

"That would be the pumpkin. At least you can hide it under the whipped cream." She leaned against the table rocking onto the balls of her feet to ease the end of the shift fatigue. The endless banging and clanging in the kitchen as the cooks prepped for the morning faded into familiarity. Their eyes meet. Hers were haunted, like a trapped animal.

"You didn't come for the pie."

"No," he cupped his hand around the mug, the hot coffee warming the thick porcelain. "I thought you might tell me about Blossom."

He'd been right, the name tag might have read Mandy, but Amanda touched the silver chain around her neck, her fingers following the links down into the open neckline of her starched, pink uniform.

"I don't know who you're talking about, you must have me mixed-up with someone else." She straightened, taking her lie to the kitchen. It was a long time before she returned with the pie. Long enough for him to watch the shadows play across the windows, the past reflecting images of him and Teonna shoved together on one side of a booth. Both aware of every touch like the burn of a match. Frank and the Chief opposite, lifting their glasses to one more bad guy off the streets. Why had the Chief been there? He'd already made detective. Five years out and a lieutenant.

That's right, the drug deal.

Jackie trying to take their order while the Chief flirted and joked.

Jackie. He'd forgotten that Jackie had ever been a waitress. Her working her way through banking school, the Chief avoiding his wife, them coming in night after night when he should have been home. Jackie – first Teonna's friend, then the Chief's lover.

Bishop tried to hold the memory, concentrating on Teonna, the deep blue of her uniform, the golden blonde of her hair, the white teeth against the pink lips. But images of the Chief, even then everyone called him Chief, and Jackie kept intruding. The Chief's teasing banter and quick smile, Jackie's haughty, come and try flirt back. The images were like slippery fish, the tighter he tried to hold them the more they slid through his fingers. He chased the laughter only to have it flop away until finally it was gone, replaced with the sound of glasses bouncing against each other as they came out of the steam washer in the back.

The mist of memories totally evaporated when Mandy dropped a plate of pumpkin pie, drowning in the promised whipped cream, in front of him. She didn't stop, moving down the counter instead. Pulling the rag out of the bucket of soapy water, she wrung the cloth out, finally slapping it onto the laminate counter top. Making circles, round and round, her muscles tightening and relaxing in a rhythm of regret, she scrubbed the same spot on the clean counter

They were close enough to talk, in the nearly empty diner she could have stood anywhere and they would have been close enough to talk.

"She was the only one who was nice to me."

Neither looked up, neither looked at the other. A part of Bishop listened, a part studied the pie. The tip of the brown custard, crusted and discolored, peeked from beneath the neon white, whipped cream product. No longer hungry, but knowing that Amanda needed to confess whatever sins she thought that she had, he pushed some of the topping off with the tip of his fork and let her ramble.

"Those other women – they didn't like me. Didn't like the things I did." She plunged the cloth back into the bucket, swirling the suds. "They were right." The lemon scented cleaning water lapped at her elbow, but she didn't seem to notice. She stared out the black window, the lights pouring out and letting nothing in.

"About a year ago, Blossom came in. Late. It was like now, dead...." She winced at her own choice of words. "I saw her Book of Shadows. We got to talking, and I told her about the spells. The bad spells."

Bits of idle conversation, in some foreign language, muffled by the swinging doors, floated out of the kitchen, followed by laughter.

"It was stupid. I shouldn't have told her." Amanda pulled her hand from the bucket, and dried it on her apron. "We compared books, spells, I had a love spell, but it needed three." She blinked back the tears glistening in her eyes refusing to let them tumble down her cheeks. Unsure what to do with her hands, perhaps realizing that they were hanging limp at her sides, she finally folded her arms around herself, hugging her waist as if her insides might escape. Slowly she swayed in a self-soothing rocking.

"A Book of Shadows?" He knew, he'd seen the book in Blossom's dresser.

Amanda stopped rocking, pulling her eyes away from the soulless window, and hunted for the bucket at her side. Finding purpose, or at least comfort, she fished the cloth out of the murky water. "Why do you care?"

He couldn't answer that. Being a cop had been nothing more than a paycheck and health insurance until Teonna, until her passion for the job had infected him, the craving for justice staying with him even after she was gone. Maybe because she was gone.

Amanda touched the necklace at her throat, the three phases of the moon medallion visible as she clutched the chain, lifting and twirling the talisman. Maybe it soothed her, maybe it told her he could be trusted.

"My grandmother gave me her book. All the things her grandmother had learned in the bayou were in there. I'd done some spells on my own, but I didn't understand them. Didn't know why you did this and not that. I wanted to know more. So Blossom invited me to the coven. She said they would help me understand the spells. Only they didn't like me."

She tried to shrug it off, brushing a loose strand of hair away from her face, but the hurt was there. "They told me the spells were wrong, that ... that someone would ... I should have listened." Amanda resumed her cleaning ritual. "I didn't think ... I'd used the spell before." She gave the cloth an extra push. "This bitch, she stole my girlfriend, so I put a misfortune spell on her. And her car broke down. Nothing bad. Her car just broke down."

Bishop stopped torturing the whipped cream, and put down his fork. Sounded like a coincidence to him. "The ME –" civilian "– Medical examiner, is ruling accidental death." His voice poured out soft, and rumbling. "Her report will come out in the morning."

This time the tears came, trickling onto Amanda's cheek. They didn't get far before she brusquely brushed them away.

"When Blossom tossed the spell into the fire," Bishop continued, "the poison ivy flash-burned and got into her lungs. You couldn't have saved her. But you did try. When you gave her CPR, you got some on your face. That's why you had on the thick make-up when I was here the other day."

Amanda touched her cheeks and lips, and then shook her head. "But there wasn't any poison ivy in the spell."

"Then you built the fire with some old branches or twigs that were lying around. Some of them could have been poison ivy. It was an accident."

"No, Virna brought the logs, she'd bought the from some place in California. Wood from a pear tree, steeped in rose oil, and then dried through twelve phases of the moon. Blossom would never have come within three feet of poison ivy. Her mother and that other witch came out all the time and made sure there wasn't any."

Time froze. A clock somewhere ticked. The air in his lungs couldn't remember if he was breathing in or out.

"You never put anything in that might harm you." Her voice was solid, and she made eye contact.

Bishop turned full-face toward her. "You knew Blossom was allergic to poison ivy?"

"Everyone knew. She wore one of those bracelets."

"I never saw a bracelet."

Amanda dried her hands on her apron. "I think she gave it to me, before the spell, we didn't want the metal in the chain interfering." She was gone and back, dropping the bracelet into his hand. Why was he reminded of Jackie's bracelet? They were nothing alike. Jackie's a thick, lacquered, designer original that had made the Chief grumble about the price of peace. Blossom's a cheap chain with a clasp, and a medical warning.

Fatigue came from nowhere, hitting him hard. "So, you and Blossom, you were best friends?" Like Jackie and Teonna had been best friends.

Amanda nodded.

"Then you know the man's name." All his muscles seemed to ache, not just his shoulder.

"She never said."

"Never? Not to her BFF?" How likely was that? What was Blossom hiding?

"He was a cop."

"A cop?" Yes, he knew that, now that she said it. "That's why she took the class. So she could see him again." Not meet him, but see him again.

"At first he pretended like he didn't know her. But she knew he did. He asked about the poison oak. They were talking when the wife drove up. Started screaming at her. Tried to run her over."

"After class? At the university." There might be a record of an incident. "So you were there?"

Amanda shook her head. "No, but Blossom told me. That's when I told Blossom about the bad spells, the ones to bring love back, the ones to cause harm ... If I hadn't told her she'd be alive."

"You couldn't have known the spell would explode in her face." But someone knew. Someone had put poison ivy into the spell. Someone had added a pinch of gunpowder.

"I knew. Every witch knows." Amanda slapped

the cleaning cloth onto the table. "The rule of threes." She leaned into her cleaning. "Whatever you send forth returns to you threefold." Amanda turned her head and stared into his eyes. But she wasn't seeing him. As if his eyes were mirrors, her soul seemed to be reflected back at her. "I knew she wanted to destroy that woman. Not just turn her husband's love away from her, but destroy her. Blossom wanted her dead, and the spell came back on Blossom."

CHAPTER TWENTY-THREE

The sun was up when Bishop finally left the diner. He could go home, shower, change, and come back. That took gas. He tapped the gauge on his dash. It jumped higher than fell back even lower. Maybe better not. In the past he would have gone to Hannah's. He still had the key. He could feel it, sharp and burrowing through the fabric of his pocket into his leg. He should give it back. When he drove by the shelter house the lights were off. A shadow moved to the back of the house. But he didn't stop to investigate. Going forward everything between them had to stay professional, no sliding back into her bed on lonely nights. He'd mail her the key.

He arrived at the station early. So did Sam. Bishop watched the lanky officer unbending from the passenger side of a Ford Escort, then pause at the station house door to wave good-bye to the little red car. As it pulled away Bishop took a long look at the driver. He didn't have to dig deep to recognize her as the bank teller from three days ago.

Sam waited for him, holding the door, and they walked in together. "How's the witch case going?"

Bishop ignored the question, and responded with one of his own. "Isn't she from the bank?"

Sam looked down, he always looked down, but this time it was to avoid any eye contact with Bishop. "Yeah."

"Is that a good idea? It could have been an inside job." Why had he said that? The words had come out without thought. Maybe to annoy Sam. Bishop led the way to the stairwell and the locker room. Besides lockers, where officers could keep a change of clothing, there were two showers. Tucked in what should have been a closet was a small room with a couple of cots where officers pulling double shifts could catch a few hours' sleep. If you jammed a chair under the door handle, the bed could be used for other things. The image of Teonna, her long hair in wild disarray, her mouth half open gasping in the thralls of passion, flashed through him like a picture on a movie screen, then dissolved to reflected light, replaced with the memory of Jackie and the Chief slipping out the door, sly grins on their faces.

"If it was an inside job, Vicki didn't have anything to do with it. The tellers don't know about the shipments until they get there."

In unison, they opened their lockers, removing the live round from the chamber of their service handguns, before stowing them. In one motion, Sam pulled his shirt over his head, and dropped it on top of the teetering pile of dirty clothing in the bottom of his locker.

"Only Jackie and the bank president knew beforehand. Everyone else found out when the couriers came."

Bishop stopped mid-button. "Outtmann said he was the only one who knew."

Sam stepped out of his pants and tossed them into the locker. "Nobody has to say what Sergio and the ME were doing in the backroom for us to know. Besides, Jackie pretty much runs the bank, Outtmann just takes credit for everything." Fully stripped, Sam grabbed his shower kit and headed to the next room. Bishop slowly followed.

Over the gush of water, Sam kept talking. "Anyway, Diane called, wanted to know if I was solving the murder. So we met for supper. To talk – you know."

Bishop knew.

"No one cares about the stolen money." Sam had to bend low to get under the shower head and rinse shampoo from his hair. "It's insured. Doesn't have anything to do with them. Outtmann's the one with his head on the chopping block. Well, not really. His grandfather owns the bank. Business as usual there, but people are curious about what happened to Blossom."

Bishop stopped washing down, and let the water rinse the soap off him. Why had Sam been talking about Bishop's case on a date? An overnight date?

"Blossom? The witch? How do they know her?"

"She used to intern at the bank, until Jackie got her fired." Sam turned off the water and stepped from the shower, water running off him in rivulets. He grabbed a worn towel from the stack, wrapping it around his waist before tossing one to Bishop. "Everyone liked her."

"They don't like Jackie?" Water caught on his scars and Bishop carefully blotted them dry. He looked up to see Sam staring and turned his back. But there were even more scars splattered across shoulders, each one a white circle that should have killed him.

Sam's razor started, the sharp buzz replacing the unasked questions in the room. "They're all a little afraid of her."

Half dressed, looking at the Sam in the mirror. "Of Jackie?"

"Diane said she gets into these black moods, and everybody ducks." Sam's eyes were disapproving as they reflected back at Bishop.

Everyone had moods, some more than others. But if Bishop knew anything about women, and being sandwiched between two sisters he could claim that he did, he'd have to say this was nothing more than hen-house politics. The bottom of the pecking order always complained about the top, whether they had reason to, or not. He tried to remember if Teonna had ever said anything about Jackie. Nothing came to mind. All he could see was Teonna standing in her blue uniform, hand on her hip holster, while Jackie stood behind laughing. And even that image seemed to be fading behind curls of smoke.

Finished removing the thin stubble of whiskers from his chin, Sam began dressing. Bishop pulled an electric razor from the top shelf of his locker. Slowly he ran the metal teeth across his cheeks.

"Murder? Did she say that? Not death?"

Sam hesitated, dropping his voice, as he yanked on a sock. "She also said that Jackie can't always find the Chief where he says he's going to be. Makes her really mad, and she takes it out on the tellers."

So? That was part of being a cop. Sometimes you changed direction. Sometimes you thought the path led north and it turned west, then twisted back to the south. The razor pulled at the skin on his cheeks. Sometimes the Chief would get in his little blue plane and fly away. To clear his head, he'd say, then laugh, that cocky, self-assured laugh you either loved or hated, sometimes both.

"How did Jackie get Blossom fired?" Bishop didn't believe it, he didn't want to believe it. Jackie and Teonna, best friends forever. The taint of Jackie doing anything wrong pushed bile into his mouth.

"Jackie said Blossom had been dipping into the drawer."

Bishop stopped shaving, the razor buzzing inches from his throat. He must have looked clueless. Sam paused, his foot halfway into his size fourteen shoe and stared over at Bishop, his dark eyes still annoyed.

"She claimed Blossom would take some of the bait money – they don't check that daily."

Bishop still didn't understand.

"You know, she would take one bill out of the bundle, they don't count every bill of the bait money every day, it just sits in the bottom of the drawer so why count and recount it? Then Blossom supposedly replaced the missing bill on payday. But Jackie did a surprise count of the drawer, fine counted everything, and uncovered the shortage. Several bills from the bait didn't match the files. You can't put back the exact same bill you took out. So they knew that the bills had been switched out. Outtmann let Blossom quit instead of pressing charges, which made Jackie furious."

Cop's wife. Letter of the law.

"But no one believed Blossom did it."

"No one?"

Sam stood, tucking in his shirt and buckling his belt. "Not even Outtmann. But you can't fight the facts."

Yet why would a girl coming into millions snitch a few bucks? So her mother wouldn't know? Because she came up short at the end of the month? Bishop knew that feeling. But dipping into the drawer? That would have made her un-bondable, she'd never be able to work another job that required her to handle money.

"So the bait money didn't match, what does that have to do with Jackie?"

"Jackie had access to all the keys, and the drawers, she could have tampered with the bait money."

Means and opportunity, but where was the motive for destroying a young girl's life? Other people had to have had access. Jackie would never do such a thing. Too many variables he told himself, emotion clouding his logic.

They left the locker rooms as the night shift started clocking out and the day shift started clocking in. Sam lead, full of energy only youth and a night of satisfied lust could impart. When they entered the office area Bishop noted that the Chief's door was closed and his light on. He couldn't help but wonder if the Chief had stayed there all night. Maybe it was good that he and Jackie were going on vacation. Let the topical sun put the heat back into their marriage. Like it had last year. They'd left as rigid acquaintances and returned like honeymooners. Maybe if he and Claire had done that – taken a second honeymoon when Teonna had come onto the scene? Maybe if they'd taken a first honeymoon?

Bishop sat at his desk while Sam headed for coffee. By rote he switched on the computer. He went through the screens entering his passwords, for an instant his mind went blank, TS+VB4evr, his fingers finished for him. The candle drawings he had made previously sat beneath the computer mouse. The cord blocking out some of the design. Bishop turned the paper. The loops and curves suddenly didn't seem as random. If he ignored the flowers and stars, and followed the stem. Bishop picked up a pencil darkening the lines. A name jumped out at him. Johnson, Rusty Johnson. He turned the paper looking for another name. Any other name. But none appeared.

Bishop thumped the end of his pencil onto the desk top. The elasticity of the eraser made it bounce and he caught it on the up motion. He felt out of sync. Nothing was right. His shoulder ached, and yet it didn't rain. Teonna drifted into his thoughts, and yet he couldn't remember the taste of her lips. Everyone knew Blossom was allergic to poison ivy, yet there it was in her spell. It could only have gotten there if someone else had deliberately put it there. No one called the chief Rusty, few even knew it was his given name, and yet there it was, a silent whisper from a dead witch. Realizing Sam stood at the desk, a cup of coffee held out to him, Bishop let the pencil drop. How long had Sam been standing there? How long had the Chief known Blossom?

CHAPTER TWENTY-FOUR

Only Bishop seemed to feel a fog fill the squad room, seeping through the closed windows and under the closed doors, thickening as the other detectives arrived. Sergio and Torres at the same time, but avoiding eye contact. Sam noticing but not commenting. Orlando, his clothes rumpled and bags under his eyes saying it had been a long night. Finally, Morris, who looked at the Chief's closed door, but didn't go over, didn't knock, just started the morning briefing off the pages he'd gotten from the desk sergeant.

The ME had determined that the Blossom Jones case accidental death, case closed. Bishop was now free to help if anyone needed it. He was up on rotation as well. The bank robbery was still an open case. Pass any calls to Sam. Starting next week several main arteries across the city would be constricted or rerouted for the Jordan Mall project. Sheets with maps and approximate dates were handed out. Sam, Bishop, Orlando were up to recertify, get out to the practice range and get it done before the end of the month. Meeting over.

Bishop went to his desk, the only one that had a clear line of eyesight to the elevators. No one liked the desk, it put you in the bulls-eye, but he had gotten so that he could identify the rumble of the machinery bringing someone up. Wheels, cables, metal moving with a smooth predictability. Before any calls came, before everyone was settled, the elevator doors swooshed open. A gaggle of women – no, a coven of witches – stepped from the elevator. Mimi led, a cling wrapped platter in front of her, Laura and JoAnn behind. Full steam ahead, she cut through the fog and made a direct path to his desk.

"Officer? Detective? Which is it?"

"Detective." Bishop answered her.

All eyes were on the platter.

"Does that make you a higher rank than an officer?"

"No, just different duties."

"I see." She looked around the room, her eyes intensely taking in every detail. When she made eye contact with Sergio he bounded out of his chair and joined the group.

"Here, let me take that for you." He commandeered the platter and placed it on his desk, then pulled back the thin plastic wrap exposing an array of baked goods: cookies, bars, and fruit breads. The sweet aroma whiffed through the squad room.

Like dogs on a scent everyone gathered around Sergio's desk.

"We wanted to thank you for all your hard work." Mimi informed Bishop while she still looked about the room. "You all have computers." She spoke to no one in particular. "Do you use them in your work? Are you watching criminals on the internet?"

A cookie in each hand and one dangling from his mouth, Sam shook his head. "No, ma'am." He inhaled the treat in one gulp. "We use them to file reports, or communicate with other officers about cases." He took Mimi to his desk to show her.

Laura gave Bishop an uncomfortable smile. "Mimi thought it would be alright. To come. To thank you."

He hadn't done anything. Blossom's killer hadn't been found. And now the case was closed, he would have to stop investigating. There would be no answers. Blossom's siren song of death, no matter how faint, would wake him in the night and he'd remember looking into her dead eyes. Not until her killer was found would she close her eyes and let him sleep in peace.

"I've gotten so much food. Mimi thought we should bring some by. For the officers." She was fumbling, an indecisive quarterback waiting for the right opening. "JoAnn made some sun tea, but it spilled in the car." The other witch was obviously making herself scarce so Laura could talk to Bishop alone, but occasionally glanced over gauging how things were going.

She paused, taking a deep breath before charging

ahead. "We're having a tree planting for Blossom, a pear tree, it just seemed right. Tomorrow afternoon. Hannah thought you might want to come."

It was his turn to something, anything. "Tea? Sweet tea?" – Maybe not that.

"You like tea?"

No, he liked coffee, but something about Sergio and sweet tea.

"It seems unreal. Only a year ago we were welcoming her to the coven. Now ..."

A year, a year and a day.

"Her full name was Pear Blossom. I thought it would make her strong and beautiful. Fruitful. That's why a pear tree." Tears welled up in Laura's eyes.

Bishop almost stood, almost took her into his arms, the need to kiss her tears away almost overpowering. But didn't. Instead he sat frozen, fighting the fog, fighting the illogical attraction he seemed to have to every woman he'd come into contact with over the last week.

JoAnn found herself ignored, or perhaps saw that things weren't going well between her friend and Bishop, and joined them. "Bring a candle." She informed him in her fairy godmother way. "We're putting them in the garden as a remembrance."

Something in the back of his brain nudged him. Something about the Chief and a ride-along civilian. Gossip, just gossip. "I can't promise anything. I have work." Tomorrow was his day off.

Laura looked away, a slight pink tinting her cheeks, a confused pain in her eyes. "Yes, of course, we shouldn't have come."

He hadn't meant to embarrass her.

Sam gestured toward the elevator. "Would you ladies like a tour?"

Mimi whipped around from where she had been studying the gun safety poster on the wall. "We could have a tour?"

Laura looked expectantly at Bishop but he didn't jump in. "Go ahead, Sam is a third generation policeman, he knows this place from bottom to top." Then he took a gamble. "But you know that. Blossom would have had a tour when she did a ride-along."

Bewilderment. None of the women knew she'd done a civilian ride-along. But would they have? Would Blossom have told them?

"I have some things to finish up here."

Before they were even gone he dug into the bottom drawer of his desk. Last year's calendar sat, stacked on top of the year before's, and the year before that's. He should get rid of them, but sometimes it felt as if the only proof he had of his existence were the five-by-eight spiral bound pages encased in fake, black leather. He flipped to the end of April. A palm tree had been doodled down the side of the page and a notation in one of the squares. Chief on vacation. A year and a day. That's how long since the Chief's last vacation. The same time Blossom joined the coven. Maybe Jackie had caught them. He flinched as if someone had hit him. Like Sonny had caught him and Teonna. Only Claire had thrown him out. Her pride wounded beyond repair. No amount of tropical sun was ever going to burn the anger out of her.

He shifted his focus. Even if the Chief had been involved with Blossom, it didn't mean anything. Even if he was the officer she'd taken the class to see, he wasn't chasing Blossom, she was chasing him. Guilt might be the reason for Blossom's silence. Maybe cornering the chief after class hadn't been enough. Maybe she took advantage of the civilian ride-along program to hound him. What could he do? Tell her to leave him alone? Put out a restraining order? He'd be a laughing stock. None of the other officers would take him seriously if he couldn't hold his own against a lovesick teenager.

Bishop clicked through several computer screens and pulled up the logs for ride-alongs. He quickly scanned the March, then April, and the first part of May for last year. No Blossom. No Pear Blossom. No Jones. He took a sip of his cold coffee, the acid burning his stomach without offering any warmth. Starting over, he scrolled back to the beginning of March. This time he went slower, not looking for a name, just looking, listening to the quiet of the squad room. No ringing phones, no chatter, no clicking of crime being investigated. There didn't seem to be any crime. Winter was gone. People had tumbled out of their house into the sunshine. The heat of summer hadn't started to fray tempers. Everyone was playing nice. Bishop inhaled the silence. Muttley and Jefferson's names came up again and again. A Tiffany Foss almost every day in March, a few in April, then nothing. Why did that name nudge him? A cloud shifted in front of the sun sending shadows through the window. Sweet tea. Sergio's sweet tea.

The elevator doors opened with their signatory whoosh of pneumatic air. Sam stood alone, the witches gone like a bad reproduction of a Shakespearian play. Sam stared at the screen of his cellphone. "They caught them."

"Caught who?" Bishop glanced up from the data base of ride-alongs.

Sam went to his desk. "The bank robbers." Everyone stopped what they were doing and turned toward Sam. He uncomfortably lifted his cell phone a few inches. "Nora texted. The leader started shooting. He's dead. They're bringing the rest back here."

Orlando straightened as if that would allow him to see the cell phone screen from the distance of his desk. "Anyone there speak Spanish?"

"Nora does." Sam went to his desk and folded his six-four frame into his chair.

Orlando shook his head, and Bishop knew what the man was thinking – like that was Spanish, some textbook grammar and a semester repairing houses with a dozen other gringos.

"They claim not to know anything."

"They who?" Sergio asked.

"The bank robbers." Sam shot at him.

The Chief came out of his office a stack of reports in his hand.

In his haste to stand, Sergio knocked back his chair. "They caught the bank robbers."

"That so?" The Chief shoved the papers he was

holding at Sergio. "You go over these reports on the Amber Alert and see if Bishop left anything out." Then went over to Sam's desk. He twisted his neck to look down at the screen, but Bishop doubted that he could see any more off the cell phone than Orlando had.

"They confess?"

Sam's thumbs danced across the phone screen. They waited. An answer came back. "Claim they don't know anything about a bank robbery."

The Chief nodded. "What you think, Bishop?"

The sketch of Blossom's candle, all hearts and stars and dreams stared up at him.

"You think they did it?"

It wasn't his case. More than anything he wished it was his case. Bank robberies were open and shut. They were all about the money. Greed had killed Esmeralda, but love, twisted and unrequited had killed Blossom. Or was it unrequited?

"Well."

Bishop stared at the Chief. When had the man gotten old? The lines on his baby face competing with his charming dimples, the lids of his bedroom eyes weighing heavy. This job did that to you. It made you old and cynical.

"If I'd just happened on a million dollars when I was thinking to get a couple of grand, I wouldn't be in an old van and poking along the back roads. Even driving the speed limit they could have been across the border by now."

"Got a point. Got a point." Everyone nodded. "Well, back to work. The Fed's will take care of it."

The Chief retreated toward his office, his feet never keeping up with the rest of him making his retreating back appear slightly hunched.

"And why kill the girl?" The words were out before Bishop could stop them. Before he even thought of the implications.

Half-way to his office the Chief turned and looked at Bishop. For an instant it was as if they were the only ones in the room. "Good question. Good question. That's why you're a good investigator, Bishop, you ask good questions." The Chief gazed around the room. "You all could learn a thing or two from Bishop here."

An embarrassed silence followed the Chief to his office. Bishop headed for the bathroom, his mind shaking. He had meant Blossom. But they had been talking about the bank robbery and it was Esmeralda that the Chief had thought he meant. And Esmeralda that the Chief had flashed and hidden guilt about.

When he came out Sam stood, leaning against the dull beige wall of the hallway, his over tall body cocked so that it had turned into all angles. He straightened and fell into step beside Bishop "There was something else." Sam dropped his voice and stared at the Chief's door uneasily. "Did the Chief say anything to you about talking to the farm workers?"

Bishop switched directions, instead of heading back to the desk area he retreated to the makeshift break room, a pair of convenience machines, one chips and candy bars, the other sodas, its cooling coils whirring against the wall. Three wobbly chairs and a tiny table, more suited to holding a vase of flowers than an officer's fatigue, sat within a step of the machines.

Sam continued in a low voice. "The day before the robbery, the Chief went out to farm where they were working and told them to move along. That he was going to call ICE."

Bishop fished the change out of his pocket. He studied the jumble of thin coins in his hand. The Garfield Falls police didn't get involved with immigration enforcement. As long as nobody was breaking any local laws they left things to the Feds. It was a matter of jurisdiction courtesy.

"And they don't normally cash their checks at the bank." Sam rested his arm on the top of the first machine. "They can't because they don't have IDs, so banks can't, shouldn't, cash their checks. Even though the checks are from Jordon Enterprises and everyone knows they're good, the workers have to go to those check cashing places and pay a huge fee."

Ask the right questions. "So why'd they go to the bank?" Bishop dropped a quarter into the slot.

"Because the Chief told them to."

The quarter hit the coin cache with a hollow plunk like a penny hitting the bottom of a wishing well.

"And Jackie told the tellers to cash the checks, even though Outtmann doesn't allow it."

Bishop found a second quarter. "Maybe he had a change of heart? Didn't like seeing them lose their hard earned money."

"No, Diane said Outtmann reamed Jackie out,

right in front of the tellers. That if the bank lost even one penny it was coming out of her pocket, not his."

Maybe that's why Jackie didn't like Outtmann, no one wanted to be reprimanded, especially in front of their co-workers. Bishop let the coin drop. He focused on the soda choices. "What did Jackie do?" Threaten to rob Outtmann's bank? Or swallow the anger and let it simmer?

"Nothing. It just keeps nagging at me."

Bishop knew the feeling. That everything looked fine, but something wasn't right. That the pieces should fit and yet there were holes, huge gaping holes.

"Your friend," he tickled the word friend so that Sam would know he meant the bank teller Sam had spent the night with, "tell you this? Last night, between the covers?"

Sam blushed. "No." Then recovered himself. "After the FBI left I went back and talked to the frontline. You know, to get a feel for how they do things at a bank."

Bishop couldn't keep the pleased smile off his face any more than Sam had been able to stop the blush. It's just what he would have done. The kid was going to be a good investigator.

"The Chief was even there."

The third quarter slipped from his fingers, hitting the others with a sharp ring. "At the bank? When you went?"

"In the parking lot. The day before the robbery. He waited until the workers had cashed their checks, then came in and took Jackie out to dinner."

Nothing unusual about taking your wife out to dinner.

"You tell the FBI all this?"

"I wanted to run it past you first."

Before Bishop could answer, the elevator doors whooshed open. Shoulder to shoulder in their dark suits and white shirts stood the two federal agents. Sergio bounded to the Chief's door and opened it enough to poke his head in. "The FBI are here."

Punching the reject button Bishop got his quarters back and followed Sam to the elevator area nearly colliding with the Chief coming out of his office, Sergio at his heels. All smiles, the Chief loped over to the federal agents.

"So you caught them. You Feds are fast. Criminals don't have a chance." The Chief slapped the back of the male FBI agent and pumped his hand in added enthusiasm. "When I went by that old factory and saw those hombres squatting there I knew they were trouble. Stopped, and told 'em to move on. We didn't want any trouble here." He turned to the female, his eyes swept over her tight figure and immobile face. "Guess I should have gone sooner."

The female's lips narrowed. "So you talked to them? When?"

"When? Well, I'm not for sure, darling. Day or two before the robbery." He stopped short. "Told them Jackie would cash their checks if they'd get out of town. Don't want any trouble here, don't want them bringing their gangs in." He looked up at the male agent's face. "You think that's what put them in the mind to rob the bank? They saw what an understaffed, easy-pickings it would be, and came back in the morning?"

"It's possible." The male agent had warmed to the Chief. Most people did. He had a manner, a way of putting you at ease and drawing you into his jocularity. "The dead woman's husband was wanted in Mexico on bank robbery charges."

"Well, I'll be." The Chief shook his head in disbelief. "You know yet which one killed the girl?" Even though Esmeralda had been over forty the Chief still referred to her as a girl.

"We have a full confession." The female agent glanced at Sam, then quickly hid her smirk. "Turner did."

Bishop doubted the corpse had confessed.

"Turner and the girl were lovers. The husband knew about it, encouraged her in fact. He had her persuade Turner into robbing the bank. After she talked," the little twist on talk told Bishop it was more like seduced, "Turner into robbing the bank, and there was more money than expected, he didn't want to share. They argued, and Turner killed her."

The Chief looked over at Bishop. "There you go. Love or money. This time it was both."

Bishop bit his tongue to keep from saying what was on his mind. Turner, the kid who drove his mother to the doctor's, who had shot out his girlfriend's tires when he'd caught her with another guy and was stupid enough to sit there crying until the cops arrived, who had agreed to mow the Chief's lawn all summer in exchange for getting out of the charges. Turner had shot his older lover, in cold blood, at close range, over money. Maybe they'd get a jury to believe it, but Bishop didn't.

"In reprisal her husband killed Turner. Then took the money and ran."

Jealousy after the fact?

"Did you recover all the money?" Sam asked the other question on Bishop's mind.

The Chief looked expectedly at the FBI agent. The man shook his head while the female scowled at Sam. "It's only a matter of time. We'll find it." She informed him.

"Of course, they spent some. Been leaving a trail of bait money." The Chief offered, nodding and bobbing his whole body as he did. Everyone except Bishop fell into agreement.

On what? Food? Gas? Did they still have the same beat-up old trucks? Had they stopped to gamble in a fantasy of turning a million dollars into a hundred million? They'd already hit the jackpot. Why didn't they high-tail it home? Cross the border and disappear?

Sergio pushed his way to the center of the group. "So now what?"

"After we're done interviewing them, ICE will come in and deport everyone. It's really an open and shut case."

The Chief grinned. "Well, now, let's go into my office and have a celebratory drink." The male agent hesitated. Nora gave him the barest shake of her head, but he allowed the chief to toss a hospitable arm about his shoulder and guide him through the glass windowed door. "Have you prepared a statement for the press?" The Chief asked.

At his office door, the Chief stopped and turned back to look at Bishop. "You look like hell, there, boy. How long since you had a day off?"

Bishop must have taken too long trying to remember.

"That's what I thought. You clock-out. Sergio here can finish the Amber report."

His arm still around the FBI's shoulder, the Chief led them into his sanctuary. No one cared if the female followed. Reluctantly she finally did, closing the door behind her.

CHAPTER TWENTY-FIVE

Bishop flicked off his computer. A bank robber. What were the odds that Esmeralda's husband was a bank robber? A trigger happy bank robber that gets himself killed the minute the feds show up. Sam rolled his chair closer to Bishop's desk, then bent down as if to pick up a dropped paper. Bishop dropped his pencil and bent down as well. Both watched the Chief's door.

"You know why the bait money was so easy to follow?"

It was a rhetorical question so Bishop didn't answer.

"It was Jackie's money."

"What do you mean?"

Sam picked up his paper. "A couple of weeks ago, Jackie brought in a stack of bills stained red on the corner. She said the Chief had spilled something on them. So she exchanged them for new and put the stained money into the vault's inventory."

"So? Wouldn't she have gone into the vault and gotten money to cash the checks." He knew a little bit about how banks worked.

Both men straightened, their eyes still watching the Chief's door.

"So, how did those bills get listed as the bait money? No one remembers changing the bait."

Easier to follow a trail of red then random numbers. If a robber didn't know which was bait, and which wasn't, he would spend the soiled money first, anybody would.

Bishop noticed Sergio staring at them, and kept his voice low. "Don't they record those numbers under dual control?"

"Yeah. But if there's a big game on, Outtmann gives Jackie his set of keys so he isn't disturbed, then he signs the control list later."

There had been a big game two weeks ago. He hadn't watched, Rock had been the guest announcer.

"That's how Diane thinks Jackie switched Blossom's money, and got her fired."

Bishop didn't say anything. Sam was right, if Jackie could change Blossom's bait money she could have changed the vault bait money.

Sergio frowned at Bishop. "Aren't you supposed to leave?"

The Chief's door opened. The woman glanced at Sam, a smug smile on the corners of her lips. They'd broke the case, they'd caught the bad guys, open and shut, justice prevailed. You'd think that would gull the Chief, but he seemed buoyant, his mercurial temperament all congratulatory, his good-old-boy smile never fading as they got on the elevator and the doors slid shut.

Bishop went home. The witch case was closed. He kept thinking of it as that, even though it was the Blossom Jones case. Smoke inhalation just like the paramedics had thought. He slept. A restless, unsatisfying sleep. Blossom's face kept popping into his dreams. Pretty little witch the Chief kept saying with sadness in his voice, his hands in his pockets, as he watched her twisting on the ground fighting to breathe.

Bishop woke, hot and alone. He gulped down the fresh spring air blowing into the room through a half-open window. The lacy curtains shifted uneasily beneath the gentle breeze. Without thought, he dressed. Then he ran, ghosts on his heels, two miles to the creek, a hundred push-ups, two miles back. He showered fighting the ache in his body, wanting Teonna, trying to catch her laughter in the cascade of water, instead getting Blossom's strangled gasps. There was no food. There was never any food. A bag of open, stale chips. The full cupboards Teonna had always provided gone.

Grabbing his keys and the stack of library books, Bishop headed out. The case was closed. Accidental death. No need for further research. At the library he checked out the latest reissue of a Louis L'Amour novel before swinging through the old neighborhood, the houses now gone, the earthmovers flattening hilltops like children pushing sand at a beach. Street

Closed signs, bright yellow, glaring in the sunlight, were already up. Utility trucks punctuated where they would be rerouting the lifeblood of the city – water, gas, electric, cable.

Instead of stopping at the grocery store, he kept going north. The care center sat on the farthest edge of town. Madeline smiled when he walked in. She was far enough from her divorce that he should be careful not to appear too friendly, yet he smiled back, letting his eyes run from her face to her feet and back again. She fumbled her stack of paperwork letting him know she had felt his interest.

"How's he doing?" That rumble, the low purr, caught him off-guard. What was he doing? He felt like a tomcat on the prowl. Had the way things gone with Hannah made him want to prove that there had never been anything between them by jumping into every available bed?

Madeline brushed an imaginary lock of hair away from her cheek. "Fine. He's never any trouble."

Bishop forced himself to back off. He wouldn't repeat the same mistake he'd made with Hannah. If he could have enjoyed one night and disappeared, but Madeline would be there the next time he came, and the time after that, expecting more each time, until he found himself facing a long aisle with groomsmen and bridesmaids on either side and a minister at the end. Or he ran as he had run from Hannah's beautiful beaded, white dress. Only this time Frank would be left defenseless, and in the middle. He could feel Madeline watching him go down the hallway. At the last door on the left, he gently knocked, one knuckled, before letting himself in. Frank laid there, his unseeing eyes staring at the ceiling, the respirator hissing life down his throat and into his lungs.

"Got a new book." The comatose figure remained unaware.

Bishop settled into the only chair, angled to catch the light from the window. A single room was more expensive, but Frank liked it better. Made it possible for Bishop to come and go at all hours without disturbing anyone else. But that's not why Bishop paid the difference. What did day or night matter to a man who drifted in time? No, it had been the former roommate's death that had made Bishop dig into his own pocket and get Frank a single room. It was as if the silent man in the bed had rallied and fought, then sank into an ache for the same release. The pain of life had been so palatable that Bishop had almost stopped coming. And that wouldn't have been right. He couldn't turn his back on Frank. He'd been Teonna's field officer and then her partner. Just as he had been Bishop's before that. Only Frank had stayed one case, one last big bust, too many. He'd been ready to retire to his house on the lake. He knew people who knew people, he'd say. He knew where secrets were buried. He'd make the city clean the place up. But if Frank knew any secrets, he held them better than a corpse.

After a few pages, Bishop looked up from the book. "Can't fool you can I?" He closed the paperback testing the weight in his hands. "You've known the Chief a long time. As long as I have." The thin novel had an unexpected heaviness that pulled against his shoulder, intensifying the phantom pain. "You worked cases together. You, the Chief, and Morris," he'd forgotten about Morris. "You broke that big counterfeit case. Your pictures were all over the paper."

He stared at the bed. Frank's thin skin held a tint of yellow whether from the lights or the lack of sunshine didn't matter, it wasn't the robust tan Frank had always had, even in the deep northern winter.

"I only knew him because of Jackie and Teonna," he flinched when he said her name out loud as if he feared the wind would snatch it and carry even that away from him. "Best friends forever." Bishop leaned back, looking to the past. "Remember when she and Jackie came to the Christmas party dressed as Santa's elves. Those little short skirts and those high-high heels."

He felt a tingle of lust even at the memory. Teonna had handed Sonny his gift from Santa, then her eyes had promised Bishop they could make mischief later. Only they hadn't. Not then. Not for a long time. Maybe Bishop would have been able to get over her if Claire hadn't pushed him into overtime helping with a prostitution investigation. Night after night standing guard as Teonna walked the street, bait in Frank's sting. Watching from a distance as she strutted and sashayed pretending to sell her wares. Occasionally, when a john got too demanding, Bishop came to her rescue like a white knight. Maybe after saying no so often, when the answer finally became yes, he couldn't stop.

"We both know the Chief was married when he met Jackie. There was that slight overlap of females." Bishop cringed when he said it. Like a pot calling a kettle black. Sometimes you got caught with your heart gone, but your feet not moving. "But there was something else. Something about Jackie and the Chief's wife getting into a cat fight."

Frank didn't answer, his eyes unblinking, staring at the ceiling, Bishop had put a Playboy fold-out up there until Madeline had scolded him, now there was a landscape of the rolling plains clipped from some magazine. Frank liked that. He was a cowboy riding the range. Occasionally a visitor would tuck a snapshot there as well and Bishop would know someone else had come by. It didn't happen often. The pictures hadn't changed in a long time.

"Yeah, that's what I thought. Gossip, just idle gossip." Like him and Teonna. People had said they were an item long before the sheets had been slid between, long before the line had been crossed. Still the catfight between the Chief's two wives nagged at him. Who had started it? How had it ended? Where there was smoke there was fire.

The man in the bed didn't blink, his blank eyes staring at the ceiling.

Perhaps if Claire and Teonna had ever met things would have gone the same way. But Claire hadn't fought for him. Her pride had been destroyed and her anger turned to a frozen glacier. He'd seen men murdered for what he had done. Bishop swallowed his guilt. Unending, like waves on a shore, the mechanical breathing of the respirator filled the room. He wished the Chief had never called him to investigate the witch case, now he couldn't let it go.

If the Chief hadn't called, the county would have declared Blossom's death accidental. No investigation. Case closed. But the Chief had called him, Frank argued. Not Hank, Hank hadn't asked for assistance, the Chief had offered it. Had the Chief known that it was Blossom lying in that field? He'd known the girl before. Perhaps known her in the biblical sense. But had he known she was murdered?

Or had it just been a ruse, getting Bishop to chase after the wind while ...?

While what? Frank demanded. Ask the right questions and you'll get the right answers.

What if Bishop hadn't taken the witch case?

He would have been home. Asleep. No, he would have been out for his morning run. Unlike the neighbors who thought they'd heard a car backfire, he knew the sound of a gun sending a bullet through the cold morning air to hit soft flesh. He would have gone to investigate. He would have found Esmeralda, the killer likely still standing over her. At the very least he would had seen the taillights disappear down the factory road. He would have been standing there when Turner arrived with the money. When the second killer arrived.

The air in the room didn't move. Too early in the year for the air-conditioning, too late for the furnace, the air had stagnated into a stuffy mix of too hot and too cold. Someone had needed him out of the neighborhood while they killed Esmeralda. Everything had been planned and orchestrated. Rob the bank, kill the girl, run with the money.

The only variable they couldn't control was Bishop.

They had to keep him away from the case.

Blossom had been a distraction.

But who? Outtmann?

Love or money, was Frank's answer.

No need for Outtmann to rob a bank, he owned a bank. His grandfather had given it to him fresh out of college. And Jackie ran it. Jackie with her master's in banking, top of her class, fetching coffee and getting reprimanded in front of her subordinates.

Not Jackie.

She had stood beside him and Teonna when Claire had thrown him out.

Not Jackie.

Between her salary and the Chief's they must make enough money. Look at everything they owned. A big new house with a fancy stone barbeque on the designer back patio. Jackie's pretty blue plane.

What kind of money did that cost? Insurance, aviation fuel, maintenance. Big vacation last year. Big vacation this year.

But the new motor home was up for sale.

Nobody makes enough money. Just because you live in a big house doesn't mean you have enough money.

Not Jackie, not Teonna's best friend. And Jackie

been locked in the vault. It would have been cold and dark with stale air, she had to have been terrified.

Bishop closed his eyes. He leaned back, resting his head against the back of the chair.

What about Jackie's fancy lacquered bracelet?

To keep the peace. An expensive bracelet to keep the peace.

Nobody gets enough love.

Except the Chief, everyone loved the Chief.

Bishop opened his eyes. Frank laid silent, the blankets stiffly tucked around him, his eyes staring forever at the rolling hills above him and the snapshots tucked half-beneath. Why had Bishop come? There were no answers here. The Chief hadn't known about the robbery when he'd called him. It was hours away. The Chief hadn't known it was Blossom whose desire for love had exploded in her face. He'd called her an old witch when he'd asked Bishop to go. Everything was a coincidence.

He followed Frank's gaze to the rolling hills. Tuffs of tall grass, swaying in the breeze. An endless horizon beaconing, the faded blues and browns and greens promising peace. A flash of color from a snapshot caught his eye. Bishop stood and reached up, taking the snapshot down. Jackie and the Chief, swimsuits and Hawaiian shirts, sitting at a Mexican tiki bar, sipping huge drinks with big umbrellas stuck in them. One of them must have stopped by and left the photo. The edges were brittle and the pigment had started to fade. Must have been here since last year.

As he reached to replace the photo, Bishop's

finger slid across the glossy print moving his gaze to the bartender. Camera shy, she had half turned, so that the camera only caught her profile, her thick, dark hair cascading down her back, a sly smile on her lips. A cat that's eaten a canary smile. He knew that smile. Knew that woman. Esmeralda.

What were the odds? He hadn't seen her next door. But he'd seen her time and time again over the last year, her dark eyes flirting with Frank. Flirting with the Chief right in front of his wife. He forced his attention to Jackie, her lips smiling, but her eyes watchful. How do you trust a man who cheated with you not to cheat on you?

And the Chief liked women. Bishop knew that about him. Had covered for him more than once. With his first wife. But never with Jackie. The Chief wouldn't have asked him. It would have been like asking him to cheat on Teonna. Some men liked the thrill of the conquest, they savored the touch of skin beneath their fingers without ever noticing the heart beating beneath. Made it easier to leave them. Only some women made it hard to leave them. Some made it impossible.

Bishop's cellphone rang. Sam.

"Yeah."

"Ever hear of Tiffany Foss?"

Bishop didn't answer.

"Meet me at the practice range."

CHAPTER TWENTY-SIX

Outside, Bishop scanned the sky with its big fluffy clouds like the painted back-drop of an old Hollywood movie, and just as unlikely to burst into rain. Although the city maintained a firing range in the basement of the station, when the weather allowed, most of the officers headed for the jointly owned county range. He'd expected the range to be empty, instead when he arrived several vehicles already sat in the dirt turn-off that served as a parking lot, a county car, and a black sedan near the entry. Alongside them was Jackie's black Mercedes, glistening with a fresh polish. The front headlight had lost the chrome ring, and the edge of the fender rippled in the intense sunlight. She must have hit something. Bishop ran his hand along the ripple. Something big. Or maybe bumped a post, been distracted and bumped a post.

Another vehicle pulled into the lot and he

straightened expecting Sam. Hank and another county boy got out. They nodded greetings with the slightest tip of the head. Hank ambled over while the junior officer got the gear out of the trunk. He noted where Bishop had been looking at the headlight.

"Hit something?"

"Looks that way."

Hank ran his hand over the ripple the same as Bishop had, then studied the headlight. He jiggled the housing and plucked a stray hair from beneath the light, holding it up for Bishop to see.

Coarse, brown hair.

"Deer." Hank informed him, proud of his knowledge.

"Deer?"

Not the dead deer out by the old warehouse.

"See it all the time. Damn things are taking over the roads."

From over the ridge, the sound of gunshots cracked the air. The other county boy waited expectantly. "You coming?" Hank asked.

Bishop looked toward the road. "I'll wait for Sam."

Hank nodded and the two disappeared over the ridge. Moments later Sam arrived. He got out of his low, white Corvette, but didn't approach Jackie's solid, black Mercedes.

"Mrs. Johnson's here."

"Looks like it."

Sam shoved his hands into his pockets. "Maybe we should go."

A glint of light among the gravel caught Bishop's eye. He bent down and picked-up a key half hidden in the dirt. Did he believe in signs? Omens? Like a cat finding a glove, or a witch reading the tarot? It was just a key, a simple interior door key, not even notched, the kind that went to a track house bedroom door. "We're here. We both have to recertify."

Bishop opened the trunk and tossed the key into his tackle box of blanks and locksmithing tools, some of them not legal. Only two boxes of bullets left. Officers bought their own weapons and ammo, and it was a long way to payday. Reluctantly he grabbed both boxes, then stuffed several magazines of 45's into his jacket pockets while Sam grabbed a locked case of weapons from his car. They headed over the ridge and down into a natural ravine, a row of sturdy trees and a mound of solid earth stopping the bullets before they could fly into some innocent foolish enough to ignore the signage and walk behind the range.

Bishop felt like he was dragging a dog on a leash as Sam reluctantly lagged behind. Hank and the county boy watched the Chief and the FBI outshooting each other. Jackie stood at the side. She held a black powder pistol, wiping down the exterior.

"Bishop." Jackie's smile was warm and friendly, just like it always was. And Bishop thought of Teonna's smile. The memory gave him a lurch and an ache in his gut.

"Sam." Her smile faded. "I'm surprised you're out here."

"Got to qualify."

The Chief seemed to finally notice their presence. He took his wife's gun, "Here, darling, you let me take care of this. You'll need to be getting back to work." He and Bishop locked gazes, just for a moment, before the male FBI hooted in pleasure.

"Ten for ten."

The Chief turned his attention back to his guest. "Good shooting. Good shooting."

The female FBI, Nora, Sam had said her name was Nora, raked Sam with her eyes, before stopping at the long range rifle he was holding. "Big gun."

The color rose to Sam's cheeks, and everyone laughed.

"Come on now boys, don't be shy. Show these government men what we can do here in Garfield Falls."

Bishop took the first target and shot off a magazine. The gun kicked back into his bad shoulder and he had to concentrate to keep from shooting wide. Still he scored perfect, every shot in the one-inch bull's eye.

Sam stepped up next. He lifted the weapon as easily as if it had been an extension of his arm. They watched through binoculars as Sam went through the line of targets. Short distance, long distance, pistol, rifle, one bullet after another within a breath of each other, like a machine tooled for precise placement.

"Maybe he takes one shot and then fires at the trees."

Sam drew a long breath, then fired, writing his name with bullet holes.

"Damn good shooting. As good as your pa." The Chief gave Sam credit.

Hank scratched as his chin. "Sam? That's your last name? I was thinking it was your first name. Where do I know that name from?"

Bishop looked up from the chamber he was reloading. The normally easy-going Sam tensed. "Common name." Bishop informed Hank, but his glance caught Hank's eye and a knit of the eyebrow sent the message to drop the subject. After a long emptiness where the birds frantically tried to fill the awkward silence, Hank let it go.

They fired off another round, the cold metal of the handgun warming with the heat of the explosive recoil. Chambers empty, Bishop headed down to the targets. Between the rain and the sunshine spring foliage had flourished threatening to take-over the narrow path. Bishop stopped. Leaves of three let them be. Sam almost bumped into him.

"What?"

"Poison ivy." Bishop gestured toward the plant lazily growing on the side of the path, its thin vine creeping up a tree stump.

Sam took a step back. "I never noticed that before."

Jackie brushed past.

Hadn't the Chief told her to leave?

"Been here for weeks. They spray one and another pops up." She grabbed the base of the plant and pulled it out, bringing up some of the roots, dirt splattering at her feet. "Maybe you'd better let Bishop change your targets."

Bishop stared at her hand, she hadn't removed her shooting glove. Unlike the leather glove most people wore to protect their hands during practice Jackie had on a dark, knit glove. Something about senseless killing of animals.

"Thought you were leaving, darling." The Chief stopped, placing his solid frame between her and Bishop. He gingerly took the plant from her and tossed it away from the path. They exchanged that look, that married look.

"I can handle myself."

"Not saying that you can't, just that it would be better if you weren't here."

Jackie tipped her head back and laughed, the sunshine piercing the blackness of her curls and warming her face. For an instant Bishop saw Teonna. Sorority sisters with the same laugh.

"You're getting to be a superstitious, old fool." She peeled off the black knit gloves she was wearing. They were new, clinging tight to her fingers. When she slapped them against each other to knock off some of the dirt, he could smell the gunpowder residue. The gloves had to be infused with the blowback of unexploded powder, the mixture of explosive and stabilizer clinging to the fibrous material.

"All right, I'll go and let you boys play." She tossed her gloves to the Chief who slid them into his pocket.

Bishop watched her head back down the path, the

little sashay to her hip, the confident strut to her walk.

"Careful, boy, I might just let you have her."

For an instant Bishop thought he was serious, then the Chief laughed, and slapped him on the back. "Let's go get those targets changed and have ourselves some fun."

The sun dropping, out of bullets, Bishop was the first to leave. Sam followed, he stared where Jackie's Mercedes had been before stowing his gun.

"You wanted to talk." Long shadows played across the gravel parking area.

"No, it was nothing."

Bishop let it slide.

"You off tomorrow?" Sam asked.

"Unless they call me."

Sam nodded and got into his sleek car, revving the finely tuned engine. The only thing Sam and his father seemed to have in common was their love of a good car. Bishop watched the taillights speed toward town.

He should have pressed Sam for why he'd called.

The car disappeared over a hill, too late now.

On the way home Bishop passed Nathaniel's. Sometimes Sam went there, on a date, or like Bishop, to get out of the house. It wasn't exactly a bar. The lights were dim, but not so low that a frog could be mistaken for a prince. There was food, good food, and the television played the news rather than sports. Sometimes the girls would put it on a sit-com. Bishop didn't see Sam's white Corvette but stopped anyway.

They'd let him run a tab. One beer, and then home. A quick glance told him there weren't any other cops there. Some nights there were. But not tonight. It wasn't a regular cop bar. Mostly it attracted construction workers looking for a large serving of good food at a fair price. On the specialty nights it got a more upscale crowd. Sometimes he would bump into his parents out on the town.

He sat at the bar and waited, watching the door as he slowly sipped his beer, the sweetness of the hops satisfying. From the reflections in the mirror, Bishop noticed a woman watching him. If he were to cast a witch in a movie she would have had the role. Tall, willowy, with a knit sweater that flowed around her in swirls of lacy cloth. Long blonde hair tumbled in luxurious waves down her back, framing her well-tanned face like the tide kissing a beach, and large green eyes balanced pink, pink lips. He'd seen her before just couldn't place where. Maybe, like him, she was an irregular regular.

She glanced away when she realized that he was staring, but an instant later she glanced back. Look, hold, glance away, glance back, lips a little parted. Bishop knew an invitation when he saw one. He felt the primal stirring of lust, but didn't move from his bar stool.

The man next to him finished his beer and flipped a five to the bartender. With a nod, he left. Before the barstool was cold, the woman was there. Bishop could feel her warmth as she leaned across the bar on the pretense of getting the bartender's attention. He could smell the woodsy, musk of her perfume.

She smiled, a come and get me smile. Bishop paused, the beer bottle half way to his lips, and from some dead place deep within, an interested smile burrowed out, and twitched at the corners of his mouth.

"Beautiful weather we've been having." She leaned forward, her necklace dangled free. A moonstone, cream and white, seeming to glow from the warmth of her skin.

Bishop felt a sharp ache in his shoulder. "Going to rain."

"Not in the forecast."

It was a bar. They were grown-ups. They went to her place. Bishop didn't take women to his house. They liked their place, their bed. Not his bed. Not Teonna's bed.

CHAPTER TWENTY-SEVEN

Bishop slowly extracted his arm from beneath the woman's sleeping body. It's not that it had been bad sex. No, it had been good sex. He just wasn't ready to stay. The lust spent, he wanted to disappear before dawn peeped through the cracks of the drapes like a voyeur. He needed to be gone before the woman in the bed woke, and things other than the sheets became tangled.

She had a name. Virna. He cringed. Vincent and Virna.

A whisper of guilt and regret nibbled at his ear, but he shook it off. No one had said anything about staying. No one had said anything about tomorrow. As he tiptoed to the bathroom, he gathered his clothes. After splashing water onto his face and chest, he looked up catching his own reflection. His face was hard, harder than he remembered it, the eyes pale, empty rocks. He turned away from the mirror, and hastened into his pants. One arm in a sleeve, there was a knock on the door.

"Vinnie?" her voice a hesitant whisper, hopeful in a childish way.

Bishop reminded himself that she hadn't been a child, even though he felt much older. He wished there was a way to escape, but there was no window he could have climbed out of, even though he wanted to.

"Yeah, just a second."

Bishop put his other arm in its sleeve, and opened the door.

Her gaze took in that he was mostly dressed, shoes in hand.

"You're leaving?"

"Work." It was a lie. He had the day off, he could laze in bed all day if he wanted.

She put her hand on his chest, sliding her fingers with their long manicured nails through his chest hair. With a bit of fantasy the little jewels glued to the tips appeared to be stars exploding across a dark sky and wisps of gray clouds. Slowly her hand moved upward, her fingertips touching his bullet scars, dipping into his pocked memories. Although it merely tickled he flinched, and she looked up at him. The question in her eyes about to leave her lips when he pulled her hand away. He pushed past her, back into the bedroom. Maybe she hadn't seen the scars in the dark of the night, maybe he had forgotten them in the heat of the bed, but they were there. And they would be there until the end of time.

He sat and pulled on his socks. He could hear the rustle of her grabbing her robe and covering herself, pulling the belt tight around her waist.

"Breakfast?"

"No, I'm fine." He stood, socks and shoes on, ready to run. "You go back to sleep. I'll let myself out."

"Be sure and lock the door behind you." Her tone had changed, the subtle anger leaving a bitter taste behind. He knew what that meant – he wouldn't be coming back. Although he hadn't wanted to, the slamming of the opportunity stung.

It was then, as he tried not to look at her, that he noticed it sitting silently in the corner. An old style broom, the twisted straw tied with twine, the knurly handle leaning against the wall. He wouldn't have thought anything of it, not if he hadn't gotten to know the witches. But now it wasn't just a decoration in the corner, it wasn't just an ornament put there one day and gone the next. He looked around the room, actually looked at all the little details that would have appeared innocent before he had entered the world of magic. At all the moons and stars stenciled on the walls, woven into fabrics, only they weren't stars, they were pentagrams. Little statuettes of black cats filled the bookshelves, some contemplative, with big green eyes, others with their backs arched and defiant. The candles that had flickered to their lovemaking weren't just pretty pillars of color and light with designs stamped on them. He crossed to the night side table, lifting one of the candles. Deep, blood red, etched with hearts and flowers, a handful of pentagrams and stars mingled in. Very much like the one he'd found at the firepit. He turned the pillar in his hand. Only this one had his name incised on it, the point of the v unmistakable and the flow of swirly loops just like Claire had done when they were first married. "You're a witch."

She only hesitated a moment. "Yes."

The tone was defensive, but it was the candle he held in his hand, the candle just like Blossom's, that put the idea in his head. "Why did you run?"

This was awkward. The sheets on the bed still tangled, the odor of sex still thick, the perfume of the candles adding an odd, floral note to the heavy musk.

"I ..." She pulled a shawl over her robe, a black shawl, finely knit in a soft yarn. "You don't remember me. I approved your loan last fall."

Bishop inwardly groaned, the realization hitting him in the gut. He'd been so focused on getting the money to Claire before Sonny's tuition was late. The regular officer had called in his supervisor who had signed off on it. The supervisor had been attractive, in another place, at another time, had he not been involved with Hannah, he would have been interested, but it wouldn't have been ethical on her part. Now here she stood.

"Funny, I noticed you." The yarn stretched where she pulled the shawl tight across her shoulders. "You were like a magnet." She took a step closer to him as if to prove her point. "You have an appeal, a strength." She might have touched him, but thought better of it, and turned away. Her shoulders sagged. "I asked Jackie about you. She said that you'd lost someone." She turned back, her eyes begging him to love her. "I was a tongue tied school girl every time you came in. And you never noticed."

He should be flattered, but he wasn't, he felt naked and exposed, she'd been watching him, she'd asked Jackie about him. Had Jackie told her about Teonna? About the mess he'd made of his marriage? That he wasn't to be trusted?

Shoving all his personal thoughts aside, he focused on Blossom. Obsessions led to murder. "It took three to cast the spell."

She didn't say anything.

"You, Amanda, and Blossom."

Still silence.

"Only Blossom ended up dead."

Virna looked everywhere but at him.

"You ran. Why?"

Her back straightened and she glared at him as if he were a fool. "I don't just work at a bank. I'm an officer. A vice-president. How would it look? Me, at a witch's coven? Everyone would whisper. Stare. And when they found out we were casting a love spell, and a girl dies ..."

How did it look that she fled?

"Tell me what happened."

Virna stomped to the kitchen and snapped on the overhead light. For an instant they were both blinded by the brightness. She got a glass from the cupboard over the sink and poured a drink from the bottle of wine they had been too impatient to finish the night before. "We waited for the moon to rise. I lit my candle. We sang, danced, I threw the picture, of that woman, the one who won't let you go, into the fire."

It hit him like a sucker punch, all but buckling his knees. She'd destroyed the picture of Teonna, the one missing from Jackie's wall.

"It didn't burn at first, just curled. She was beautiful. I can see why you loved her." Virna stared into the blood red wine. "Her eyes went last. Those accusing eyes." She knocked back the wine like it was whiskey.

"You stole Teonna's picture." His hands had curled into fists.

"No. Jackie gave it to me." She stared at the bottom of the empty glass. "I, we, I asked her about you. She's normally not friendly. But she talked and talked, and then wanted to know about the coven."

"Jackie's a witch?"

"No. But she knows I am. When she found out about the spell, she gave me the picture. And your scarf. The gray plaid one you would wear when you came in to cash your check." Her eyes held that longing of a hungry child coveting someone else's ice cream cone.

He remembered looking for the scarf, a gift from Sonny on Father's Day, deciding that he had left it at a crime scene, or perhaps the morgue. "Jackie knew about the spell?"

"Yes." Unable to meet his eye, Virna turned away. "She helped me take the scarf apart so I'd have thread to tie your hair into a bundle. She even gave me the hair. I knew it was yours: short, salt and pepper."

Jackie helped her. He'd trusted Jackie and she'd betrayed him. He felt the edge of what he'd done to Claire. It hurt like a knife coming under the ribs and straight into the heart. He choked back the pain and forced his emotions to disengage. "Tell me what you did the morning Blossom died."

"We started the fire. I went first. Burned the picture so that she'd release you. Then tossed the hair into the flames and said the enchantment so that you'd come to me. I remember thinking that burning hair smelled awful. That maybe you put some conditioner or gel on it." She looked at him, the pain in her eyes palatable. "But you don't, do you."

He didn't answer, waiting, letting the silence, only a clock whirring the seconds away, grow until it nudged to her to talk some more. She ran her hand over the smooth finish of her kitchen table. Her eyes watching her hand. "Nothing seemed odd or strange. No explosion, no smoke. When the hair was done burning, Amanda motioned Blossom to go next. So she lit her candle." Virna paced, she glanced out the window at the blackness of the night broken by a single streetlight. "A wind came up. Blossom threw bits of her desire's sock into the flames, but they didn't burn, not really, more like they melted, and bits blew off in the wind."

High polyester content.

"Amanda stepped forward. I think she was going

to say something about Blossom doing the spell backwards, that she should have thrown the glove in first. But before Amanda could say anything Blossom threw the glove into the fire."

Virna touched her throat, her long fingers with their jeweled tips strangling her words. "It exploded. I've never seen anything like it."

"She'd added gunpowder and it flash burned. Did she think it would make for a good show?"

"We never added gunpowder."

Amanda had said the same thing, so how had it gotten there? "Maybe she added it and you didn't know. Like you didn't know that the logs you were burning were poison ivy branches."

Virna shook her head. "We mixed the spell ingredients together. Everything we did took three. One to unbind, one to join, and one to hold. And we used special logs, not wood that we found lying around. We wanted pear wood. It had to be dried a special way. None of us could do it. Then I found this woman in California who would sell us a few logs, but she wouldn't mail them to me, someone had to go and get them. All the way to California. I mentioned it to Jackie and she offered to fly out. Said she needed to get away and that it would be a lark."

"Jackie?"

Virna stood, unsure. "This isn't how it's supposed to turn out." She braced herself, her eyes pleaded with him. "When the spell exploded and she died, I knew that you would come. I couldn't stay. I couldn't ... meet you... like that. You cast the spell, but you don't control how the bidding comes about."

He understood. "Like wanting a million dollars thinking you'll win the lottery. Instead your child dies, and you get a huge insurance settlement."

All this, all the candles, the chanting, the aligning of stars and signs, all this for him. He should be flattered, but he wasn't. He felt like a child who discovers the circus is not only hot and smelly, but that they beat the bear to make him dance.

"Tell me about Blossom and the Chief."

Virna sucked in her bottom lip. "They'd had a relationship when she interned at the bank two years ago. You know how the Chief is – all honey, and pretty thing, all harmless."

"Until a sixteen year old girl without a father obsesses about him." Bishop thought of Blossom, yes, she was the Chief's type, sweet as cherry pie. "And Jackie found out?"

"The Chief flew Blossom to his cabin. They were going to spend the weekend when she brushed against some poison oak. She almost died. I guess he panicked and flew home without her. Laura called me. I took time off and went out with her to get Blossom. It wasn't hard for Jackie to put two and two together. Before we got back Jackie had done a surprise cash count on Blossom's drawer. The bait money was all wrong. It looked as if Blossom had been stealing from the till and putting the money back later. If Mr. Outtmann hadn't intervened Blossom would have gone to jail."

So Jackie had been out for blood. "Why did she

help you with the spell?"

Virna looked surprised at the question. "I don't know. Jackie's been, well, different, since last year, since her and Chief got back from Mexico."

"Different? How?"

"Nicer."

"So nice that she flew out and got special logs for Blossom to use in a love spell to steal her husband?"

Virna laughed, a quick one note laugh that never left her chest. "Not that nice." Virna looked over at him. "Jackie didn't know about the others, just me."

"And she gave you her glove? For you to catch me? Doesn't quite fit the spell."

"I gave Blossom the glove. I was leaving the bank and Jackie dropped it on the way to her car. She didn't notice, didn't look back."

No, she wouldn't have. Not for an inexpensive shooting glove.

"So I picked it up thinking I would give it to her in the morning, then I thought how perfect it would be for the spell."

"And you gave it to Blossom?"

"Yes."

If Jackie had worn that glove out target shooting it would have been infused with gunpowder, could have been caked with poison ivy. But how could Jackie have known Virna was going to give it to Blossom? He could hear Sam's voice in his head. No one has to tell you what Sergio and the ME were doing in the back for you to know.

CHAPTER TWENTY-EIGHT

The sun was just showing the glow of its sleepy head when Bishop pulled into his drive. He stared at the empty house next door. Everything was askew. His shoulder ached and yet it didn't rain. Teonna drifted into his thoughts and yet he couldn't remember the taste of her lips. The FBI solved the Chief's case and while he should have been annoyed, the Chief was elated.

Instead of going for a run, Bishop headed for the basement. A lone bulb hung by a cord and cast odd shadows across the room. A row of wooden shelves, original to the house, framed a work area. Squeezed among the disarray of tools and jars holding nuts and bolts was an old wooden cigar box. He didn't smoke, never had, but when Sonny was born, when the baby had had fair skin and gray eyes, and Bishop had known for certain the child was his, he had gone out and bought cigars. It was tradition. Good, lavish cigars in a fancy walnut box. The money taken from his someday college fund. And Claire hadn't said anything about the expense.

He hadn't opened the box in a long time. He sat on the stairs holding it in his hands. It wasn't heavy. It should have been heavy, the keeper of all his memories, memories he carried like a burden. He brushed the dust from the smooth finish and opened the lid. On top was Teonna's badge. After fifteen years it looked new, shiny even in the dim light of the basement.

He lifted it out, the pin in the back pricking his thumb and he remembered the first time that he had seen her. Feet planted in a wide stance, hands on her hips, head tipped up, a don't mess with me gleam in her eyes. Jackie taking her picture. When had that been? Academy graduation? The two of them dissolving into laughter. Their voices blending together so you could not tell which belonged to which. Frank had stopped and nudged him. They'd both looked, admiring the healthy, sleek beauties the way you would admire an expensive, fast car. Claire had come up behind, baby on her hip, one glance and she'd dismissed Teonna and Jackie as little more than children, before handing him Sonny, wet and cranky from sitting in the sun through the long ceremony. Teonna had noticed him – him and the baby – some women liked men with babies.

The box tipped, and a small object thumped against the side, the gold catching the light. His wedding ring. Bishop closed the box. Everything came with a price. Blossom had paid the ultimate price for love. What price was Jackie paying to keep the Chief? Had she thought through that Virna needed something for a love spell, that Blossom's mother was in the same coven as Virna, that Blossom had come back into the Chief's life, had been in the parking lot talking to the Chief after he'd spoken to the criminal justice class, that Blossom just might be casting a spell of her own.

Jackie had dropped her glove where Virna would find it. Did she drop the glove thinking Virna would give it to Blossom? Did she know the smoke would make Blossom ill, might even kill her? It was a long path for a jury to follow. He needed more, something, someone else.

Bishop called Sam, even though it was merely dawn, he wasn't surprised that Sam was awake.

"What about Tiffany Foss?"

Sam didn't hesitate, didn't need to search his memory. "Remember what you said about the bank robbery? About how I shouldn't be dating Diane because it could be an inside job?"

Bishop climbed the stairs, he remembered.

"Well, I ran a background check on her."

Filling the pot with cold water, he started coffee.

"She came up clean."

What did it have to do with Tiffany Foss?

"I ran a background on everybody."

Through the phone, Bishop could hear a door open and shut.

"Didn't find much, the usual. Mr. Outtmann

drives too fast."

Like he cared about Outtmann's speeding record. "Get to Tiffany Foss." He reminded Sam. The rich aroma of coffee exploded into the room when Bishop lifted the can's thin plastic lid.

"She filed a restraining order against Mrs. Johnson."

Bishop remembered the picture on the kiosk. Have you seen Tiffany Foss? Beautifully exotic with caramel skin, and slanted eyes. Sweet tea. "Against Jackie, not the Chief?"

"No, Mrs. Johnson. Right after that Tiffany disappeared."

There was more, something left unsaid, the words dangling in the air. He filled the filter, the grounds a rich brown like potting soil.

"She got the restraining order because Jackie threatened to kill her. Seems she and the Chief were, you know."

He knew.

"When he moved on, Tiffany didn't. She called Jackie and told her about the affair, thinking Jackie would throw the Chief out."

Bishop pushed start on the coffee maker. Like Claire had thrown him out. No explanation, no discussion, no second chance.

"But, according to Tiffany's roommate, Jackie went nuts." Sam paused, they both knew it was hearsay. "According to the roommate, Jackie trashed Tiffany's credit rating, vandalized her car, and threatened to kill her if she came within a hundred yards of the Chief."

An escalating history of violence.

"So, Tiffany hired an attorney to sue for harassment, but then never showed for the trial date."

"Because she'd disappeared?"

Again, Sam hesitated. "According to the roommate, Tiffany went to meet the Chief in Mexico."

"He just calls, and says meet me in Mexico?" The first drips of coffee hit the pot, sizzling in the cold of the early morning.

"Yeah."

"And Tiffany went?" Love had a way of clouding common sense. Love and money.

"Suitcase gone. Ticket used."

Bishop moved the pot and inserted a thick mug beneath, catching the stream of strong, black coffee. "What about the return ticket?'

He could almost hear Sam slapping his forehead. "I didn't ask. You think she stayed down there?"

In a shallow grave in the desert? "Yeah. Who took the harassment report?"

"Morris."

His shoulder throbbed. The Chief and Morris went far back. Pounded a beat together. Things happened on patrol, things that bound two officers together tighter than wedding vows. Things that made a man look the other way when he shouldn't. "Let me handle it."

"Morris buried the report."

Sam wanted more than answers. Morris had pointed his finger at Sam's father when evidence had gone missing. Morris had testified at the trial.

"Remember the day of the bank robbery? How Morris called in sick?"

Bishop burned his tongue taking a sip of the coffee too soon.

"He wasn't sick."

It happened. Sometimes you just needed a day off.

"His wife called it in. Took him to the hospital. He was having an anxiety attack."

How did Sam know that? Nurses. Sam and nurses.

"So I talked to Shirley. She never called the Chief about the silent alarm."

"He must have heard the call to Jefferson and Muttley."

Angry silence came from the other end of the phone.

"Stay out of it." Bishop warned him. "You know how it'll look."

"I'm just doing my job."

"No, you're not. You're trying to find a reason to make Morris look like a liar." Gingerly this time, Bishop took a sip, the black adrenaline rushing to his heart. "If Tiffany was doing civilian ride-alongs with Jefferson. We start by talking to him."

"I'll meet you."

"No."

There would never be proof that Jackie had intended to kill Blossom. But murder had a way of cascading, one crime trying to cover another. When had Jackie hit that deer? Was Esmeralda the mess the

Chief was trying to clean up?

"Do you still have the tapes from the robbery?"

"Yeah."

"Look at the day before. At Jackie's car. Was her headlight damaged?"

It took two phone calls to locate Jefferson. He'd picked up a double and was heading out for traffic patrol. Bishop met him at his squad car. The big man smiled until Bishop asked about ride-alongs.

"Tell me about Tiffany Foss."

The larger officer tightened his jaw in resignation. He looked around at all the listening ears. "Not here."

They crossed the parking lot to the corner. Muttley had seen them and followed. The two partners exchanged looks. They remembered her. They'd known this was coming. Finally the big officer took a deep breath. "What you want to know?"

"Everything."

"Could have happened to anybody." Jefferson defended without Bishop making any accusations.

"Hell, a girl like that," Muttley justified, shifting his weight from one leg to the other. "Looked like a million bucks of stolen money and all hot to get herself a badge."

Bishop kept his mouth shut, the less he said, the more he'd learn.

"She was waiting in the briefing room while we got the paper work together."

Again Muttley interrupted. "When we got back the Chief was there."

"He'd just been passing by, but you know the Chief, can't ignore a pretty face."

"The two of them hit it off. I mean, really hit it off." Muttley overemphasized the really making it into an innuendo.

"He did a couple of patrols with us." Jefferson proceeded in his matter of fact drone. "They'd sit the in back laughing."

"They'd sit in the back doing everything except the one thing they both wanted to do." Muttley added. "Got so that I'd hope for a call just to get out of the car and away from the steam."

They looked at Bishop to see if he understood. He understood. "What happened?"

Jefferson started, "You know how these things go-"

"– hot and fast," Muttley finished.

Jefferson gave Muttley the look, the sour why do I put up with this stare. "One side always burns out before the other."

"The Chief started ducking her." Muttley gave Bishop a wink and a quick nod. "Why buy the cow?"

"Anyway," Jefferson hurried his words, "She threatened to sue the city. Even had a lawyer. Claimed Jackie was harassing her. Then, poof, she was gone."

"Gone?"

"Gone." Muttley gestured like a magician on the stage, nothing up his sleeves.

"The lawyer even came by to see if we'd talked to her."

"The Chief thought she might have gone to

Mexico with a new boyfriend."

Both men stared uneasily at Bishop.

Their story was stupid and lame, which made him believe it. "And she's never turned up." Sometimes he didn't like being right. "Any leads?"

Jefferson shook his big head. "We passed everything to Morris."

"Not Orlando?" He was the expert at finding missing girls.

"No. The Chief said Morris."

And Morris buried it.

Bishop's phone rang. Sam.

"Jackie turned in an insurance claim the day of the robbery. Said that she'd hit a post. On the tapes, her car is fine when she left work the day before, but you can see the damage when she pulls into the parking lot the day of the robbery. And there was blood on the fender."

It could have been any deer.

"Call your friend at the bank. See if Jackie's there." They needed to talk.

Bishop headed back to the station, the first shift had arrived. The Chief would be there. Jefferson and Muttley had disappeared while he'd been talking to Sam. Just as well, anything they'd say would make them look stupider. When Bishop reached the door his phone rang. Sam.

"Jackie's at the bank. She has an insurance check for the damage to her car and wanted to cash it before going on vacation."

Bishop headed back to his car.

"But Outtmann won't let her. They're in his office. No, guess she just left. Diane says she slammed every door."

"Why wouldn't Outtmann let her cash the check?"

"Checks made out to the insurance company not her. Rumor has it she owes too many people too much money."

Bishop knew the feeling.

"Did she say where she was going?"

"The airport."

Bishop didn't understand.

"Her and the Chief are leaving for vacation."

"Today?"

"Yeah."

"When does the flight leave?"

"Not taking a flight. Jackie's flying them."

In her little blue plane the color of the Chief's eyes. No baggage check that way.

"Call the airport and see when they're scheduled to take-off." Soon would be his guess.

The airport was on the other side of town. Through the city was shorter, but the county roads were faster. Bishop went west around the city, out past the upscale neighborhoods, down the twisting Dumonte Road, the manor house's flags fluttering. He turned down a gravel sectional spinning his wheels on the loose rock and spitting out a plume of dust. By summer it would be a hot hollow of dirt the animals would bathe in to escape the flies and mosquitoes. Not like the little tropical island the Chief and Jackie were going to. That would be an oasis of water and palm trees.

His phone rang and Bishop pulled it from his pocket. Sam. "Roger says they just got there. The Chief's doing a flight check."

"See if Roger can stall them."

Bishop hit the siren. He flew to the airport, passing on the shoulder when he had to. He went beyond the aging facility to the private hangers. Silencing the siren, he slowed. There was the Chief's car outside a small Quonset hut, the steel siding curving to form a dome. Jackie sat in the car, freshening her lipstick, while the Chief walked around the plane doing the final inspection. One of the airport personnel stood near-by, gabbing.

Bishop pulled his car between the plane and the runway. Both men scowled at him, but the Chief recovered first, putting on his good-old-boy charm like a second skin.

"Miss me already, there, boy?"

"I need to talk to Jackie."

There was a flicker, his wanting to talk to Jackie wasn't unexpected.

Jackie got out of the car, slamming the door, but instead of joining them she went round to the trunk and opened it. The Chief watched her and Bishop watched the Chief.

"Considering your track record with women, I might need to know what this is about." The Chief pulled his attention away from his wife and back to Bishop, seemingly waiting for an explanation.

"It's about Blossom Jones." Or was it about Esmeralda? Or Tiffany Foss? No, Blossom was the one who'd burrowed into the Chief's heart.

When the Chief's hand fell lightly on his gun, Bishop almost missed Jackie coming up behind him. He fainted right and the tire iron she had aimed at the middle of his head glanced off one side. Still he fell to the ground, his ears ringing.

"What about Blossom?"

The Chief was looking at his wife, not at Bishop, a hurt dog furrow in his brow.

"The little slut. You just couldn't keep your pants zipped."

"Darling, that was long over." The Chief's eyes held a moist plea.

"Was it? Then why was she in the bank, looking for you, looking all innocent? Why did she have your number?"

"They don't mean nothing to me." He shook his head. "I see a pretty girl, it's like an addiction, you understand."

On unsteady feet, Bishop stood, leaning against the plane wing. Jackie opened her purse, pulling out her 9mm handgun. She pointed it indecisively, first at the Chief, then at Bishop, then back toward the Chief. "No, I'm done understanding. She called you, only she got me. Well, I got her, didn't I."

He filled in the information for the Chief. "Virna told Jackie about the love spell that the witches were planning on doing. Jackie knew Blossom was a witch and guessed that she'd take part in the spell." Bishop shook some of the ringing from his head. "Virna needed something of Teonna's to burn in the fire, but the only thing she had was Teonna's picture. Jackie reasoned that Blossom needed something of hers to burn in the fire, so she deliberately dropped her glove where Virna would see it and pick it up."

The Chief stared at his wife in disbelieve.

Bishop kept pushing. "She knew Blossom would throw the glove into the fire. So she soaked it in poison oak resin. When Blossom burned the glove for the incantation she had to be standing over the fire, inhaling the flames."

He could tell by Jackie's reaction, not even a flicker of surprise or denial, that he was right.

"My, but aren't you the clever one. Teonna always said that about you."

"You knew Blossom had been exposed to poison oak before, when the Chief had taken her to the mountains two years ago, for her sixteenth birthday. He panicked, left her, her mother called Virna."

"It wasn't hard to figure out." The gun tipped toward the Chief.

"You switched bait packs in her drawer to get her fired." Bishop tried to keep her off-balance. Maybe she'd drop her gun and give him an opening.

"It was easy, easier than I expected."

"You had excess to all the keys, all you had to do was get her drawer combination. Is that when you decided to rob the bank? When you saw how easy it would be?"

"You don't know what my life's like. Bad enough

you had to chase every skirt the wind blew," She shook the gun at the Chief. "But at work? My work!"

Had to be uncomfortable. Jackie's pride would have gone beyond wounded. It would have been raw and bleeding.

"You killed her?" The Chief eyes teared over.

Bishop wasn't surprised that had Chief loved Blossom. She'd been fresh and young and sometimes the job got to you. Sometimes you needed to feel the innocence, or you fell apart.

"You pig. After all our planning, after leading Gregg to think of ordering the money for the other banks. You..." she sputtered her rage exploding in her face, the carefully applied foundation of deep bronze, and powder of shimmering dust, cracking. "You have to go and bonk that little slut."

The gunshot startled Bishop, but not as much as the bullet must have surprised Jackie. Her eyes widened like a child who actually got a pony for their birthday. Chest, chest, head. Three shots, rapid session. The force of the bullets hurled her backward to the ground.

The Chief stood, the smoking gun steady, his eyes burning with cold fury. "You're the slut I should have stayed away from."

Bishop had been right. Two MO's. Two shooters. He waited. The Chief wouldn't miss, not at this close range. At least it would be fast.

"There's your killer, Bishop. Love or money, isn't that what Frank always said. Well, for her it was both. She killed Esmeralda. Didn't want to share the money.

Left the body for me to find. Threatened that the next time she caught me she'd kill us both. Guess not."

He used the barrel of the gun to motion Bishop away from the plane.

"I'll kill you as well, stand back."

Bishop stepped back. The Chief hefted the huge duffle bag, grunting as he tossed it into the passenger's seat.

"What happened to Tiffany Foss?"

The Chief paused. "You know about her too? Always said there wasn't a crime you couldn't solve. Put in a barbeque pit just to cover-up that little mess Jackie made."

He stood, stance wide, shoulders back, an advertisement for strength and virility. No wonder women chased after him. No wonder Jackie was consumed with jealousy.

"You could come with. There's nothing here for you. Teonna's gone. Frank's mostly gone. We could lie in the sun, drink all day, have us women that smell like coconuts and lime."

Bishop didn't move.

"No, you're too noble for that." The Chief gave a quick nod of good-bye. "Good knowing ya.'"

When he turned his back to get into the plane, Bishop dove for him. The Chief had been expecting it. He twisted, slamming the gun butt across Bishop's face. His knee rammed into Bishop's gut, knocking him breathless to the ground.

"Don't be a fool. What makes you think I won't kill you?" The Chief gestured toward his dead wife, the bloom of blood spoiling the brilliant white of her sundress. "I killed her."

"She deserved it. I don't."

That made him pause. The Chief liked to talk, and Bishop needed him to keep talking until Sam got there with the cavalry.

"What? No sins, Bishop?"

Cautiously, Bishop stood, staying back from the unwavering gun.

"Claire might have a thing or two to say about that." He laughed. "But you held out for a long time. Longer than I did."

The gun tipped away. Bishop dove low. He knew he couldn't beat the Chief. It was like wrestling with a bear. A younger, stronger bear. The gun butt pounded against his back. An elbow jammed between ribs making Bishop grunt in pain.

"Give it up."

His knees buckled and the only thing holding him up was the Chief. White, white teeth grinned in his face. The pounding on his back stopped and the gun, a circle of steel with a dark center of emptiness, pointed towards him. So much for the cavalry.

The bullet whizzed past his ear. The buzz like an angry hornet.

Red appeared on the Chief's chest. Blood exploded into Bishop's face and eyes.

This time it was Bishop holding the Chief up. His hand clutched Bishop's shirt. The eyes flared, his soul fighting to stay. There were too many sins for him to not be afraid. The last breath rattled as muscles tightened and released arrhythmically.

Bishop looked up to find Sam standing there, the hot sniper rifle still in his hand.

"I thought he was going to shoot you."

Bishop pushed the body away and stood, staring down at his old friend's lifeless body.

"So did I."

CHAPTER TWENTY-NINE

Bishop woke to light streaming in the care center window. He hadn't intended to stay the night. Frank's respirator hissed contentedly. The television in the corner babbled endless repeats of reports passing as news. Pictures of the Chief, Jackie, the pretty blue plane, flew past before fading into memories, the prediction of a summer drought overtaking the headlines. Standing, Bishop shook off the aches of sleeping in a chair. When he reached to switch the television to a music only station a new picture of the Garfield Falls police building flashed on screen and he stopped.

"Interim assistant chief of police was announced today by the mayor's office."

On the station steps a group of people assembled, waving and smiling for the camera. Bishop recognized the mayor. And the man next to him, the one shaking his hand. A knot formed in Bishop's stomach.

Juniorcowski. His beautiful wife Claire at his side. Their three children, Lexi and Tobias respectively hanging back, Sonny even further back, with his hands in his pockets and a sullen face. Junior turned and shook the hand of the first well-wisher on his right. Sergio.

Bishop took a deep breath. Bruises he hadn't felt yesterday told him he should have gone to the doctor. Nothing they could do. Nothing that could be done. He'd lived with pain for a long time. This was nothing new.

He took the long way home, going through the upscale subdivision. He passed the Chief's house, a for sale sign already on the lawn. Farther down the road was Claire's house, the prefect lawn, the lace curtains blocking out the harsh effects of the summer sun to come. Farther east was his last stop, then he would consider the case closed.

When he knocked there was no answer. The garage doors were open and he went through to the back where he knew that he'd find her, digging in the new garden, a straw hat keeping the sun off her face, gloves protecting her hands as she transferred small seedlings from their germination pots to the ground. Blossom's mother knelt down to the cool damp soil. She tipped the starter perennials into her hand. Using a gardening trowel to make a small hole, she carefully placed the flower into the dirt, then tapped potting soil into the hole and up the stem, supporting the plant.

He watched, until she finally felt his presence and

turned around. "Bishop."

She wasn't surprised.

He didn't know what to say. She had to have seen the news. An officer had to have come by and told her.

"Thank you."

He wanted to make light of it. "It's my job."

"Yes."

She didn't like his job.

"I never asked, do you have children?"

"A son."

He thought of Lexi, then buried the suspicion, there was no reason to go there, it would just cause more hurt. And with Junior taking over the Chief's job, he'd be seeing more of Claire and Lexi.

"You don't have a wife do you, Bishop?'

He'd rather not say. It was better not to get involved with civilians. They never understood the stresses and disappointments that went with a cop's life.

Laura, Mrs. Jones, looked up at him. "You don't have to answer. I understand that it's hard to let go. But when the time is right ..." She left the thought dangling.

He thought of Teonna. Would the time ever be right to let her go?

"Will you get me one of those candles?"

Bishop went over to the potting shed bench. An array of candles sat patiently waiting for their turn to contribute to a spell. The vast array of colors winked back at him each one coo-ing pick me, pick me.

"Which one?"

"Anyone."

He hesitated. He knew what she was doing, casting a spell for him, not that he believed. Red was love so he avoided any candles with shades of red from pink to salmon to burgundy Green was money He should pick money, but a little blue candle, deep jewel blue, like an azure summer sky, and then a little white one, seemed to bounce into his hands. She could choose.

Laura took the candles, weighing them in her hands and coming up even. "Hmm? Perhaps both?" She set the candles on the ground, between the freshly planted flowers. It looked cold and barren to him. Bishop picked up a handful of little glass beads sitting on the potting table. He scattered them randomly around the candles. They caught and reflected the sunshine, little mirrors in the dirt. Laura looked up at him. She didn't smile, didn't say anything, but Bishop felt a weight lifting from his shoulders.

The phone in his pocket rang.

Shirley.

"Dead body."

"Give me ten."

"I'll give you five."

I hope you enjoyed *Bishop Bewitched*, you might also enjoy *Bishop to Queen's Knight*, the other book in the Garfield Falls series. In it Bishop jeopardizes his career investigating the cold case of a missing teenager.

Please consider leaving a review at your favorite book discovery site. Even if it's just a sentence or two, your kind words could help another reader find just the book they've been looking for.

For more about me and my writing check out my website: BartennMills.com.

VANILLA
LIES

A 1985 mystery

By
Bartenn Mills

Prologue

"Make yourself comfortable." Marley dimmed the lights, lit a cluster of candles, and put a blank cassette into the recorder before he hobbled back to his seat. He faced the woman across from him already settled in a red Queen Anne's chair as if she were a queen herself. Her attitude clearly said that not only did she know she was beautiful, but, like Lolita, she had always been beautiful, her creamy skin flawless, her blonde hair a loose tumble framing the classic features of her face, her body thin and leggy.

Yet she was broken. A closer examination of her face revealed multiple fine scars of repeated cosmetic surgeries. There was the whisper of unevenness in a nose smashed so often it was now beyond repair. Even her perfect white teeth were false. And that was only on the outside. Inside there was no beauty, there was a hard brittle shell protecting the frightened little girl who thought pain was love and hurting was normal.

"So what do you want to talk about?" He settled his legs easing them into a straight, casual appearing position.

"Nothing. My life's boring. Nothing's happening."

"Really? How are things with your new boyfriend?" He watched her closely. In the dim light she was more likely to reveal the little bits of herself she wanted to hide, but it was also harder for him to know if it was the flicker of a candle or a true emotion.

She shifted her shoulders in a disinterested shrug and looked away from him. "Everything's fine."

"How does it feel to have a normal relationship?"

At that, she made a brittle, nasal noise that could have been called a laugh. "He's using me."

"What makes you say that?"

"Because he's nosey. He's a nosey reporter."

"Did he hide that from you before you let him move in?"

She picked the arm of the chair, then seductively tipped her head to gaze at him, her lips parting in a sexy pout. "No."

Marley had sat across from one too many broken women to be distracted by a little sexual come-on. "What is he nosey about? About your coming here?"

"He wants to know about the book."

Although he tried, there was no way to cover his surprise. "You've talked to him about your book?"

"No."

But he could read the lie as easily as a ghost goes through walls. He waited, letting the falsehood hang in the air over her, until Trudy confessed.

"Yes." She sighed before rallying into anger. "He just made me so mad. He starts in with his big education, and quoting some Dante thing about lust being a deadly sin, and how smart he is, and I'm not."

"Does he hurt you with words instead of blows?"

"No." Then honesty won. "Yes."

"Is that why you wanted him to move in?"

"Maybe, maybe part of it. When we fight I feel more alive." She watched her fingers worry the threads on the arm of the chair, relentlessly fraying the fabric. "And ... and ... having him there makes me feel safe."

Marley forced himself not to lean forward. "He hurts you, but he makes you feel safe?"

"I'm afraid about what will happen when the book comes out."

"That people will look at you differently? That they will know all your secrets?"

"No, that he'll kill me." She turned her head and stared him full in the face. There was no coyness, no little girl flirt, no using sex as a cover for her true emotions. This was honest, the raw truth, that since the first time she'd waited in the dark listening for steps outside her door she had feared he would kill her.

And she had a right to be afraid. Marley couldn't tell her that she would be safe. He had felt the pain, the fear, the blows, and the wishing that you could die. He wanted to tell her to think of herself first. There would be consequences, but no one had ever been put to death for not delivering a manuscript. Yet all he could think of was the eloquence of her words. If they gave one person hope, one person strength, stopped one person's fist, any price was worth it.

"You don't have to put your name on the book," he said instead. "We have plenty of time to change things enough so no one will be able to identify you."

She shook her head, sending her beautiful curls into a seductive dance. "No. It's my name that will sell." She leaned back, a determined set to her jaw. "I want to take this book and shove it down his throat."

Marley nodded. So did he. "Wrath."

"What?"

"Wrath, it's another of the deadly sins. It's the one that broke your nose."

She laughed, a real laugh this time. "No, I think that was someone's fist."

Her tension eased, and the rest of the session went well. By the time she left all thought of burying the book was gone. Marley saw her to the door, leaning heavily on his slim metal crutches. He shut off the tape recorder and opened the drawer to put the cassette next to the black, three and a half-inch computer floppy disk already there. The disk contained Trudy's manuscript, painfully written as a declaration of emancipation from her past.

He picked up the solitary disk. She was right, without her name on the book no one would care, it would just be one more scholarly thesis on abuse. On impulse, he opened another drawer and pulled out a stiff cardboard disk mailer. He wasn't sure why. Some compulsion. He could make another copy off the computer. This one he wanted far away. Somewhere safe. He tapped his pen on the desktop. But where? He could mail it to himself. Let it sit in the post office box. No, even that didn't feel safe enough. It needed to be with someone he could trust, and he thought of Jane. He'd thought of Jane too much since the last writer's conference, her luminous eyes and quick smile haunting him. He wanted to wrap his arms around her and weep at her innocence and let it drain away his pain. But that was never going to happen. She didn't belong in his world. And that was exactly why the disk would be safe with her.